She hugged the side of the road and careened around a bend. Then she saw it—a pearl-gray automobile parked half on the asphalt and half against the roadside underbrush.

She jerked the truck to the left as a man holding a cell phone to his ear stepped onto the road. In the instant before she swerved on two wheels away from his vehicle, she noticed the man's eyes—large, round and filled with terror.

A loud crash followed by the screech of rent metal and the squeal of her own brakes made Helen's heart thud against her chest. She glanced in the rearview mirror. The man was nowhere to be seen. Had she struck him? She jumped out and ran toward the sedan.

"Hey, mister!" she called. "Where are you?"

"I'm in here."

Helen walked hesitantly to the gaping hole that had been the driver's door. She peered into the car's interior at the tasseled tops of a pair of oxblood loafers and the twin peaks of bent knees encased in perfectly pressed tan chinos. "You okay?"

The knees parted and an ashen face rose from the passenger seat. "I don't think I'll ever be okay again in my life."

Dear Reader,

To those of you who read Claire and Jack's story in *An Unlikely Match*, I'd like to welcome you back to the island community of Heron Point, Florida. To those of you visiting Heron Point for the first time in this book, I hope you will enjoy this quirky little town as much as I enjoyed writing about it.

It's autumn and change is in the air in Heron Point. The citizens are hopeful about the future, and some of them are falling in love. The leading lady of this story, Helen Sweeney, is not the typical heroine. She's tough and strong and struggling to make her way in a male-dominated profession. And when faced with the most important decision of her life, whether or not to raise the child growing inside her without its father, she shows a vulnerable, humbling side of her character, as well. I hope you enjoy Helen and Ethan's journey to a happy ending.

And for those readers who have asked me if Heron Point really exists, take Florida route 24 west until you hit the Gulf. There, among the cedar trees, you'll find the closest thing to it.

I love to hear from readers. Please visit my Web site, www.cynthiathomason.com, or e-mail me at Cynthoma@aol.com. My address is P.O. Box 550068, Fort Lauderdale, FL 33355.

Sincerely,

Cynthia Thomason

AN UNLIKELY FATHER
Cynthia Thomason

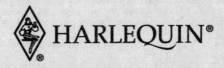

HARLEQUIN®

TORONTO • NEW YORK • LONDON
AMSTERDAM • PARIS • SYDNEY • HAMBURG
STOCKHOLM • ATHENS • TOKYO • MILAN • MADRID
PRAGUE • WARSAW • BUDAPEST • AUCKLAND

ISBN 0-373-71345-2

AN UNLIKELY FATHER

Copyright © 2006 by Cynthia Thomason

www.eHarlequin.com

Printed in U.S.A.

Books by Cynthia Thomason

HARLEQUIN SUPERROMANCE

Don't miss any of our special offers. Write to us at the following address for information on our newest releases.

Harlequin Reader Service
U.S.: 3010 Walden Ave., P.O. Box 1325, Buffalo, NY 14269
Canadian: P.O. Box 609, Fort Erie, Ont. L2A 5X3

This book is dedicated to my favorite
hero/fisherman, my husband, Walter,
who was literally my "left-hand man" while
I recuperated from a broken wrist.
All is forgiven, honey, even though
I suffered this injury when you took me fishing.

CHAPTER ONE

At EIGHT-THIRTY WEDNESDAY morning, Helen Sweeney waited for Maddie Harrison to raise the window shade on the door of Heron Point's only medical office. As soon as Maddie changed the sign from Closed to Open, Helen got out of her scarred old Chevy Suburban, walked inside and strode to Maddie's desk. The receptionist looked up and smiled. "Good morning, Helen. What brings you here? Is something wrong with Finn?"

"No, Pop's all right. It's me who needs to see Dr. Tucker."

"Sorry, hon, but the doc's out of town. Won't be back for three days. I'm only here for a couple of hours to finish some paperwork." She searched Helen's face as if she could come up with a diagnosis by just looking closely. "It's not like you to get sick, Helen."

"I'm not sick, Maddie, but I do need to see the doctor."

"Well, like I said…"

"I know. Three days." Helen twisted her fingers together, a habit she had when she was nervous, which wasn't often.

Maddie came around the desk and took Helen's elbow. "Sit down, dear, before you do something stupid like faint on me." She led Helen to a chair, forced her onto the wooden seat and sat down next to her. "Tell me, what can I do?"

Even though she knew no one was in the waiting room but her and Maddie, Helen still scanned all four corners of the office. She looked out the windows, stared at the door. She figured she could trust Maddie, and since Doc Tucker was away, she was going to have to. She turned toward the older woman and said, "If I tell you something, you have to abide by patient confidentiality, right? Just like if I told Doc?"

Maddie patted Helen's clenched hands. "I don't know about the official rules, Helen, but I do know if you tell me something you want kept a secret, I'll go to my grave with it." She smiled. "Now, is that good enough for you?"

Helen nodded, swallowed, then plunged ahead. "Since Doc's not here, I guess I need one of those things from the drugstore. One of those…" She couldn't even say the words.

"Do you need a prescription?" Maddie asked. "Because if you do, I can't give you one without Dr. Tucker's say-so."

"No. It's over the counter. I need a…pregnancy test."

Maddie fell silent for a moment before uttering a simple, "Oh."

"I can't go buy it myself," Helen said. "Within a half hour, everyone on this island would hear about it." She stared down at her hands, stilled now by the pressure of Maddie's comforting hold. "I can hear it now, 'poor ol' Helen. Now she's gone and got herself pregnant. And no husband.'"

Maddie leaned closer. "Do you want me to buy the test for you, hon?"

Helen looked up. Relief washed over her, and finally, the spasms that had gripped her stomach since she'd stepped into the office stopped. "Would you, Maddie?"

She nodded. "You betcha. I don't suppose anyone in town would waste gossip on me. Five grandchildren is

about as close to mothering as I'm ever going to get again."
She stood up. "You answer the phone till I get back. And
tell any walk-ins that Doc'll be back on Saturday."

Helen agreed, gave Maddie a twenty-dollar bill and
watched her go out the door and turn in the direction of
Island Pharmacy. And then she paced. Buying the test was
only the first round.

MADDIE HANDED THE white plastic bag to Helen. "I put your
change in there, along with the test."

Setting the bag on the desk, Helen knotted the two
handles together at least a half-dozen times. Anyone who
tried to see inside would have to have X-ray vision or a
machete. "Thanks. Did Frank ask you any questions?"

Maddie smirked. "Of course. I swear that pharmacist
thinks he's got the right to know everyone's business."

"What did you tell him?"

"That my daughter was coming to town, and she asked
me to pick up the test." Maddie shrugged. "Heck, the way
that girl reproduces, it could turn out to be true."

Helen tucked the sack under her arm. "I appreciate this.
You're a good friend."

Maddie stared at her as if she wanted to ask something.
But she settled for saying, "It's still quiet. Do you want to
talk anymore?"

"No. I've got nothing to say, yet. I'll see what this test
shows and then, if…well, I'll make an appointment with
Sam if I need to."

Maddie put her hand on Helen's shoulder. "Okay. No
need to get yourself upset unnecessarily."

Helen headed for the door. "Thanks again for buying this."

Maddie returned to her chair behind the desk. "Good luck, Helen. I don't know what to wish for. Babies are awful sweet gifts, but in your situation, the responsibilities you've already got…"

Helen gave her a weak smile. "I know." As she walked to her truck she analyzed what her situation was, exactly. She was thirty years old, unmarried and tied down to a job that demanded more from her physically than was expected of most men. She wasn't complaining. But heck, if this test turned out to be positive, wasn't fate asking more than she could give? But who said life was fair?

She tossed the sack onto the passenger seat and started the truck. As she rumbled down Island Avenue, she repeatedly stole peeks at the innocent-looking plastic bag rustling in the breeze coming in her open window. Pregnant. It wasn't possible. Donny used protection. They were careful. She raked her fingers through her hair a couple of times. She didn't even want to think about how Donny was going to take this news if the test was positive.

Helen could have driven narrow Gulfview Road blindfolded. She'd lived with her father all her life in a two-bedroom cottage next to their private dock that jutted into the Gulf of Mexico. And she'd traveled the two-mile journey into town more times than she'd like to admit. Her world had always been this island, these few acres, these twisting, palm-lined roadways.

Once away from the moderate traffic of midisland, she pressed her foot to the Suburban's accelerator and mindlessly cruised toward home and the task she had to face when she got there. She hugged the side of the road and careened around a bend, feeling the shocks of the old truck moan in protest as she leaned into the curve. And then she saw it—a pearl-gray automobile parked half on the asphalt and half against the roadside underbrush.

The driver's door of the sedan opened as Helen approached, and a pair of trouser-clad legs swung from the interior. She jerked the truck to the left as a man holding a cell phone to his ear stepped onto the road. In the instant before she swerved on two wheels away from his vehicle, she noticed the man's eyes—large, round and filled with terror.

A loud crash, followed by the screech of rent metal and the squeal of her own brakes, made Helen's heart thud against her chest. She turned her wheel sharply to the right, buried the hood of the Suburban in a thatch of sabal palms and thrust the gearshift into Park. For one brief second she folded her arms over the top of the steering wheel and dropped her head to her wrists. "Oh, shit."

She glanced in the rearview mirror. The gray sedan was visible, but there was no man standing beside it. Had she struck him? Was he lying in the middle of the road? Did he still have the damn cell phone so she could at least call 911?

She heaved her shoulder against the driver's panel, mumbling a few obscenities under her breath about the rusty old hinges that required a body slam to open the truck door. She jumped out of the vehicle and ran toward the sedan, which was a hundred yards down the road. Before she reached it, she saw the driver's side door halfway between the car and her truck. It rocked innocently on the pavement like a delicate wing ripped from the body of a great silver bird.

Without pausing, she sprinted the rest of the way to the car, relieved that she didn't see a body sprawled on the road. "Hey, mister!" she called. "Where are you?"

"I'm in here."

Slowing her pace for the first time, Helen walked hesitantly to the gaping hole that had been the driver's door. She peered into the car's interior at the tasseled tops of a pair of oxblood loafers and the twin peaks of bent knees encased in perfectly creased tan chinos. "You okay?" she asked.

The knees parted and an ashen face lifted from the passenger seat. Deep brown eyes stared at her with numb shock. After a moment, the man squinted and exhaled a burst of air. "I don't think I'll ever be okay again in my life," he said in a hoarse whisper.

"At least you fell back into the cár instead of onto the road," Helen said. Spotting his cell phone, she picked it up and examined the keypad to see that the battery light was on. "You need an ambulance?"

"No, I don't think so."

She reached into the car between his thighs. "Here, give me your hand."

He did, and she pulled him upright. Once his feet hit the road, he gaped at the mangled mess in the car's framework that had once connected the driver's panel to the rest of the vehicle. "The door's gone," he said.

Helen pointed down the road. "No, it isn't. It's right there."

He leaned out. "Oh, right. My mistake."

Deciding the guy wasn't hurt, Helen held the phone toward him. "You might need to use this."

He remained motionless while she set the phone in his hand. "I was sort of trying to use it when you dissected the car," he said.

She wiped her damp palm along the pocket of her shorts. "Yeah, I saw you with the phone. You lost, or something?" Scrutinizing his automobile, which she now noticed was a Lincoln Town Car and would probably cost about a million bucks to fix, she added with a mental wince, "You're new to Heron Point, right? That would explain why you'd pulled over in such a dangerous place."

His eyebrows arched in astonishment. "What do you mean, 'dangerous'?"

"This is a busy road. All the locals know you can't just park your car on the side like you did." She shrugged her shoulders with all the bravado she could muster. "Makes you a target for oncoming traffic."

He stood up, towering over her by several inches. "Oh, sure. A target for any vehicle that barrels around that curve at sixty miles an hour." He nodded toward the Suburban, which was idling like a tethered dinosaur, smoke hissing from its radiator. "And, by the way, that death trap of yours is the only car that's come down this *busy road* in the last ten minutes. I should know. I've been waiting to hail the first vehicle that showed up." He wiped a drop of sweat from his forehead and stared at it on the back of his hand as if he'd never perspired before. "Just my luck, you were driving it."

Helen tried to recall the details of her pitiful auto insurance policy. She knew she didn't have coverage on the Suburban. Why would she? That tank could survive anything. And she seemed to recall that her liability coverage had a deductible equal to the payoff of a winning lottery ticket.

Lately, Helen's meager savings account had suffered some major hits. The future didn't look much better if that pregnancy test came up positive. Certain that her best course of action was to maintain a tacit innocence, she shoved her hands in her pockets and rocked back on her heels. "So, you had car trouble even before—" she glanced from the Lincoln to the dismembered door "—this happened?"

"Yeah. I rented this thing in Tampa, exactly—" he checked his watch "—one hour and forty-five minutes ago. It ran beautifully for eighty miles and then conked out on your deserted stretch of Heron Point superhighway."

Helen leaned against the hood of the Lincoln. "Tough break. A car this fancy should get at least a couple hundred miles before breaking down."

He smiled grimly and looked at the pad of the cell phone. "At least we agree on something. I was just calling Diamond Rental to come pick up this two-ton pile of misery when you decided to make my complaint a bit of an embarrassment. I think the rental company might question the validity of my claim, now."

He started to dial, but paused and said, "Maybe you ought to get your insurance information. And I suppose we have to report this to the police."

Oh, great. Just what she needed. It'd probably be Billy Muldoone who'd swoop down upon the scene with his siren blaring and his features cemented into a condescending sneer. He'd write her up faster than the women of Heron Point turned him down for dances at the Lionheart Pub. In the pit of her stomach, Helen sensed a tingling of panic—the second time today. She didn't like the feeling, though she figured she'd experience it again while she waited for the pregnancy-test results. But right now she needed to calm down so she could plan a course of action for this current disaster.

"Ah, sure," she said. "I'll get my insurance card from the truck." She walked to the Suburban and lifted the hood to make sure none of its parts had been crippled. Thank goodness the steam had cleared and the engine hiccuped with its usual congestive rattle, telling her its internal workings were A-okay.

"Any damage to your vehicle?" the new guy called to her.

She looked over at him. "A busted headlight." Then she flashed him a little smile, hoping to distract him from following accident protocol to the letter. "Guess you'd better get your insurance information, too. Last time I replaced a headlight in this beast it cost me twenty-five bucks."

He held up a card between his thumb and index finger. Naturally, he already had his card ready even though he'd probably determined he was the injured party.

Helen scribbled a phone number on a scrap of paper and walked back to him. Ignoring a persistent niggling of guilt, she said, "I forgot my wallet. Here's my number. How can I reach you?"

He pulled a business card from his shirt pocket and held it out to her. "I'm staying at the Heron Point Hotel temporarily," he said. "You can leave a message if I'm not in."

She stepped closer to him and reached for the card. When she took it, he wrinkled his nose and jerked his hand back. "What's that smell?"

Well, great. Barely an hour ago she'd been cleaning the bait well on the *Finn Catcher,* getting the boat ready for its next charter trip on Friday morning. She hadn't bothered to change clothes before running into town for a quick visit to the doctor, and now she noticed a few glistening fish scales still stuck to her cargo shorts. Fishy smells didn't bother her.

She'd grown up with them, but that obviously wasn't the case with this pressed and polished out-of-towner.

She slipped the business card into her waistband. "It's fish."

"Fish?" He said the word as if he needed a zoology textbook to figure out what she was talking about.

"This *is* an island," she said. "We are surrounded by the little creatures."

He stared at his hand but at least had the decency to chuckle a little in a self-deprecating way. "Of course." Then he abruptly changed the subject to one she definitely wasn't interested in. "I guess I'll call the police now."

She pointed a finger at him. "You do that. I'll wait in my truck."

She walked away from him, got behind the wheel of the Suburban and backed out of the palm thatch. Then, without so much as a backward glance, she peeled down the road. It was the coward's way out. Helen knew that just as she knew she wasn't getting away with anything. Maybe he'd call that number she gave him and have a nice little chat with the old guy who repaired fishing rods in town, but the decoy wasn't going to get her out of trouble. Everyone in town, and especially the police, knew who drove a rusty old Suburban.

So, it was only a matter of time until she had to face up to what had happened here. Helen frowned at the package on the passenger seat. But first she had to face something a whole lot more important.

APPARENTLY FINISHED WITH his inspection of the damages, the muscle-bound cop leaned against the Town Car and rested his elbow near the retractable sunroof. "So, what did the driver of the other car look like, Mr. Anderson?"

Ethan stared at the police officer who had arrived a few minutes ago heralded by earsplitting sirens and flashing lights. Ethan had considered the entrance a somewhat over-the-top reaction to what he'd called a "minor traffic accident" when he'd phoned in the report. Pad in hand, and his eyes narrowed in that officious scowl police officers seemed to perfect, the cop had sauntered all around Ethan's car, and its missing door fifty yards away.

"What did she look like?" Ethan repeated.

Officer Muldoone removed his arm from the top of the car and prepared to write. "It was a female, then?"

"Right, yes," Ethan answered. He held his hand just under his chin. "She was about this tall."

"About five feet, five inches?"

"Give or take. She was skinny. No, thin. Not too skinny." Now that Ethan thought about the daredevil driver, he decided she was actually quite pleasantly proportioned. She was slim all over, though her breasts were certainly full enough to satisfy any man's standards. And ignoring this woman's better features under that ribbed tank top had been impossible.

"Anything else you remember?" the officer asked. "Hair? Eyes?"

Funny. Ethan remembered both quite well. "She had light blond hair." He wiggled his fingers around his own head. "Strands of it stuck out every which way, some short over her forehead, some longer, reaching her shoulders." He felt his skin flush when he realized he must sound like a Manhattan hairdresser. "That's not important," he said. "She's a blonde."

Muldoone wrote.

"And she had blue eyes," Ethan added. "I remember that distinctly."

"Sounds like Helen Sweeney," the officer said. "Was she driving a noisy old Suburban with rust spots?"

Ethan nodded, experiencing a totally unexpected attack of guilt. The ID had been too easy for the cop. But why should Ethan feel guilty? The car rental agency had specifically informed him that he'd need a police report when they sent a tow for the Lincoln. Heck, he was only doing what he had to do. Besides, the kooky lady could be here defending herself if she hadn't shot down the road, leaving him in her dust.

"And it was a hit-and-run, you say?" Muldoone asked. "That would be Helen's MO. She ran down a mailbox last month, and we didn't know who to blame until a new box showed up at the victim's house two weeks later with a note of apology. Signed H. S."

Helen's MO? The cop was behaving as if this woman had a rap sheet. Ethan scrubbed his hand down his face. "To be completely honest, officer, it wasn't truly a hit-and-run. Helen, or whoever did this…"

The cop let loose with a sputter of laughter. "Oh, it was Helen."

"Anyway, *Helen* did hit my car, but she didn't immediately run. She stayed quite a while, actually. She made certain I wasn't hurt." When he remembered Helen's initial reaction upon finding him flat on his back in the car, Ethan tried to make her seem more sympathetic to the officer. "In fact, she offered to call an ambulance."

"Big of her." Muldoone chose not to write that information down.

"What are you going to do?" Ethan asked.

"I'm going out to the Sweeney place when I leave here. Helen just lives a mile up this road. I'll issue her a ticket for reckless driving, and she'll have to face a county judge. He may take her license, this time."

Wonderful. Here he was, his first day in a new town. He was here to get the residents' cooperation and to get them to accept that Anderson Enterprises was coming in and would most definitely make an impression. And what had happened? Before he'd been here an hour he'd had a literal run-in with a local and stood to make an enemy of her if she lost her license. Not a very auspicious beginning.

"To be perfectly honest, Officer," he said, "maybe I shouldn't have been parked where I was. The car is half on, half off the road."

Muldoone smiled and flipped the cover over his notebook. "Don't let her get to you, Mr. Anderson," he said. "You can be sure Helen will give the judge that little detail. If I were you, I'd stick to your story. If not, you could end up losing *your* license. Helen has a way of turning the tables."

The officer headed toward his patrol car. Before he got in, he turned back to Ethan and said, "What are you going to do now, Mr. Anderson? You want me to call headquarters? I've got the only patrol car, but I can have my partner come out on the golf cart, pick you up and take you back into town."

Oh, right. Ethan remembered the head of security for Anderson Enterprises telling him that Heron Point cops rode around on golf carts. As much as he wanted to see that, and as much as he wanted to get out of the heat, Ethan declined the offer. "I've got to wait for the tow," he said.

"I could be here as long as two hours. You're kind of remote on this island."

"Suit yourself. I'll probably see you when I'm coming back from the Sweeney place."

Officer Muldoone got in his car and drove away. Ethan swatted at an aggressive dragonfly, got in the Town Car and turned on the air-conditioning. Most of the cool breeze went out the gaping hole where the door had been, but Ethan didn't care. He didn't suppose Diamond Rental was going to say much about the car returning without a full tank of gas.

WHEN SHE HEARD the knock on her door, Helen looked out the front window and swore. "Oh, hell."

Her father silenced the Sweeney's fifteen-year-old yellow Lab and wheeled around in his chair. "Who is it, Helen?"

"It's Muldoone," she said.

"What in the world does he want?"

"I clipped somebody on Gulfview Road today," she said. Seeing the worried look on her father's face, she added, "It was no big thing, Pop. The other guy's fine. Our truck just got a scratch."

"And you didn't tell me this?" Finn asked.

The pounding on the door increased, and Helen turned the knob. "I knew there'd be time enough." She opened the door. "Hi, Billy. Nice day, isn't it?"

"Not for you, Helen." He handed her a ticket. "Reckless driving. Again. You'll have to make a court appearance on this one. About six weeks from now."

She took the ticket. "I'm probably busy that day, but I'll try to squeeze it in. By the way, how's that guy, the one who got in my way?"

Muldoone sent her a strange look, one that hinted he was amused by her question. "You don't know who you hit, do you?"

"No." She hadn't bothered to look at the business card, which right now sat on the bathroom counter. "Who is he?"

"Ethan Anderson," Billy said smugly. "Does the name ring a bell?"

It did. Almost as if the bell were clanging against the side of her head with the intention of deafening her. "The guy from Anderson Enterprises."

"Oh, yeah. And you sure taught him a lesson about Heron Point hospitality. If he doesn't hightail it back to New York on the next plane, he'll at least avoid you from now on."

Could this day get any worse? Now she'd hit the one man people in Heron Point were looking to as a financial savior.

Sticking his head inside the front door, Billy said, "How's it going, Finn?"

"It'd be better, Billy, if you hadn't given us that ticket—and that news."

Helen closed the door a couple of inches. She had to get rid of Billy. She had to go down to the edge of the water and scream as loud as she could where no one would hear her. "Okay, then, boys," she said. "Enough chitchat."

Billy stubbornly leaned his two-hundred-pound frame against the jamb, preventing her from shutting him out. "Hey, Helen, you still going out with that folksinger?"

"Sure am. We're as cozy as a pair of fleas on a dog's ear."

He moved a toothpick from one side of his mouth to the other. "You let me know when you break up. You still owe me a date."

Helen couldn't remember the debt, but even if it were true, there was no way Billy Muldoone was going to collect. "Right. You'll be the first person I tell." She shut the door and collapsed against it.

"I don't know what's worse," Finn said. "The ticket you just got or the fact that an Anderson has finally showed up in Heron Point."

Helen had never understood her father's resentment of anyone associated with Anderson Enterprises, and she'd grown tired of asking him. Finn would tell her when he was ready. "My money's on the ticket," she said. "You're the only one in town who hasn't been looking forward to Anderson's arrival."

Finn frowned. "You okay? You weren't hurt in that little mishap, were you?"

"No. I'm just dandy." She stared down at the ticket in her hand. That, and the bad impression she'd made on Ethan Anderson weren't the most disturbing pieces of information she'd gotten today. In fact, they weren't even a close second and third. The absolute winner in the bad-news category was that eight-letter word printed in blue on the plastic wand in her bathroom. It said, *pregnant.*

CHAPTER TWO

At ELEVEN O'CLOCK THURSDAY morning Helen parked the Suburban behind the Lionheart Pub and entered the establishment through the back door. She'd been up since seven preparing fishing tackle for her charter trip the next morning, but she'd put off coming into town until she knew Donny would be awake. His last set at the Lionheart didn't end until nearly two o'clock, and he liked to sleep in after performing late.

Helen hadn't come to see him play last night. He'd called during his first break to ask where she was. She'd tried to sound cheery, as if nothing was wrong. She'd said she was tired and would see him the next day.

And now that she was going to face him, she didn't feel any more confident about telling him the news than she had the day before. She'd hoped that a quiet night alone with her thoughts would result in a clear plan for what she was going to do about the pregnancy, but that hadn't happened, because her decision depended heavily on Donny's reaction. Now, as she came through the Lionheart's kitchen, she pondered the two conclusions she'd come to sometime in the middle of a restless night. She would tell Donny today. He was the father. He deserved to be the only

other person she confided in. And for now, she would think
of her condition in terms of the clinical word *pregnancy.*
She refused to think of herself as having a baby. That was
too intimate. Too conscionable. And certainly, until Donny
reacted as she hoped he would, too scary.

Vinnie, the Lionheart's luncheon cook, looked up from
a bubbling cauldron of spaghetti sauce as she walked by.
"Hey, Helen, it's kind of early for you to be here."

"Hi, Vinnie. I could tell what you were cooking all the way
over at the *Finn Catcher* this morning, and had to see for
myself if it tasted as good as it smelled." She took the spoon
he offered, dipped it in the pot and slurped a healthy portion.
The rich tomato sauce settled in her stomach like a lit fire-
cracker, and reminded her that two cups of coffee and a
helping of garlic probably wasn't a fit breakfast for a pregnant
woman. "Yep, just as I thought," she said. "Delicious."

He smiled with pride. "Come back for lunch. I'll make
sure you get a big helping."

She laid her hand over her stomach. "I'll hold you to
that. Is Donny outside?"

"Yeah, hard at work as usual."

Helen knew what that meant. Donny spent most of his
waking hours building his sailboat. Luckily, the vacant lot
between the Lionheart and the Heron Point Hotel was large
enough to accommodate the twenty-nine-foot hull that
he'd lovingly assembled in the three months he'd been on
the island.

She went through the public area of the bar without
being noticed by the few patrons inside, walked out the
front door and looked at the sandwich sign standing under

a front window. While she gathered her courage for what had to be done, she silently read the advertisement she knew by heart.

The Lionheart Pub proudly presents the mellow folk styling of Donovan Jax. Six nights a week beginning at nine o'clock.

In the time he'd been here, Donny had seemed to fit in with the varied population of Heron Point. At least folks came to the Lionheart with enough regularity for Helen to believe they liked his singing. The only person who didn't seem to take to the town's most recent performer was her father. But getting Finn to admit to liking anything new on the island was always a challenge.

Helen descended the two steps from the porch to the sidewalk and strode around the side of the building. Donny was there, a kerchief around his forehead and his shoulder-length brown hair tied with a bit of twine at his neck. Dust motes rose in the sun as he sanded the bow of *Donovan's Dawn,* the vessel he'd promised would take the two of them around Key West and into the eastern Caribbean.

Helen watched him work for a moment. She noticed especially his strong arms, since he was wearing a T-shirt with the sleeves cropped off at the shoulders. His muscles flexed with each smooth, practiced swipe of the sandpaper—muscles as finely tuned to this task as they were to playing a guitar. His devilish green eyes narrowed as he studied the results of his labor before his full, sensuous lips rounded and he blew a puff of sawdust into the air.

He looked up, saw her leaning against the building and gave her a cheeky smile. "Hello, cupcake. How long you been standing there?"

She walked toward him. "Long enough to know that I'll be glad when this thing is finished and I can see if she'll really float."

"Oh, she'll float all right, if I have to swim underneath her holding her up the whole time." He picked up a rag and brushed wood specks from his damp arms. "I thought you had a charter this morning."

"Nope. Wish I did." Any day Helen didn't have a fishing trip was a day she didn't make any money. "Got one tomorrow, though."

"Good. Then you can help me today."

"Yeah, how?"

He pointed to a stained foam cooler a few feet away. "By tossing me a beer."

She pulled a bottle from the melting ice and threw it to him.

"Have one for yourself," he said. "Once you start sanding, you'll find out how hot that sun is today."

A beer sounded good. Maybe it would help relax her. Helen reached into the ice again and withdrew a tempting bottle. She wrapped her hand around the cap and started to twist, anticipating the hiss of carbonation that always tantalized her taste buds.

Wait a minute, a voice inside her head cautioned. *What are you doing? A woman who's having a... A woman who's pregnant isn't supposed to drink alcohol. Isn't that what you've heard? Isn't that why you've always pitied those poor females in the heat of summer who are sweating for two without benefit of a little cold fermented malt grain?*

Slowly, certainly reluctantly, Helen lowered the bottle back into the cooler.

"What's the matter?" Donny asked. "It's close enough to noon, even for you."

She wiped her wet hand along her shorts. "It's not that. I just changed my mind."

"Suit yourself." He held up a roll of sandpaper. "Anyway, if you're sticking around for a while, you might as well tear off a piece and start to work on the deck rail."

She walked closer to the boat, but didn't reach for the sandpaper. "Donny, I have to tell you something."

He set down the roll and went back to work. "Okay, go ahead."

She watched him a moment longer, listened to the sound of the rough-grained paper on the already smooth teakwood. For a minute, her skin tingled as if he were abrading her body instead of the sailboat. She rubbed her arms briskly. "Donny?"

He glanced up, squinted, returned his attention to the task. "What?"

"I'm pregnant."

He stopped sanding. Her heart skipped a beat. For a few torturous seconds, he glared at her over *Donovan's Dawn* with extraordinarily wide eyes, and Helen waited for his next words to restart her breathing.

He dropped the paper and planted his elbows on the railing. "What did you say?"

"I just found out yesterday. I took one of those tests. It was positive."

He shook his head as if denying it would make it so. "That's impossible."

"No, only nearly impossible. Anyway, remember Friday night two weeks ago after we... Well, didn't you say that something didn't seem right, that maybe there was something wrong with the condom?"

"Oh, hell, that was just talk. Besides, it was after your friend's engagement party. We were too juiced to know what we were doing."

She felt the grip of shame in the tightening of her stomach muscles. The reminder of her overindulgence at Claire's party was still enough to make her cringe in mortification. She was too old to excuse such irresponsible behavior anymore. Getting drunk and stupid was just, well, stupid.

"It doesn't really matter, does it?" she said. "I'm pregnant and that's a fact."

At least he didn't argue the indisputable. He simply draped his hands over the side of *Donovan's Dawn* and mumbled something. She thought she heard the word *damn*.

"What are you going to do?" he asked after a moment.

The wording of his question stunned her since it seemed as if he'd completely left himself out of assuming any responsibility. By asking her what *she* was going to do he was, in effect, telling her to do *something*.

She fought an escalating anger. Finn always told her she tended to act without thinking, to strike without having a justifiable target. She wasn't going to do that, this time. She'd just dropped a bomb on Donny's plans, on their plans together. He had a right to be defensive, confused.

"My first thought was to tell you," she said calmly. "You're the father, so obviously you have a stake in what happens with this ba…pregnancy." She looked into his eyes and spoke with clear intent. "What do you think *we* should do?"

"Well, hell, I don't know." He rubbed his hand along the railing of the sailboat. His touch seemed gentle, caressing, even more than when he made love to her. "We have plans, Helen. When I got the boat done, we were going to take her around the Keys, sail all the way to the Turks and Caicos Islands, just you and me."

"Plans can change, Donny. Life happens." She'd never told him that his idea had been impractical from the start, anyway. Maybe deep down she'd hoped they could sail away just the two of them, but she knew it wasn't going to happen. Maybe some people believed in fantasies, but not Helen Sweeney.

Donny took a long swallow of beer and wiped his mouth with the back of his hand. The eyes that focused on hers were cold and distant. So were his words. "I don't know, Helen. I'm forty-two years old. I can't wrap my mind around the idea of a kid and a mortgage and a college savings account."

Her eyes burned and Helen cursed her frailty. She wasn't going to cry. "I know it's a shock, Donny. It is for me, too. I still can't believe it. But it's happened, and we have to…" Her voice hitched. Damn. She couldn't go on, so she sat on the cooler, dangled her hands between her knees and took a deep breath.

At least a minute passed, the longest minute of Helen's life, until Donny came around the boat and stood in front of her. When he laid a hand on her shoulder, she brushed at a stubborn tear and looked up at him.

"It'll be all right, Helen," he said. "You tell me what you want, and we'll make it work. If you want to go through with this, have the kid, I'll stand by you. If you decide on a different course, I'll be there for that, too."

Her body went limp with relief. She covered the hand that still curled over her shoulder. "We don't have to get married," she said. "It's enough to know that you'll be here."

"Sure. Don't worry about me. You've got more important things to think about. We'll still sail the boat. It may just take a little longer than we'd planned." He crouched down in front of her and took her hands. "So, you're going to have it? That's what you want?"

Her lips quivered. Stupid hot tears spilled down her cheeks faster than she could wipe them away. But it was okay. They were tears of gratitude. For the first time, she allowed herself to think of the little seed growing inside her as a human being, not a condition.

Donny smiled. "I guess that's my answer." He stood up. "You go on home now. Aren't you supposed to be resting?"

She let him pull her up from the cooler. "I'm fine," she said. "In fact, I'm better than fine."

"Atta girl." He turned her around and nudged her toward the Lionheart. "I know you've got a charter in the morning, but are you coming back tonight for the first set, at least?"

She smiled over her shoulder. "I'll be here."

She felt the warmth of his gaze as she left him and climbed the steps to the entrance to the bar. Everything was going to be okay. She held that thought all afternoon as she prepared for Friday's trip into the Gulf. She believed it as she drove back into town that night. Her confidence grew with each breath until she arrived at the Lionheart at nine o'clock and realized that only a few cars sat outside, far fewer than normal. She didn't really worry until she parked a block away from the pub and walked to the front door. The sandwich sign was no longer sitting by the entrance. That could only mean one thing. The great Donovan Jax was no longer playing at the Lionheart Pub.

"I DON'T KNOW MUCH, Helen," the owner of the Lionheart said a few minutes later when she sat at the bar, nursing a Coke.

"He just left without any explanation?" she asked.

"Yeah, well, he said there was an emergency. He apologized for leaving me with no entertainment, packed his bags and took off."

There was an emergency, all right. Someone without a backbone was about to become a father. "I suppose this is pointless to ask, Stan, but did he leave a forwarding address?"

Stan shook his head slowly while wiping his perfectly clean bar. "Sorry, Helen. I think it's lousy of him to walk out without letting you know."

She swallowed the rest of her drink and slid the glass across the bar. "Don't waste your sympathy on me. Donny and I weren't getting along, anyway. I was about to end it. Probably would have tonight if he hadn't bolted."

Stan draped the damp rag over the sink behind the bar. "Maybe he sensed that and left before you broke his heart."

Helen got down from the stool. "Right. I have to get up early, so I'm calling it a night." She headed for the door, but stopped and turned around. "One more thing…"

"What's that?"

"*Donovan's Dawn.* I noticed the sailboat is still in the vacant lot. Did Donny say anything about it to you?"

"Yeah, he did. Said he'd send a mover to pick it up as soon as he could. I expect in the next week or so. I can keep a watch out there. You want me to try and get a location where the boat's going?"

"Never mind. It doesn't matter now." She walked out onto the porch and paused in the overhead light. Knowing where Donny went really wasn't important. Everything had changed in the last few minutes, and once again Helen had to face a grim reality. Planning a future with Donny had been a ridiculous dream, anyway, and was best ended quickly. Now, without Donny's support, Helen knew she couldn't raise a kid and keep the *Finn Catcher* going and take care of Finn. She barely made enough money to keep her family going as it was, and she couldn't do any more. So this little bean inside her belly was the sacrifice she'd have to make.

She went down the steps, but stopped at the street. So, if this was her decision, why the hell had she ordered a Coke? She could be in the Lionheart right now, tossing back Wild Turkeys like there was no tomorrow. But she'd ordered a damn Coke.

She stared down at her flat stomach before closing her eyes to the image that had been stuck in her mind all afternoon. *Little bean.* What did it look like after two weeks? She remembered a picture in a high-school biology book. It looked like a lima bean. A tiny round speck, one a person could barely see without a magnifying glass. It had no heart, no brain, no sense that its mother was contemplating…

"Aw, hell." Helen went back to the door of the Lionheart. She had a bit of time to wait and hope for a damn miracle.

Stan looked up and saw her at the door. "You forget something, Helen?"

"No, I just changed my mind. It wouldn't hurt to ask the boat mover where the *Dawn* is going. In the next few days

I might think of something Donny left behind. Something important I'd need to contact him about."

"I'll keep a watch," Stan said. "If I find anything out, I'll let you know."

Helen didn't walk to the Suburban. She went into the vacant lot and stared at *Donovan's Dawn*. The boat's teak sides shone in the moonlight, testament to the weeks she and Donny had worked so hard. That had been a ridiculous dream, too, thinking she could take weeks away from Heron Point and sail around with Donny. Helen hadn't been away from home for more than a couple of days in her life.

She'd been born in Micopee thirty miles away, and from the time her parents had brought her to the little cottage she still shared with Finn, she'd been as much a part of Heron Point as the giant cedar trees, the dozens of pelicans that squatted on all the old pilings, the sea itself. But the Gulf was ruled by the tides, so even the water moved to and from Heron Point more than Helen ever had. Maybe if Finn hadn't lost the use of his legs, maybe if her mother hadn't run off, maybe then Helen could have gone to college, made something of herself. But not now. And if she had this baby, not ever.

A cloud covered the moon, and suddenly the *Dawn* was a great hulking shadow of unfinished business just like Helen's life. The sailboat stood on her supports, mocking Helen for believing in her, for believing in Donny. Finn was right, after all. Helen didn't have a lick of sense when it came to men. She fell too fast and didn't take long enough getting up before letting it happen again.

Well, not anymore. This time it wasn't just her heart that

was stomped on. This time the betrayal left her with a mountain of guilt about what she planned to do and a seriously wounded self-respect she'd never faced before. It wouldn't be so easy to put the last three months out of her mind. This time it hurt.

Anger coiled inside her until she thought she would explode. Finding no outlet, she clenched her fists until her nails dug into her palms. She started to walk out of the lot, but when a shiny silver can by her feet caught her eye, she picked it up and rolled it between her hands. An innocent beer can. A weapon, a release. She hurled it at the sailboat. It pinged against the polished surface, hit the ground and rolled to the end of the lot. Tension ebbed from Helen's shoulders. It felt good to fling her anger at the only tangible reminder left of Donny's deception. She went to the garbage bin, picked up another can and threw it, too. Then another. Then many more.

She might have continued until the ache in her throat faded and her tears stopped flowing, except she heard men's voices coming from the street behind her.

"Helen? Is that you?"

She froze. Just what she needed. Jack Hogan, Heron Point's new chief of police and the man her best friend Claire was going to marry in a few weeks. She spun around and stepped into the shadows. "Hell, no, Jack. It's not me, but I'll clean up this mess somebody else left." And then she saw who he was with and she couldn't seem to speak another word. Her mouth dried up. Her lungs were incapable of drawing in air.

"That'll be fair enough," Jack said. He was still in

uniform and she figured that technically he could nail her for vandalism. "Are you okay?"

"Dandy." She stared at the sky, the dirt beneath her feet, anything but Jack and the man he was with, the town savior she'd nearly decapitated yesterday.

"It looks to me like somebody was picking on an innocent sailboat," Jack said.

"Yeah, right. Not so innocent when you're looking at it through my eyes. I see someone's face very clearly on the side of that boat."

Jack smiled. "I heard about Donny leaving. Sorry. But like I told Claire, you can do better."

She huffed her opinion of his conclusion but mentally thanked him for saying it.

He turned his attention to Ethan Anderson. "I'd introduce you to our local fishing guide, Ethan, but I know you two met accidentally yesterday."

"Yeah, we met," Helen said. "Ethan sort of got in my way." She managed to smile a little at the guy who was still dressed like he'd just gotten off the plane, in pressed pants and a blue oxford shirt. "You don't need to arrest him, though, Jack. I'm not pressing charges, and I think he learned his lesson."

"That's generous of you," Ethan said. He switched a foam takeout box from one hand to the other.

"Dinner?" she asked.

"Dessert."

"Ethan and I just ate over at the Tail and Claw," Jack said. "He's waiting for a rental car to get here from the Tampa airport."

Ethan looked at his watch. "It's nearly ten o'clock. I'm only going to give them another few minutes."

"I guess I'll go on home, then," Jack said. "You going to the hotel?"

For some reason, Ethan looked at Helen as if she could contribute something to his answer. "I think I'll wait out here a little longer," he said. "Tell Claire hi for me."

"Will do." Jack started to walk away. "Oh, by the way, Helen, Claire said if I saw you, I should remind you about Thanksgiving dinner. She's planning to cook up a feast, and obviously she's counting on you and Finn to come."

Thanksgiving? Right now, the holidays were the furthest thing from Helen's mind. "When is it?"

"Same as always, I suppose," Jack said. "Fourth Thursday of November."

"Oh, right. And what's today?"

Jack chuckled. "The third Thursday. Gives you a week to mark the calendar."

He said goodbye to Ethan and headed toward his vehicle. And Helen thought how lucky Claire was to have found someone like Jack. Solid. Dependable. And very rare.

After a moment, she turned toward Ethan. "Good luck with getting that rental car delivered. In a way, I feel somewhat responsible for you standing out here waiting for it."

He smiled. "No offense, Helen, but once the new car arrives, I'm going to stay as far away from that truck of yours as I can."

"No offense taken." They stood without talking in the gloomy silence of a battlefield littered with beer cans. Helen figured she ought to start picking up the mess she'd created, but before she took a step, she heard the subtle squeak of the foam restaurant container.

Ethan held it out to her. "Do you like chocolate cake?"

ETHAN DIDN'T VERY often feel as if he walked a thin line between boardroom executive and idiot, but that's exactly how he felt right now. What was he doing, standing here with a peace offering for a woman who'd been doing her best in the last two days to destroy two perfectly fine modes of transportation?

She peered over the edge of the box. "You're giving me your dessert?"

He shrugged an indifference he didn't feel and said, "Seemed like the quickest way to soothe the angry beast. I have to wait out here for my car. You're here, too, and there are still a few cans in that trash bin."

Her lips twitched. He hoped it was a hint of a smile and not the beginning of a snarl. And then she said something that in his experience was a predictably female reaction. "I'd do most anything for chocolate." She stuck her thumbs in the waistband of her jeans and nodded down the street. "Come on. I'm not eating standing up."

He followed her a block to where her Suburban was parked. She stepped up on the front bumper, turned around and sat on the truck. He noticed a slash of flesh through a slit in the knee of her denims. She patted the hood beside her and said, "There's room."

He looked at the seriously faded steel, taking in the gritty remains of road dirt, and, considering her occupation, who knew what else, and stared down at his perfectly pressed beige Dockers. And he remembered that during his tour of Heron Point today he hadn't seen a business that was essential to a Manhattan male's lifestyle—a dry-cleaning establishment.

She must have correctly interpreted his reluctance because she sort of smiled again and then gripped the edge of her shirt cuff and wiped a small circle beside her. "Don't worry, Princeton," she said. "In all my years in Heron Point, I don't recall anyone ever catching something from the hood of a truck."

Princeton? He thought about correcting her and saying he was a Harvard man, but didn't think that would earn him any points. And that's what he was here for, after all—to establish a good working relationship with the locals. For some reason, his father, head of Anderson Enterprises, had decided to invest in this quirky Florida island by buying an old, run-down resort, and he'd sent his son to see that the renovations went smoothly.

It helped that Archie Anderson's chief security officer, Jack Hogan, had been in town a month longer than Ethan and had become something of a superhero to the two thousand people who lived here. In fact, Jack had even decided to stay once he'd fallen for the town's mayor. But Ethan needed to relate to these people on his own, one at a time, if he had to, and despite the way he and Helen had met, he didn't mind starting with her first.

He placed the toe of his Italian loafer on the bumper, hoisted himself up to the hood, and admitted to a grudging admiration of the old truck. The metal didn't even groan when he sat his clean chino-covered posterior on top of it.

He handed the box to Helen. She took out the fork, poked through a quarter inch of creamy icing and brought up a wedge of cake to her mouth. While she chewed, she handed him the utensil. "There's only one fork," she managed to say. "I can always light a match and sterilize it between bites."

Any sympathy he'd begun to feel for this teary-eyed woman who'd dropped a can in front of Jack like a guilty delinquent vanished. Helen Sweeney was about as vulnerable as a barracuda. And just as alien to a Manhattan guy who'd never been closer to a fish than the city aquarium. Unfortunately, what was unfamiliar was almost always fascinating, as well. And Ethan couldn't take his eyes off Helen's smart mouth as she chased a trail of frosting with the tip of her tongue.

"Never mind," he said, taking the fork and cutting a piece of cake for himself. He swallowed, licked the fork and handed it back to her. "See? I can be as daring as the next guy."

She huffed, dug into the dessert again, and, quite unexpectedly, Ethan found himself wondering what it would be like to share more than a plastic fork with this woman.

CHAPTER THREE

FINN WAS ALREADY in the kitchen at six o'clock the next morning when Helen padded in on bare feet. He looked up at her and frowned. "What time you get in last night?"

"A little before eleven. I had a few janitorial services to perform in town, but I'm fine. Don't worry."

He gave her a questioning stare before wheeling to the kitchen table with a quart of milk. "I've got your cereal and toast ready. I'll cut up some fruit."

"Thanks, but mostly I want coffee." She responded to a scratching on the screen door and went to let the dog in. The Labrador lumbered into the room, his arthritic back leg stiff as it always was in the mornings. "Did you give Andy his pill?" she asked her father.

"Not yet, but there's a chunk of liverwurst on the counter."

Helen stuffed a large pain pill into the meat and molded a sort of liverwurst cocoon around it. Andy walked over to her, opened his mouth and accepted the treat without being coaxed. Helen bent down and kissed the top of his golden head. "That'll get you through another twenty-four hours, big guy," she said.

"I'll fix you some lunch to take with you," Finn offered.

Helen shook her head. Every time she had a charter, Finn asked her if he could fix her a lunch. And almost every time, she said no. "I can't eat when I'm out there, Pop. You know that. I'll eat when I get back."

"I know what you say, but you should take a sandwich along just in case."

She poured herself a mug of coffee and sat. "Look, Pop, you know what it's like. I'm going to rig lines, cut mullet and bait hooks for four hours. It's not all that conducive to a hearty appetite."

"No, I guess not. Eat your breakfast."

She stared at two bars of shredded wheat floating in a sea of milk. Her stomach turned over. Surely she wasn't going to suffer from morning sickness. Life couldn't be that cruel. She pushed aside a glass of orange juice in favor of a small bite of cantaloupe. It settled in her digestive tract without much of a revolution and gave her courage to try the cereal. She knew she had to eat. She wouldn't see food again until after noon.

"How many are going out today?" Finn asked.

"Six. A group of accountants from Tampa." She saw a glimmer in Finn's eyes and quickly worked to extinguish it before he attempted a matchmaking scheme. "Never mind. I saw a couple of them last night in the Lionheart. Balding and overweight."

"You can't blame me for hoping." He sipped his own coffee. "I heard, you know."

Her gaze snapped to his and panic gripped her. Just what had he heard? The really big news nobody knew but her and Donny? "Oh, yeah, heard what?"

"About Donny leaving."

She relaxed, spooned up another piece of cereal.

"Pet was over last night," Finn continued. "She told me the rat left the Lionheart without even telling you goodbye."

The efficiency of Heron Point's gossip trail didn't surprise Helen. Claire's aunt Pet had been Finn's special companion for six years. She worked in a café in town and heard every bit of news that circulated around the small community. Besides that, she claimed to have psychic abilities, a talent that Helen had witnessed on more than one occasion. Pet probably knew about Donny leaving town before he'd thrown the first pair of socks into a suitcase. "It's certainly no secret," she said, adding to herself that she'd better avoid Pet or this pregnancy might register on a psychic radar screen.

"I'm sorry, Helen. I know you fancied yourself having some sort of future with that guy. But I knew he was bad news."

She concentrated on a slice of toast which she'd already smothered with three layers of jelly. "So you told me— many times."

"Ha! As if I can tell you anything. But I keep trying, at least. What kind of job is singing, anyway? Fly-by-night if you ask me."

"With Donny it's more like fly-by-day, but it doesn't matter. You won't catch me extolling his virtues any longer. I'm not sure he ever had any in the first place."

"So why did he take off?" Finn asked. "Did you and him have a fight?"

She pressed a hand over her stomach, a gesture she'd repeated quite often the last twenty-four hours. "Actually, no. I think Donny was finding Heron Point a little too crowded."

"Too crowded? What the hell's wrong with that man? We've got room to breathe in this town. This is a paradise for anyone who doesn't like cramped spaces."

Helen smirked. "Yeah, well for some men, even the addition of one more person can be intimidating."

Finn was silent a moment. "I guess I know what he means there. I've been thinking about the invasion of the Anderson clan myself. First, Jack Hogan…"

Helen paused, her spoon hanging from her hand. "You still don't like Jack?"

"I don't want to, but he's okay when you get to know him. I guess I'll have to tolerate him living here."

"Now that he's chief of police, I suppose that's very generous of you. I think he might arrest you if you tried to have him tarred and feathered."

He went on as if she hadn't spoken. "But that other one, the fella that knocked the headlight out of the truck…"

Helen dropped the spoon against the side of her bowl but didn't bother correcting Finn's version of the accident. "What about him?"

"He's an Anderson. That's a whole different story."

She leaned forward. "You know, Pop, if you ever hope to get any sympathy from me about this whole secretive thing you've got against Anderson Enterprises, you've got to give me a little more to go on. I talked to Ethan Anderson awhile last night. He's not so bad. He's kind of nice and polite. And cultured. He's not like the men around here. He cares about more than the arrival of the next beer truck."

Finn propped his elbows on the table and stared at her over his clasped hands. "You're not getting any ideas about him, are you? I can't see my daughter with an Anderson."

She practically laughed out loud. "Yeah, Pop, I'm just his type. I plan on letting him sweep me off my feet and whisk me out of this town with diamonds on my fingers."

"Don't even talk like that, Helen. I know I don't have much control over what you do, but I'd fight to my last breath to keep you out of the clutches of an Anderson."

She stood and carried her dishes to the sink. "For heaven's sake, Pop, will you please tell me what this is about? I can't even imagine how you know these people."

He wheeled away from the table. "I suppose I'll have to tell you if you've got your sights set on this fella."

"I do not have my sights set on him! Nothing could be further from reality than me with Ethan Anderson."

"Well, good."

"So you'll tell me?"

"We'll see."

"Fine, but not today. I've got a lot on my mind that requires a good bit of thinking. As curious as I am about this little intrigue of yours, I've got my own problems to take care of for now. Not to mention six accountants from Tampa."

Finn looked out the door to the porch. "Here comes Rusty. He's a good boy. Wish he was more your age."

"You're hopeless." Helen waved out the door to the kid who served as her mate on the charters. "Be right out, Rusty. You can check the rigging on the lines." She kissed Finn on his forehead. "Is there anything you need before I go?"

"I'm good."

"Okay, but here's some advice. If you're so anxious to matchmake, why don't you think about working on yourself? Pet's a fine woman, in case you haven't noticed."

"I've noticed. Quit pushing me."

"Ditto for me." Helen scratched Andy behind his ears, grabbed her coffee and her heavy-duty sneakers and headed out the back door.

"Don't forget to collect from those bean counters ahead of time," Finn called after her. "They're obsessed about getting their money's worth. I don't want them reneging if they don't catch anything."

"Right.' Helen walked toward the *Finn Catcher.* It was true what she'd told Finn. She had some serious thinking to do. Three or four charters a week barely kept the business in the black. She certainly couldn't support another mouth on what she currently brought in. And what if she couldn't keep up the strenuous work demanded of her when she was in the last months of the pregnancy? And what about when the baby was born? What would she do with an infant if she had to spend hours every day out in the Gulf? Leave it with a sixty-eight-year-old man in a wheelchair who nodded off when the wind changed direction?

The only way she could rationalize having this baby was if the charter business suddenly picked up. And that wasn't likely to happen. Things hadn't changed in Heron Point since she'd been born, except to maybe get worse. '

Unless they were about to change now....

Helen hopped onto the boat deck. She stared out over the Gulf while Rusty chattered about tackle and bait, wind speed, and all the things that should have mattered this morning but suddenly didn't. Her thoughts were on Ethan Anderson. Everybody in town seemed to think the re-opening of Dolphin Run, and Ethan and his father were the answers to Heron Point's financial problems. But as Helen watched a van pull up in front of the cottage and six men with large-brimmed hats and coolers get out, she wondered if Ethan could be the answer to hers.

ON FRIDAY AFTERNOON, Helen drove into town and parked near the Wear It Again shop on Island Avenue. The weekend crowd had started to pick up as it did every Friday. Heron Point's quirky, anything-goes lifestyle, great seafood restaurants and unique shoreline drew visitors to the island in large numbers for a couple of days of kicking back.

Like Helen with her fishing charters, the artists and gallery owners with establishments on Island Avenue made their living from the tourists. While the two-day influx of population often cramped the styles of the permanent residents, everybody recognized that weekenders were the lifeblood of the community.

Helen looked up and down the avenue. As usual for a Friday, sale signs had appeared in shop windows, and merchandise dotted the sidewalks in pleasing displays. One of her own posters advertising *Finn Catcher* Charters sat in the window of Wear It Again, the vintage clothing store owned by Helen's friend and Heron Point's mayor, Claire Betancourt.

Helen stepped inside the shop to the welcoming tinkle of dolphin chimes. Claire's nine-year-old daughter, Jane, scampered to the door, her bright brown eyes peering out from under the brim of a great straw hat laden with silk flowers. She twirled around in a circle. "Hi, Helen, what do you think?"

Helen put a finger over her mouth and stared pensively. "Positively divine, dahling. You've been invited to tea, have you?"

Jane giggled. "No. For pizza. Jack's taking us later."

"Even better." Helen glanced around the shop. "Is your mom here?"

"You bet," Claire called from the entrance to the dressing rooms. Stylish as always, her honey-blond hair pulled back into a sleek upsweep only her perfectly oval face could flatter, Claire took a hanger from a rack and handed the garment to SueAnn, the clerk who helped out on weekends. "Take this back to the second room, will you? Tell the customer I think it would look great on her."

SueAnn left and Claire came over to Helen, slid her hand through Helen's elbow and walked her to a pair of bar stools behind the checkout counter. "What's up? You want to go for pizza? Jack's treating, and I happen to know that Pet's taking dinner to Finn from the café, so you don't have to fix anything."

"I don't know. Maybe," Helen said. "Mostly I'm just here on a fishing expedition."

"Oh, really?" Claire looked around at the dated garments that filled her racks and shelves. Many of them had once belonged to celebrities. "You suddenly have an urge to splurge on a bit of Hollywood memorabilia?"

Helen laughed and looked down at her faded scoop-neck yellow T-shirt and olive-green cargo shorts. "No, but I'm fishing for information."

"Oh, well, that's free—if I have any to give."

Helen came right to the point. "What do you know about Ethan Anderson?"

Claire's eyes sparkled. "Oh, Ethan. I know he's rich, but doesn't act it. And he's handsome and can't help it."

"He's not wearing a ring," Helen said. "So I assume he's single."

Claire grinned at Helen. "Thirty-two and never been married. But from what Jack tells me, you know more about him than I do. I understand you gave him a rousing welcome to town the other day."

Helen smirked. "So, the legend of Helen Sweeney lives on."

"Absolutely. Especially since Archie Anderson told Jack to watch out for his only son while he's in Heron Point and keep him out of harm's way. Poor Jack. Ethan hasn't made it easy for him to play protector. He arrived in town without telling anyone, and when he'd only been here for a few minutes, his rental car was victimized by a drive-by mangling."

Only Claire could get away with such blatant teasing. Helen laughed. "It's not like I was aiming for him."

"I know that. Sometimes, honey, it just seems like bad luck follows you around."

That was an understatement. Helen shook her head. "You don't know the half of it. So why does the golden boy need watching over, anyway? He doesn't seem like the type to have his own bad-luck shadow."

Claire waved her hand in a dismissive gesture, and focused her attention on the day's sales receipts. "Oh, who knows? Jack tells me Archie is paranoid about crackpots taking advantage of his money and power. He thinks half the world is out to get him or a member of his family." She returned her gaze to Helen. "There's probably some truth to it."

Helen sensed there was more to Claire's simple explanation than she was letting on, but she didn't probe. "Yeah, potential trouble is everywhere, even in Heron Point, as we learned the hard way."

Claire glanced at her daughter. As Jane tried on hats, a haunted veil clouded Claire's eyes. Helen had seen a similar desperate look once before on Claire's usually placid face. No one in Heron Point would ever forget when Jane was put in danger a month ago. Though, thanks to Jack, there was a happy ending, the incident made everyone in town open their eyes to the possibility of threats, even in their isolated little paradise.

."So, why the interest in Ethan?" Claire said, returning to the more comfortable topic that had brought Helen into the shop. "Of course, I heard about Donny, the creep. Ethan's not like that. He's a gentleman…."

Helen held up her hand. "Stop right there. You're as bad as Pop."

Claire faked an innocent expression. "Whatever do you mean?"

"I'm through with men for a while, at least in the way you're thinking. Finn's right. I seem to lose all capability for rational thought when I'm around the opposite sex. Besides, I know better than to go after a man who probably dates glamorous New York women who make me look like something they scraped off their boots."

Claire gave her a scathing look. "I hate when you talk about yourself that way." She fingered a strand of Helen's limp hair. "You're gorgeous, don't you know that?"

"Right. In a she's-got-potential kind of way. But relationships aside, I would like to get to know Ethan better, for a purely practical reason."

Claire smiled. "You need another buddy, Helen?"

"Sure, who doesn't?" She sighed, knowing she'd have to level with Claire if she planned on enlisting her help. Claire was too smart to con. "Actually, I'd like him to see me as someone other than a fishy-smelling, hell-on-wheels delinquent, if that's possible."

"It's entirely possible. And you think I can help you accomplish this goal?"

Helen rolled her eyes before returning her attention to Claire's skillfully applied makeup and expertly chosen clothes, elegant yet fitting to a Heron Point environment. Claire had it all, and Helen needed some of it.

"Who else?" she said. "For heaven's sake, Claire, look at you." She swept her hands down her sides, encompassing the total ragtag package that was Helen Sweeney. "And then look at me."

Giving Helen an exasperated look, Claire said, "No problem. I can have you looking so adorable that Ethan—"

"Stop right there," Helen said, tamping her natural curiosity to hear the rest of Claire's sentence. "I already told you. I'm not going the adorable route. I couldn't if I wanted to. This is business."

Claire sat back and studied her friend. "Okay, but I've got to ask, honey. If you're not interested in romance, then what *do* you want from Ethan?"

Helen took a deep breath. She'd known Claire would ask this question, especially since hearing that Jack had vowed to keep Ethan safe. Besides that, as mayor of Heron Point, Claire would be concerned for the welfare of the man who could raise the tax base so the town council could purchase another ambulance, a fire truck, make repairs to the roads and better secure the shoreline. But Helen wasn't about to whine to Claire about her problems. Because of Donny, Helen had reconfirmed her previous belief that most men were louses, and she was often too stupid to avoid them. Now, because of her current unplanned circumstances, it was time to start thinking of Helen Sweeney. She needed to safeguard her own future, and the future of the Lima Bean if she decided to keep it snuggled in her belly.

"I want a mutually beneficial relationship with him," she said. "I want him to notice me as a serious businesswoman in this town because I intend to approach him about a financial proposition."

"A business arrangement?"

"Here it is in a nutshell, Claire. I want the charter business Ethan could throw my way once the resort is reopened. And I figure he's more likely to be agreeable to a business arrangement if he finds me a little more pleasing to his eyes. If you've taught me anything, Claire, it's that a woman who has mastered the traits of…" Helen could hardly say the words since they were so alien to her vocabulary, her way of living. "…of grace, confidence, attractiveness, can accomplish a lot more than one who just bullies her way through life because she knows how to run her mouth. I haven't cared much about any of that until now. But now it's important."

"Why now?"

If you only knew. If I could only tell you, but I can't, because I don't know how this story is going to end. "You know the charter business just keeps my head above water," she said. "Finn and I aren't getting anywhere. But Ethan and Anderson Enterprises have brought opportunity to Heron Point. Other business owners in town know that and plan to take advantage of it. Why shouldn't I?"

It was very simple, really. Other women used their wiles to get what they wanted, why not Helen Sweeney? But first she had to find those feminine traits that must be hiding somewhere underneath her coarse exterior. All Helen needed was more business and more money, which would lead to a way out of this horrible moral dilemma she'd found herself in.

Men had tromped on her all her life, and she had the emotional bruises to prove it. Now she had the chance to maybe come out the winner in a relationship. And who would get hurt, anyway? Not Helen, who, for the sake of the Bean, was determined to keep her emotions under control for once and regard Ethan Anderson only as a means to an end. Even if she learned a few tricks from Claire, and managed to grab Ethan's attention for a while, when the resort was up and running and his work here was done, he would simply dust off his Dockers, get on with his life and forget Helen Sweeney ever existed.

Helen would just have to ignore the fact that Ethan was so darned good-looking, and so, for lack of a better word, *nice*. She could really fall for a guy who was so unlike any of the men she'd dated in the past. But talk about a worthless fantasy! Helen could never interest Ethan for the long haul. He was a Manhattan penthouse and she was a cottage by the Gulf. He was a Montblanc pen and she was a fishing rod.

So she'd forget his obvious attributes and approach him on a purely rational level. And she'd have what she needed, for once, a way to support her family thanks to a few extra fishermen willing to pay three hundred bucks for a trip into the Gulf. And he'd still have what he'd always had—houses and cars and an enviable New York lifestyle.

Claire's voice brought her back from where her wishful thinking had taken her. "So, that's what this is all about? You want Ethan to take you seriously as a businesswoman and send you customers?"

"That's it. I just need an image improvement course to make it happen."

"Okay. I don't have any doubt that we can make Ethan notice you," Claire said. "Let's do it." She stood up and headed to the back room. "It might be fun. Who knows what will come of this?"

As soon as Claire disappeared into the back, the shop door opened. Jack came in, followed by Ethan. And Helen groaned. After all her elaborate scheming here she was, face-to-face with the man again, and she was still plain old Helen, a woman with a serious problem and only one hope of solving it.

Jane ran up to the man who would soon be her stepfather. "Are we still going for pizza, Jack?"

"As long as you're still picking up the tab, kiddo," he teased. He looked at Helen. "Why don't you come with us?"

"Oh, I don't know…"

"Of course she will," Claire said, entering from the back room. "You'll come too, won't you, Ethan?"

Helen stared at him, tried to decipher the unreadable look on his face. Her confidence plunged. How was she going to make herself interesting to this man if he couldn't even stand to sit across from her in a pizza joint?

Just when she was certain that half a piece of chocolate cake was all she would ever get from Ethan Anderson, he hitched one shoulder and said, "Sure, why not?"

It wasn't a rousing victory, but it was better than nothing.

CHAPTER FOUR

PETULA DEERING'S SEVEN-YEAR-OLD compact car rolled to a stop in front of the weathered cedar cottage at the edge of the Gulf. Pet got out and headed to the front door. "Three times a week," she mumbled. "For the past six years I've parked in the same spot and walked up this sidewalk at least three times a week." She stared at the old cement slabs under her shoes. "Even the cracks are the same. They've gone unpatched for six years."

Pet had moved to Heron Point to get away from routine. All her life, she avoided the ruts that trapped so many people while life passed them by. She'd even changed husbands three times, burying the last one and sending the first two packing. Yet here she was, crazy about a man who kept her tied to an emotional string, never moving forward, yet never letting go.

But in the last few weeks she'd sensed change in the air in Heron Point, and she'd begun to long for the old excitement in her own life. People in town were enthusiastic again, hopeful, and Pet was feeling it, too. Unfortunately, her biggest challenge was to get Finn Sweeney to accept that change was good, because it was way past time he admitted that he should change his twenty-five-year bachelor status and ask her to marry him. That's all she wanted, really—a firm commitment from the man she adored—and she would have all the excitement she needed.

As she approached the entrance to the cottage, Andy stood up from his spot in front of the fireplace and ambled to the screen door. He emitted a low-pitched whine of welcome when she came inside and swished his great golden tail in anticipation of her attention. While she patted his head, it occurred to her that too often there was more life in this arthritic old dog than there was in Finn. Well, maybe she could do something about that.

Finn wheeled his chair around from in front of the television and smiled. "Hello, beautiful."

He always called her by some form of endearment, and she loved that about him. She was fifty-nine years old and certainly no longer beautiful if she ever had been. But she was interesting looking. She kept her platinum hair long and tied with ribbons and leather and fancy clips. She wore ankle-length, flowing garments that masked her middle-age flaws and accentuated her still-positive qualities. She kept her lavender eyes, which Finn said either beguiled or bewitched him, depending on her mood, sparkling with penciled outlines in shades of pink and sapphire.

"Hello, handsome," she said as she walked between Finn and the television to deposit her enormous tote bag on the sofa. As she passed, he grabbed a fistful of gauzy skirt and pulled her back onto his lap. She landed with a low chortle and nuzzled her face in the crook of his neck. "It's a good thing you don't have feeling in these legs or you'd be hollering about my weight."

"Ha! I'd never complain about that. Besides, I've got feeling where I need it, and you are lighting my fire, woman."

She laughed and stood up. Okay. There were still moments of pure excitement in her life after all. "Hold that thought, old man. I've brought your dinner from work. I don't want you passing out from lack of nutrition."

She spread the top of her bag and took out a sack from the Green Door Café. "Snapper sandwich, fries and coleslaw," she said. "It was the special today."

Finn had already returned his attention to the television. "Damn news," he said. "Damn Republicans. I miss Walter Cronkite. At least he could deliver the news without depressing the hell out of a person."

Pet warmed his dinner and brought it out on a tray with a glass of iced tea. He turned off the television and began eating. "So, any news from town today?" he asked.

This was her chance. "Oh, you bet. Since that fella from Anderson Enterprises arrived, everybody's talking about the reopening of Dolphin Run."

He grunted, dipped a fry in ketchup. "Bunch of damn fools to get all riled up over an Anderson in town."

Pet ignored him and pressed on. "Everybody's making plans," she said. "The town council's talking about sprucing up Island Avenue. Larry hired a contractor to give him a quote on fixing up the Green Door's outside eating area. He wants to expand and add new lighting, maybe some of those outdoor heaters so we can keep the patio open even in the cold months.

"Claire hired a couple of guys to paint the town hall. She's picked a nice shade of peach. And I saw new porch furniture at the Heron Point Hotel today." Pet took a sip of her iced tea. "It's exciting, Finn. Really it is. Change is good, you know. Keeps us young."

Finn stared at the television as if he hadn't turned it off, his way of avoiding eye contact with her, she supposed. "Not if it means Archie Anderson is coming to town," he said. "That kind of change will ruin Heron Point, you mark my words."

Being a self-proclaimed spiritual person, Pet didn't rise to anger quickly. She'd found it easy to maintain a calm sense of being in Heron Point. This little town made hibernating bears out of the most aggressive beasts. But she was angry now. She set her tea glass on the floor, crossed her arms over her knees and leaned so close to Finn that he actually jerked back a couple of inches.

And she blasted him. "Finn Sweeney, I am sick of hearing you spew all this negativity about Archie Anderson. For over a month now you've berated the man and his company without offering one bit of concrete evidence to support your contempt." She sat back and let her gaze wander slowly over his features from the top of his head to his shoulders. "There's a bad aura about you, has been for weeks. You're under a psychic cloud, while everybody else in Heron Point is standing in the sunshine."

His face pinched up, so for a moment his bushy gray eyebrows seemed to connect with his moustache and beard. A hairy monster about to explode. "You don't like it, Petula, there's the door."

"You'd like that, wouldn't you? You'd like me to leave you alone to stew in the cauldron of discontent you're trying to brew up for this town. Well, it's not going to happen because I'm not going anywhere unless it's out to

Dolphin Run to do a little investigating of my own. I guarantee you I can walk inside that big ol' place and sense what's going on as fast as you can snap your fingers." She snapped her own in front of his face to prove her point. "I'll find out if there are ghosts around that run-down resort. I don't need you to tell me."

His brows drew together in a threatening frown. "You stay away from Dolphin Run."

"I will not. At least not until I get some answers from you."

He stared at her, his gray eyes glittering. Just when she thought steam might come out of his ears, he said, "All right then, Petula, what're the damn questions?"

Now she was getting somewhere. "How do you know Archie Anderson? Why do you hate him? What did a big financier from Manhattan ever do to you, a fisherman from Heron Point? What connection do you have with Dolphin Run? How…"

He held up a hand. "Hold your horses, Pet. You're making my head spin." He took a deep breath.

She waited.

He clasped his hands in his lap and stared at them a full minute before speaking so softly she had to strain to hear him. "Forty-seven years ago a boy drowned off the dock at Dolphin Run. And a twenty-one-year-old man tried to save him and nearly lost his own life in the process. And it was all Archie Anderson's doing." She gasped. He looked up into her eyes. "And that's just the half of it," he said.

THE ENTHUSIASTIC PARTY of five meandered among the Friday-night crowd the two blocks from Wear It Again to the Pepperoni Pit, Heron Point's only pizza restaurant. Helen lagged behind Jack, Claire and Ethan, and walked with Jane. They kept up a lively discussion about school and boys and Claire's upcoming wedding to Jack. Tonight especially, Helen enjoyed Jane's company, maybe because the idea of having a child of her own was not as remote as it always had been.

Plus, there was another advantage to walking behind the other adults. Helen decided right away that she liked the view of Ethan's back as he moved through the crowd. Having abandoned his neatly pressed pants for a worn pair of jeans and a navy-blue-and-white knit shirt, he looked almost like a local tonight. Traces of Manhattan still defined him, however. His shirt was tucked into the waistband and, in Claire's shop, Helen had noticed an embroidered emblem over his pocket. That simple knit garment had probably cost as much as Helen spent on clothes in an entire year.

Ethan was shaped nicely, too. Not like the muscle-bound cycle types who showed up in Heron Point on weekends. And not like the wiry, skinny men who lived in town year-round and drank beer and shot pool in the local taverns. No, Ethan was sculpted like a fine work of art, broad across the shoulders, narrow at his hips, rounded at his quite admirable buns. If he made money for Anderson Enterprises by sitting at a computer or attending high-powered meetings, he obviously made time for fitness, as well.

While she stared at him, he turned toward Jack, said something that made them both smile and raked his long fingers through his light brown hair. The style was neat and trim, just long enough for strands at his neck to brush the collar of his shirt. His profile was nice, too. A well-defined nose and chin, a slightly sloped, strong brow. Helen hadn't been able to study these details the night before when they'd sat in the dark on the hood of her truck eating cake. And the day she'd smashed his car she'd been too nervous to give him more than a quick once-over. But now, in the soft rays of the setting sun, Helen liked what she saw.

She shook her head to keep her thoughts from wandering in a dangerous direction. "Stop it, Sweeney," she said. "You made a promise to yourself, remember? No more…"

"What did you promise?" Jane asked.

Helen pressed her lips together and reminded herself that she was talking out loud. "Ah, pizza," she said. "I promised I wouldn't eat pizza for a while." She laughed. "I never should have promised that, now should I?"

They were coming to the entrance of the pizza shop, and Jane skipped ahead to her mother. "Heck, no."

Ethan held the door, and Claire and Jane went inside. Since Heron Point was packed with strangers, Helen didn't expect to see anyone she knew. The townies usually stayed home on Friday nights, at least during the dinner hour. Which explained her shock when she stepped into the doorway and bumped into Maddie Harrison.

"Helen! I've been looking all over for you." Holding her pizza box in one hand, Dr. Tucker's receptionist grabbed Helen's elbow and dragged her away from the door to stand in the middle of the sidewalk.

Helen groaned. What luck. When a woman was keeping a secret of enormous proportions, the last person she wanted to see was the only other human being in town who knew anything about it. She freed her arm from Maddie's grasp. "Sheesh, Maddie, you've got quite a grip for a grandmother."

"That's exactly why I have it. Because I *am* a grandmother. I haven't lost one of the little scamps yet." She pierced Helen with a concerned glare. "Why haven't you made an appointment to come back to the office?"

Helen glanced at the door, which Ethan still held open. Claire had poked her head outside, and both of them were staring at her. "Maddie, now isn't a good time," she hissed, jerking her head toward the door. "And smile, will you? With that look on your face, Claire will think you're telling me I have only two weeks to live."

Maddie dropped her voice to a whisper. "But I'm worried about you. First you come to me to buy the test. Then I hear you've been in a terrible accident."

"It wasn't like that…"

"And now, look at you. Pale, washed out. Your hair's got no shine to it."

Helen shook her head. "Thanks, Maddie. That's just what I needed to hear tonight." She looked at her evenly tanned forearm. "I'm hardly pale. I was on the Gulf for five hours today."

"Well, never mind. What did you find out?" She leaned in close. "Are you?"

Helen debated telling the truth for about two seconds, and then realized Maddie would find out anyway. "Let me put it this way. You probably should get me in to see Doc Tucker one day next week."

Maddie's bright red lips rounded as if she were singing the "Hallelujah Chorus." "How exciting!" She immediately reined in her outburst. "Of course, that's only if you're happy with the news."

"I don't know," Helen said. "I haven't decided for sure what I'm going to do."

"Okay, but you should start prenatals just in case. You don't want to take any chances."

"Okay, fine." Helen looked at Ethan, who gestured inside the restaurant. "Go ahead," she called. "I'll be right there." He stepped inside. Helen breathed easier and grasped Maddie's free hand. "You can't tell anyone, Maddie. Remember, you promised."

"I know. I won't tell. But if you need someone to talk to about this, I'm an expert."

It was a nice offer, and Helen was glad to get it. Some secrets were too big to carry alone. "I'll call you on Monday. We'll set up an appointment."

Maddie nodded and started to walk away. She'd only taken a couple of steps before she turned back around. "That fella…the one who was standing by the door just now."

"Yes?"

"Would he be the father?"

"Heavens, no! That's Ethan Anderson. He just got into town."

"Too bad. What a nice-looking young man." She frowned. "Then it must be that scoundrel, Donovan Jax, who I heard left town."

Helen didn't confirm or deny the accusation.

Maddie smiled down at Helen's tummy. "Don't worry, little one. You've got good strong genes on your mama's side. Gotta go, Helen. Pizza's getting cold." She turned and headed down the block, and Helen followed her friends into the Pepperoni Pit.

She found five chairs crammed around a table for four. The only empty seat was next to Ethan. When she saw the coy expression on Claire's face, Helen knew at once who'd masterminded the seating arrangement. She slid in beside Ethan and bumped her bare leg against his hard, denim-clad thigh. She scooted a couple of inches away. "Sorry."

He gave her an odd smile and rephrased her statement from the previous evening. "I've never heard of anyone catching anything from a pair of jeans."

A waiter brought a Coke for Jane and a pitcher of beer, which he placed in the middle of the table. Jack picked it up and poured, first into Claire's glass and then aimed for Helen's. She placed her hand over the top.

Jack laughed. "Now I know there's a full moon. You don't want a beer?"

"No. Not tonight." When he continued to hold the pitcher above her glass, she knew further explanation was necessary. Helen Sweeney never turned down a beer. "I'm still suffering from the mortification of my behavior at your engagement party."

"You were just having fun," Jack said.

Yeah, and look where it got me. "Sometimes, Jack, I have a little too much fun."

He poured into Ethan's glass. "Okay. Suit yourself."

Jane found a friend, borrowed a few quarters and went off to play video games. Jack draped his elbow over the back of his chair and said, "So, Ethan, you talk to Archie today?"

"Sure did. He hasn't stopped complaining that you're not working for him anymore."

"He's got some good men around him. And I'm here when he decides to come to Heron Point. By the way, do you know when that will be?"

"A couple of weeks. And believe me, he expects miracles before then."

Helen tucked that bit of information away. The great Archie Anderson was coming to the island to personally check out his new investment. She'd have to remember to tell Finn, or maybe not. Considering Finn's reaction to any mention of Archie's name, maybe it would be wiser not to warn him of the arrival at all. She relegated that decision to a later time because Jack's question had presented the opportunity for her to ask about the resort and plans for its reopening. "What are you going to do with Dolphin Run?" she said to Ethan.

"I'm starting tomorrow with a cleaning crew," he answered. "Mostly because I'm moving in on Sunday."

Jack raised his eyebrows in obvious alarm. "What? You're leaving the hotel? You didn't tell me that."

"I don't tell you a lot of things, Jack," Ethan said, with what seemed like forced teasing in his voice. "My rental car arrived late last night and I actually drove into Micopee all by myself this morning." He shot Helen an amused look. "Made it all the way there and back without getting a scratch on the new ride, too."

"You should have told me about your plans to move, though," Jack said.

"Seems to me I just did."

"Great."

Helen broke the uncomfortable tension between the two men with another question. "All right. You're having the place cleaned. Then what?"

"I'm meeting with a county engineer tomorrow. He's going to check out the building, make sure it's structurally safe." He looked at Jack again. "While Jack was still on Dad's payroll, he made certain the building was safe as Fort Knox with all the wires and security codes and hidden cameras. I just have to know that a guest won't fall through the second-story floorboards once we open up."

"I've never even seen the place," Helen said, thinking she might wrangle an invitation. She wanted to scope out the old building, see how many rooms it had, how many guests and potential customers for her charter business it could accommodate. "It closed before I was born."

"You'll have to stop by then," Ethan said. "How about tomorrow? You might have to dodge clouds of dust, but I'll be there most all day."

That was easy. Helen noticed Claire's suggestive smile and spoke before her friend accepted the invitation for her—one she unfortunately would have to turn down. "Can't tomorrow. I've got two charters, morning and afternoon."

"Oh. Too bad."

"What about Sunday?" Claire said. "You don't have two charters then, do you?"

"Ah, no. Only one in the morning."

Ethan took a swallow of beer. "Great. Like I said, I'm moving in, so I should be there. I'll leave the gate open so you can drive in without busting it down."

Helen snickered and Jack continued to look worried. "Is that such a good idea, Ethan? Leaving the gate open?"

"It is if you've seen Helen drive."

Even Jack laughed at that, and while the men were distracted, Claire kicked Helen under the table. *Come over before you go,* she mouthed. Helen figured Claire was arranging her first attempt at a Sweeney makeover.

"You'll have to come to our place for Thanksgiving, Ethan," Claire said. "Helen and her father will be there. Helen makes the best cranberry-orange relish."

It was a good thing the pizza hadn't arrived yet, or Helen would surely have choked on it. Before she could comment on the blatant lie, Ethan's cell phone rang. He glanced at the screen and stood up. "That's Dad now. I'll take this outside."

As soon as he'd walked away from the table, Helen speared Claire with an accusatory glare. "What did you tell him that for? I can't make any kind of stupid relish. I can barely fry an egg."

Claire grinned. "Relax. I'll make the relish. You're the one who wants to impress Ethan with the new you. Why not start by at least pretending you can cook?"

Jack looked from one to the other. "What's going on here?"

Luckily no explanation was necessary because the waiter arrived with two giant chrome pedestals overflowing with pizza crust. Ethan returned in a couple of minutes and sat down.

"Trouble?" Jack asked.

"No. Everything's okay, but Archie did say something kind of surprising."

"Oh? What?"

"Claire had just mentioned Helen and her father coming over for Thanksgiving…"

"And?" Jack prompted.

Ethan looked at Helen. "What's your father's name?"

"Finn."

"I thought so. Dad just asked me if I'd run into a guy named Finn Sweeney. I immediately connected the name with yours, of course. How do you suppose my father has heard of Finn?"

Helen set her slice of pizza on a paper plate. "I haven't the faintest idea," she said. "But lately that has been the million-dollar question."

ETHAN COULDN'T GET his father's interest in Finn out of his mind. Even after Jack paid the tab and everybody split up to go their separate ways, Ethan still wondered. He followed Helen out of the restaurant. "Do you need a lift home?" he asked.

"No. I drove my truck."

"Where'd you park? I'll walk you."

Her eyes widened in astonishment for just an instant, and he thought she might dismiss his offer. Maybe walking a woman to her car wasn't such a priority in Heron Point, but Ethan was from Manhattan. Things were different there. And besides, it was early, and he didn't mind hanging out with her a little longer. Among other possibilities, maybe they could come up with an answer to the Archie-Finn mystery.

"It's close by," she said.

He walked beside her down a narrow alley that ended after a couple of blocks at the Gulf. Her vehicle was parked near the corner, close to Island Avenue where the crowds still lingered. A few couples strolled past them heading for the water. When they reached her truck, Helen stopped, leaned against the hood.

"You feel like going a little farther?" Ethan asked, patting his abdomen. "I wouldn't mind walking off a little of this pizza."

She stuck her hands in her pockets, hunched her shoulders.

"It's too cold, isn't it?" he said, realizing the temperature had dropped since the sun set.

"It's fine," she said, pushing away from the truck. "Let's go."

They walked in comfortable silence for a minute until he said, "So what do you think is the connection between our fathers?"

"I wish I knew. I can tell you this much, Finn doesn't seem to like your dad."

The bluntness of her answer caught Ethan off guard. Nearly everyone in his circle of acquaintances liked Archie—or at least respected him. "That's odd," he said. "Do you know why?"

"Haven't a clue. But Finn will tell me when he's ready."

"When might that be?"

"With Finn, you never know. He keeps stuff inside."

Ethan frowned. Like father, like daughter. He was just thinking that Helen was about as unreadable as a blank page. Deciding he wouldn't get any more info from her tonight, he changed the subject. "Tell me about your business. Do you run the charter boat by yourself?"

"Basically. But the law requires that every public charter company has at least one mate on board. It's a good idea. In a typical trip there's too much work for one person to handle."

They reached the shore and Ethan looked out at shimmering waves that rolled from a limitless horizon to wash up on the sand. "How far out do you go?" he asked.

"It depends where the fish are. As far as we need to. At least a mile, sometimes five or six."

"What do you do with the fish you catch?"

"We operate a catch and release boat. None of the fish we bring in can be mounted as trophies. We let the fishermen haul them on board, we take their picture and then release them. If the fish is a good-eating variety, we'll sometimes bring it home, clean it and sell it to one of the restaurants in town."

Ethan wouldn't know one fish from another, but he did enjoy snapper and grouper when it was offered on a menu. "That sounds like a sporting way of doing things," he said. "So how do all the taxidermists stay in business?"

"We don't have one in Heron Point, probably because we're the only charter company in town and wouldn't send them any customers. We just don't think it's the right thing to do."

She shivered, hugged her elbows close to her sides and pushed her hands deeper into her pockets. A cool wind blew off the Gulf. The temperature away from the protection of the buildings was at least ten degrees colder than on the avenue. Ethan wished he had a jacket to offer her. She couldn't know that to a New Yorker, this was like a balmy summer night. He wrapped his hands around her arms, rubbed his palms over her skin. "You're freezing. We'll go back."

"That's probably a good idea," she said through chattering teeth.

He was forced to release her as they turned away from

the water. They'd nearly cleared the sand when they had to skirt around another couple sharing a passionate kiss. The lovers were oblivious to anyone else on the beach.

Pretending great seriousness, Helen said, "That's week-enders for you. No shame."

Ethan laughed, leaned close to her and caught a whiff of something nice, lemony and salty at the same time. Fresh, not bottled. He liked it and thought about putting his arm around her, using the chill wind as an excuse. But instead he said, "I don't know. Maybe the weekenders have the right idea."

All at once she seemed to draw away from him, stiffen, becoming a defensive version of the easygoing woman she'd been just a moment ago. Surely she hadn't taken offense at what he'd said. He didn't mean anything by it. Not really. She walked more briskly. When they reached her truck she stepped away from him, pulled her keys out of her pocket and said, "Thanks."

"You're welcome. I'll probably see you Sunday, then."

"I'll try to make it. I don't always know how long the charter will take."

"Okay. I'll be around if you decide to come over."

She got in the truck, started the engine and pulled out of the parking space. With a skillful snap of the wheel, she turned the lumbering vehicle around and headed out of town.

Ethan watched until her taillights faded in the distance. Then he made his way back to the hotel. Even after spending a couple of hours with Helen, he realized he didn't know a whole lot more about her than he had when he'd walked into Claire's shop earlier. But his interest in her had grown considerably.

HELEN DIDN'T STOP shivering until she turned onto Gulfview Road, and she knew her reaction had nothing to do with the temperature. She was still scolding herself when she pulled into the driveway at her cottage. "Watch yourself, Sweeney," she said. "The idea is to cement a working relationship with this guy, not to fall for him. You've got enough problems without letting your imagination run wild over Ethan Anderson. At least with Donny, you thought there was a chance he might stick around. You know this one won't."

She stepped onto the shellrock drive and slammed the truck door. "Sure, he seems like a nice guy," she said. "But how many times have you fallen for an act like that?" She stomped to the back porch door and yanked it open. Andy peered up at her from the hardwood floor in the kitchen. "Hello, mutt," she said.

She knelt down beside him and rubbed the thick fur at his neck. "We Sweeneys are a stupid lot, aren't we, big guy? I keep butting my head against a wall thinking some guy is going to really care about me and what I want, and, with a half-dozen doggie beds around this place, you keep sleeping on the floor. Gluttons for punishment, that's what we are. Too stupid to learn and too old to start over."

CHAPTER FIVE

ETHAN KICKED OFF HIS SNEAKERS, sat on the edge of the bed and took his cell phone out of his pocket. He pressed the single number that connected him to his father's private line in his Manhattan residence.

Archie Anderson answered on the second ring. "Hey, son, I'm glad you called back. I just got some disturbing news from Jack. He says you're moving into Dolphin Run on Sunday."

Mentally cursing Jack and the pipeline he always kept open to Archie, Ethan managed to answer in a calm voice, "That's right. I told you earlier when we talked. I'm having the place cleaned tomorrow and checked for structural problems. If everything looks okay, I'm moving in. Taking charge of the renovations is why I'm here, after all, so it only makes sense for me to live there."

"Well, sure, but I would have hoped for a little more notice."

Ethan shook his head, tamped down an angry reaction. "Why? So you can get a team of security men over there first?"

Archie responded with a nervous chuckle as he always

did when confronted with Ethan's insistence on independence. "We've been over this. I feel better knowing…"

"…knowing you've got me under twenty-four-hour surveillance? Come on, Dad, this has gone on long enough. You've got to let go of the past. I'm thirty-two years old, able to take care of myself. You've given me this responsibility. Let me handle it my own way."

"I *am* letting you handle it. I've got all the confidence in the world in you. Having a little security around the place has nothing to do with my faith in your ability to do the job you've been sent there to do."

"Right. And it has everything to do with your own paranoia," Ethan pointed out.

"It's not paranoia when the unthinkable already happened once. Then the fear is real, and the caution is justified."

Ethan had tried for twenty-two years to put the terrifying incident from his childhood where it belonged, locked into a dark corner of his mind where he wouldn't have to face it every day. Yet, despite his best efforts, Archie kept reminding him of it with his team of security experts who shadowed Ethan whenever he was out of town. "Dad, we've been over this. I was ten years old, a target for opportunists."

"Adults get taken, too, Ethan. It happens all the time."

The image of that dark, dank basement flashed through Ethan's mind. The filthy rags that bound his wrists and ankles to a rusted iron headboard, the stench of the mildewed mattress, the crumbs of a half-eaten bologna sandwich molding on the single table. Two weeks of hell, two weeks when he didn't think he'd ever see his parents or his sister again. Two weeks when he'd believed his fate was sealed, and he'd begun to pray that his captors would end it quickly. Even a ten-year-old kid knew death was better than a living hell.

Ethan blinked hard, rubbed his fingers over his forehead. "Look, Dad, I didn't call you to talk about this."

"I know. You never want to talk about it—or at least listen to me talk about it."

"I called to ask you about Finn Sweeney."

Archie's voice rose a notch. "Why? Have you met him since I last spoke to you?"

"No, nothing like that. But I have met his daughter."

"His daughter?" Archie paused as if he were reaching into the well of a memory. "That's right. I remember hearing that Finn got married, that he had a kid. What's she like?"

Ethan considered his answer. How could he explain Helen Sweeney? Bold, unpredictable, reckless? Certainly unique. Maybe he should stick to physical characteristics. Blond, blue-eyed, strong and wiry yet soft in all the right places. Despite the adjectives that popped into his head, he merely said, "She's nice."

It was a simple, uncomplicated answer that said nothing at all, so he added, "She runs a charter fishing business down here."

"That figures," Archie said. "Finn was a great fisherman. I guess his daughter helps him."

"She's out there on the water," Ethan said. "I even got the impression that she does most of the work. I'm assuming her father's getting up in years."

"He's a year younger than me," Archie said. "So, tell me. Is she pretty?"

"Helen? Yeah, I think you'd say she's pretty. Not in a New York kind of way, though. She's not sophisticated. She's more, well, unaltered. She doesn't try hard to look good. Doesn't have to. She has a natural appeal, if you know what I mean."

"I know you more than answered my question," Archie said. "Are you dating her?"

"No, of course not. She knows Jack and Claire, and we all had pizza together tonight."

"With Finn? Was he there?"

Back to Finn again. "No. Like I told you, I haven't met him. But Helen and I, we thought it was awfully coincidental of you to call during dinner and ask about him tonight. How do you know Finn Sweeney?"

"Let's just say I used to know him. It's a long story."

"Dad, it's only eight-thirty on a Friday night. I've got lots of time to hear it."

"I'll tell you when I come down there. For now, it's enough for you to know that Finn and I were acquainted way back in the fifties when my family used to vacation in Heron Point. We stayed at Dolphin Run, and Finn worked there and lived nearby."

Ethan let his father's words sink in but drew his own conclusion. "Here's what I'm thinking, Dad. You bought Dolphin Run not just because you met Mom there, but because you have some sort of connection to Finn Sweeney. And you've really aroused my interest."

Archie huffed. "I'll say it again. I bought Dolphin Run because I met your mother there. Because of Charlotte I've always felt a bond with that place, that island. Call me a sentimental old fool, but now that your mother's gone…"

"Stop right there, Dad. I know you might be sentimental, but you're certainly no fool. There's more to this purchase than just an attempt to keep Mom's memory alive."

"It's a great property," Archie said. "You've seen it. You agreed with me that it's a good investment. Once it's fixed up again, it'll bring in decent revenue, and it's a good place to entertain clients. Distinctive, out of the way…"

"Dad…"

"Okay, okay. To be honest, I might have a couple of fences to mend with regard to Finn. That's all I'm saying tonight on the subject."

Ethan knew Archie well enough to accept when a discussion had been closed. "All right. I'll talk to you tomorrow after the engineer has been out."

"Fine. In the meantime, you take care of yourself. Watch your back and let Jack do his job."

Ethan laughed, though he was tired of every conversation eventually returning to the same old topic. "Have you forgotten already? Jack's job is chief of police of Heron Point, not head of security for Anderson Enterprises."

"Right. And I'm still not happy about it. Good night, son."

"'Night, Dad." Ethan disconnected, propped a pillow against the headboard and reached for the television remote. Before he began channel surfing, he thought about what his father had said. What could Archie have done to a simple fisherman in Heron Point that still bothered him to this day? And what if Finn Sweeney didn't want to be reminded of the past? Ethan knew better than anyone that his father had a knack for dwelling on the darkest moments of a person's life. And how much did Helen know about their fathers' connection? She'd said earlier that she had no idea how Finn knew Archie. So how would she feel when Archie came to town and old wounds were reopened?

All at once the potential problems associated with renovating Dolphin Run after all these years looked a lot more serious than just fixing a few loose floorboards and updating some electrical wiring.

ON SUNDAY AFTERNOON, wearing only a bra, panties and a large towel, Helen let herself be led from Claire's frilly bedroom to her private bath. She sat on a vanity bench in front of an ornate gilded mirror and studied the ultra-feminine decor which consisted of dainty floral wallpaper, an artificial ivy dripping from a ledge over a claw-foot tub and colorful glass bottles in an open hutch stuffed with pastel towels. "You know, Claire, in the three years I've known you, I've never been in this room," she said.

"I'm glad you're seeing it now, then," Claire said. "I've come to the conclusion that it's a bit fussy for a man's taste, and since Jack and I are getting married, I may have to consider converting it to a room more sensitive to form and function."

Helen smiled. "I can help you there. Our bathroom at the cottage should give you some ideas about eliminating the fancy trim. Our decor is limited to a pair of medicine cabinets. A tan one decorated with fish for Finn, and a yellow one decorated with fish for me." She picked up a bottle of bath oil and sniffed the contents. "Mine has prettier fish, though."

Claire laughed. "Good. I'll need some tips." She aimed a spray bottle filled with water at Helen's clean hair before plugging in a hair dryer. She raked her fingers over Helen's scalp, pulling damp strands into different patterns as she checked the effect in the mirror. "I think a smooth style around your face will flatter those fabulous cheekbones."

"I'm in your hands," Helen said. "All I ever do with this mess is wash it, go in the sun and hope for the best."

Ten minutes later Helen's angle-cut hair fell in a soft pageboy from her chin to her shoulders, and Claire had moved on to makeup.

"Not too much," Helen said.

"Of course not. You don't need much. Some eye shadow, a bit of coral-colored blush, lipstick and of course mascara." She stepped back from the mirror when she was finished and gave a nod of approval. "There, what do you think?"

Helen lifted her chin, turned her face from side to side. "I like it," she said, surprising herself with the honest reaction. When she'd left for Claire's today after her charter, she'd expected to tolerate her friend's makeover attempts, thank her for the effort and resign herself to leaving for Dolphin Run as an only marginally improved Helen Sweeney. She hadn't expected to appreciate the silky feel of her hair against her neck or marvel at the glow a little expertly applied color added to her naturally bronzed skin.

"You look great," Claire said. "Now clothes." She ducked into her bedroom and returned with a floral sundress with a full skirt and pencil-thin straps holding up a fitted bodice.

Helen gawked, tried not to choke. "You're kidding, right? Me...in that?"

"It's gorgeous," Claire said.

"Yes. And it's you."

"Why can't it be you?"

"Because it just isn't, and even a guy who's only seen me a few times will know it." She frowned. "Besides, it's a party dress, not the look I'm going for."

Claire pouted in that charming way she had. "Oh, all right."

She carried the dress back to her closet and Helen followed. "Don't look so glum," she said, picking up the small duffel bag she'd carried in earlier. "I brought something to wear."

"Okay, let's have a look. Except for my engagement party, when you showed up in slacks and a jacket, I've only seen you in blue jeans or baggy shorts with enough pockets to hold a week's worth of groceries."

"Oops. Then don't get your hopes up." Helen unzipped the bag, fully expecting that Claire wouldn't be impressed with her choice of clothing. She brought out a white cropped blouse with capped sleeves and a light blue ribbon woven through a V-shaped neckline. Not exactly business attire, but for a Sunday afternoon, it was a compromise between frilly and serious. It might not be up to Claire's standards of femininity, but to Helen it was like donning a ruffled pinafore.

Claire held it up. "What are you talking about? I like it. It's cute."

"Okay. But now…" She reached in the bag again and removed a pair of denim calf-length pants. "I know. Jeans. But at least they're new. Just picked them up last week at Wal-Mart. And they're me."

Claire examined the jeans and then shook her head in a

gesture of giving in. "I suppose if you use your imagination, they could be considered a little sexy."

Helen raised her hand. "I'm not trying to be sexy, remember? I want Ethan to take me seriously."

Claire nodded. "Honey, you have to be noticed first. This outfit will work. The blouse will show off some midriff and the jeans will emphasize your flat tummy."

Yeah, while it's still flat, Helen thought, knowing that if she didn't decide pretty soon about the Lima Bean, her abdomen was going to puff out like a bloated grouper. She slipped on the clothes, stood in front of a full-length mirror and stared. She certainly hadn't achieved an uptown executive appearance, but for a fishing guide, she looked pretty good. "I guess I'm ready," she said. "Just my luck Ethan won't be there like he said he would."

"He's there. I know for a fact. Jack was at Dolphin Run an hour ago checking on things, and Ethan was right where he said he'd be."

"Hello, there. Anybody home?"

At the sound of Pet's voice, Claire went to the bedroom door. "Good. They're back. I can't wait for them to see you. In here," she called.

Pet and Jane entered the room.

"Wow, you look nice, Helen," Jane said.

"You sure do," Pet agreed. "Just a couple things missing." She took a delicate bracelet from the pocket of her skirt and hooked it on Helen's wrist. Sterling silver bell charms tinkled gaily. "It's important to make an alluring, mysterious sound," she said.

To attract a business associate? "I don't know about that."

"Trust me. Wear it. Getting a man's attention involves

more than just one sense, Helen. Now we've taken care of two of them. Sight and sound." She pulled a vial of liquid from the same pocket, removed the cork and upended the bottle on her fingertip. Waving her finger under Helen's nose, she said, "What do you think? I've been steeping lavender herbs in water for the last hour and this is the result."

"It's nice," Helen said.

She dabbed a bit behind both of Helen's ears and stroked a moist stripe down her breastbone. "That takes care of smell. Only two senses left. Touch and taste, and although I have a few suggestions I could give you, I suppose we'll have to leave those up to you and Ethan."

Helen shook her head. "There won't be any touching…."

"This is from me," Jane said, bringing her hand from around her back. "It's a dried sprig of lemongrass. Aunt Pet says you put it in your underwear for good luck."

Helen tucked the herb into her bra and then looked at each of the three women who had contributed to her trans-formation. Each face beamed with pride. "Oh, heck," she said. "I guess there's not much point in reminding you that the purpose of this visit is business?"

Pet and Jane tried not to giggle. Claire said, "Frankly, Helen, we're hoping for more."

"Then prepare to be disappointed." As Helen headed for the door, she stopped and spoke to Pet. "If you're going to see Finn later, you might want to avoid telling him about this. He wouldn't be too pleased knowing I'm going to see Ethan."

Pet nodded. "You don't have to worry about me telling him. I know well enough how your father feels about anybody named Anderson. It's a lot of silly nonsense, if you ask me. Even if Finn holds a grudge against Archie, that shouldn't affect his opinion of Ethan. I never believed the sins of the father passed to the son."

Helen had crossed the threshold, but something in Pet's tone made her spin around and face her. "What did you say about a grudge? Pet, do you know what this longtime animosity is all about?"

"What? No. I don't know anything."

"Yes, you do. Finn told you, didn't he? He told you why he hates Archie."

Pet's face wrinkled with concern. "You go on now, Helen. I couldn't tell you even if I did know something, and I'm not saying I do." She tapped a finger against her bottom lip. "Still, I'd sure like to go over to that inn sometime and see what my instincts tell me."

Helen grabbed her arm. "Ha! You do know! Well, never mind. I'll get it out of Pop myself. I don't have the persuasive techniques you have with him, but I have my ways. But it will have to wait." She smiled at Claire. "Even the new, improved Helen Sweeney can only handle one man at a time."

HELEN TREMBLED WITH a totally unexpected attack of nerves as she approached Dolphin Run. To buy time, she took her foot off the Suburban's accelerator and allowed the truck to creep along the road to the formidable iron gates. She'd passed the barricaded property many times without giving its existence much thought. But today was different. Today she was going inside.

And knowing about a mysterious connection between Finn and Archie and Archie's sudden purchase of Dolphin Run, she couldn't wait to see for herself what existed beyond the tall fence.

Still, her curiosity was tempered with anxiety about facing Ethan Anderson again. Even though she had a new hairstyle, and she was clean, fragrant and tinkling with silver bells, she was the same old Helen. Underneath the artificial trappings, the real Helen Sweeney was at home on a fishing boat. And while she considered herself an equal to any man in Heron Point, she knew she was completely out of her league with a worldly, educated man like Ethan.

Having reached the driveway, she masked her trepidation with a burst of courage and turned in. Ethan had said he'd leave the gates open for her, so she'd assumed she would proceed onto the property with no trouble. Unfortunately that wasn't the case. She braked the Suburban in front of wrought-iron gates that looked like they could be shielding a crocodile-filled castle moat. And just as forbidding were the two large males who guarded the entrance.

One of the men came to the driver's window. "Good afternoon," he said.

Helen placed her elbow on the truck door, met his surprisingly nonthreatening stare and said, "Hello yourself."

"May I see some ID?"

No one on the island had ever asked for Helen's identification before. But of course everyone in Heron Point already knew who she was. This muscle-guy in black with the dark sunglasses had no idea who was violating his space. She reached for her purse and wondered why Dolphin Run needed a security checkpoint. Nobody other than the occasional homeless person had bothered the place in the last forty-plus years. Reluctantly she withdrew her driver's license from her wallet and handed it to the Unflappable Hulk.

He studied her picture, glanced at her face and handed it back. "Mr. Anderson is expecting you, Miss Sweeney." He motioned to the other castle guard, who pushed at the center of the gates, causing them to yawn open with a rusty groan. "Have a nice day now," the guard said to her as she drove through. The gatekeeper waved as she passed by.

She continued down a palm-lined, crushed-shell lane until the truck broke through the untended landscaping and faced a pleasing three-story structure with a half-dozen gabled windows peeking out of a sloped tin roof. The color of the inn was mostly nondescript, but Helen could detect enough of the original paint in the faded siding to determine that it once had been a cheerful yellow.

She angle-parked between two late-model, six-passenger Chevrolet sedans at the base of a large wraparound porch. After taking a deep breath and staring at a massive double door stained a dark walnut, she got out of the truck. She hadn't taken two steps before the door opened and Ethan came out.

"Helen, you made it. I wasn't sure you would." He hurried down the steps, took her hand and held it a bit longer than was necessary. His slow gaze swept from the top of her sleek new hairdo and ended at a pair of sling-back sandals Claire had insisted she wear at the last moment. He said the most complimentary thing she could have hoped for. "Wow, look at you. Didn't you have a fishing charter this morning?"

She combed her fingers through her hair, experiencing renewed confidence when the strands fell around her face just as Claire had coaxed them to. "Sure I did," she said. "I just decided to wash my hands before coming over."

He laughed. "Well, you look great."

"Thanks." So did he. Wearing a pair of casual navy shorts, a print shirt with the tails out and deck shoes, he seemed as relaxed as he'd been since arriving on the island. They stood a minute without speaking until Helen pointed to the cars next to the Suburban. "Is one of them your new rental?" she asked.

"Yeah, the red one is mine." He smiled. "The rental company claimed they didn't have another Lincoln."

"I guess the other car belongs to those pro wrestlers at the gate."

Ethan rubbed his hand over the nape of his neck. "Yeah. About those guys... I guess I should tell you that there are two fullbacks at the back of the property who came with them." He tried to smile as if the situation were amusing, but Helen sensed he didn't find it so. "It wasn't my idea," he said. "They were sent from the home office to sort of secure the place for a while."

Helen recalled Jack's negative reaction when Ethan announced he was moving from the hotel into Dolphin Run. Ethan had downplayed Jack's concern, but apparently he was still being "protected," as Claire put it, whether he liked it or not. Mostly Helen wanted to know why Jack and Anderson Enterprises felt Ethan needed protection. There was a story here and Helen was as curious about the details as she was about the puzzling Legend of Finn and Archie.

Ethan took her elbow. "So, you ready for the tour?"

"Absolutely. Lead the way. I've waited thirty years to see this place."

ETHAN HAD STOPPED believing Helen would come. As the hours ticked away, he'd experienced the most inexplicable disappointment that she wouldn't show. And he'd taken out his frustration on everyone around him. He'd been less than courteous to Jack and the men Archie sent to watch the inn, and he'd been especially curt to his father—not that Archie didn't deserve to hear how Ethan felt about the hired muscle. And then Helen arrived, climbing out of that old truck and looking like, well, looking like Helen but even better. And none of those earlier irritations seemed to matter anymore.

There was definitely something different about her today. Ethan had noticed right away. She looked cute and feminine in a blouse that allowed a lacy bra to peek through and showed a slash of tempting flesh above a pair of tight denims. Plus, she was attentive to every little detail he showed her about the inn. And, if he stretched his imagination, he could even convince himself she was truly interested in him.

The other times he'd been with her, he'd gotten the impression that she merely tolerated him as the outsider who might eventually, after months of training, adapt to Heron Point life about as well as a fish would to a leash. But today she actually seemed to like him, and, for some reason, earning the admiration of this woman was suddenly very important to him.

"So that's the downstairs area," he said when they'd toured the lobby and the dining room and ended up in the kitchen. "All the rooms need updating, of course."

She lingered by a worn scrub table, which sat on a scarred planked floor under unforgiving florescent tube lights. "The appliances probably need to be replaced," she said. "But I like the furniture in the dining room. There's a store in

Gainesville that specializes in fifties and sixties furniture. That retro style is experiencing a kind of revival now."

"Really?" He leaned against a wood countertop and stared at her. Listening to Helen talk about furniture gave him an idea that served two purposes, one that would benefit the inn, and the other that would allow him to spend more time with her. "Do you go to that store often?"

"When I can. Mostly I just like going to Gainesville. It's a nice little town. At one time I thought I might live there."

The only reason Ethan had ever heard of the north central Florida town was that it was home to the University of Florida. "Did you go to school there?" he asked.

She waved off his question and focused on the floor. "You're kidding, right? You don't need a college education to bait fishhooks."

He leaned over so he could see into her eyes. "I think there's a lot more to you than fishhooks, Helen."

She smiled shyly. "Yeah, there is. I know my way around an outboard motor, too. Now, what about the upstairs?"

He gestured to the back staircase, which led from the kitchen to the upper floors. "Sure, but keep in mind that most of the furniture up there is pretty beat-up. It's all going to be changed."

He followed her up the stairs and took her into the first guest room. It had a terrific view of the Gulf from the front window, and Helen walked over for a look. She leaned on the sill and breathed in the salty air. "Nice," she said before turning her attention to the furnishings with the same appreciative eye she'd used in the dining room.

"These old dressers could be brought back to life," she said. "You might want to keep the original look of the inn for some of the suites. Maybe create several themes that carry from room to room, like a sixties' theme, a country-inn theme, maybe even a rustic-ranch theme."

He stared deep into her eyes and saw something far removed from the tough, physical existence of a charter boat operator. He saw the wheels of creativity turning. "That's a great idea," he said. "In fact, I've come up with a plan in the last few minutes since you mentioned that store in Gainesville."

Her eyes widened with interest. "Really? What?"

"I need someone to help me make this place appealing again. You could take me to that store, recommend purchases, advise me on decorating."

She stared at him as if he were speaking a foreign language. After a moment, she shook her head. "I don't know anything about decorating. I was just thinking out loud."

He took a couple of steps closer to her. She inched back until she was pressed against the windowsill. The sun, now low on the horizon, cast her hair in a golden halo, while the blue of the Gulf water created a pastel backdrop to her coppery skin. For a moment it seemed as if she were veiled in gauze, somehow surreal. She reminded him of a Monet painting of a beautiful woman blending with a perfect sunset, and he told himself to thank his sister for dragging him to the Museum of Art every year.

She inhaled a quick, sharp breath. The breeze swept her hair from her shoulders. Ethan reached for her, held her arms. "Be careful," he said. "You're awfully close."

She swallowed and tensed in his arms, but he didn't let go. Releasing her was the furthest thing from his mind.

"I'm always careful," she said, and then pressed the flat of her hand against her abdomen. "Well, almost always."

"Like now?"

"I'm not too sure about now."

"I really do need someone's advice on fixing this place up."

"You need Claire. She has impeccable taste, and I'm sure she'd volunteer…."

"No. I need you, Helen. Definitely you."

CHAPTER SIX

HE WAS GOING TO KISS HER. His hands were firmly clasped around her arms. His gaze, as intimate as a touch, connected with hers in a way that made her stomach muscles tighten. His breath was warm on her face, igniting a slow simmer in her bloodstream that could not even be put out by the breeze coming in the second-story window. Helen swallowed and realized that just an hour ago when she arrived at Dolphin Run, if anyone had told her that Ethan was going to kiss her today, she would have flatly denied it, while at the same time secretly hoping that he would.

Her eyes locked on to his—deep brown and flecked with golden sunlight.

Don't be a fool, Helen, she warned herself. At least don't be the same old fool you've been for years with men. This time was going to be different, remember? In fact, Ethan just offered you the perfect opportunity to work with him, so take advantage of it. Be his decorator, even it you don't know silk from burlap. A business relationship is what you want, isn't it? This is supposed to be your chance to save your company, build a future for you and the Bean. So, damn it, Helen, don't let your emotions take you where you have no business going. Don't let him take you in his arms, no matter how tempting those arms may be.

So why, after all that sound advice, did her face slowly tip up, her lips part, her eyes begin to close. *You've got to stop this from happening. Don't be "that girl," that Helen Sweeney whose parade of lovers and losers could stretch across the deck of the* Finn Catcher. *Don't...*

Too late. His lips were on hers, and they were soft, moist, gentle. They moved over her mouth with such sweet intensity she had to trap a moan of pleasure inside her chest. It was a perfect kiss—warm, a wee bit hungry and filled with the fascinating potential of pleasures to come. And the wonder of that kiss worked on Helen as Ethan deepened his exploration of her mouth. He lingered on her lips, teased, tasted, until Helen's mind swam with all the possibilities. If a man did this much with his mouth, just what could he do with...

His cell phone? Her eyes snapped open. With his lips still pressed against hers, he muttered, "Damn. I guess I'd better get this."

He pulled away, and Helen felt the loss. One minute his mouth was tempting hers. The next, the salty spray of the Gulf tingled on her lips. Her breath escaped in one long, frustrated sigh as he reached into the pocket of his shorts. He stared at the screen, pressed a button and grumbled, "What is it?"

His eyes narrowed. "A woman? Here? What does she want?" A pause. "I didn't order any pictures. What's her name? Hold on." He pressed the phone against his shirt front and spoke to Helen. "Do you know anyone named Missy Hutchinson?"

The sublime dizziness of a moment ago was replaced with cold, harsh reality. Helen nodded and tried to hide her opinion of Missy behind a flippant answer. "Oddly enough, your gatekeeper has our Missy Hutchinson pegged. She is indeed a picture seller. Only don't call her that. She prefers photographic immortalizer, slash cultural engineer." Helen couldn't hide a frown. "She owns one of the galleries on Island Avenue."

Helen leaned out the window and glimpsed the BMW that belonged to one of Heron Point's wealthiest women. Just as Missy always managed to maintain a respectable distance from Helen, the BMW sat far enough away from the Suburban so rust mites wouldn't attack her car's pristine gray exterior. "Missy's here all right, and you'd better see her. She won't go away."

"I'll be right down," he barked into the phone and flipped the cover shut. He raked his fingers through his hair. "Sorry."

"No problem."

"About that kiss…"

It was wonderful, she thought, but said, "Yeah, what about it?"

"I guess it came across as a little impulsive."

"You're apologizing?"

"No! I just thought maybe an explanation was necessary. I'm not usually so rash."

She scooted around him into the middle of the room. "Right. If you get those urges just talking about dressers and tables, we'd better avoid the topic of mattresses."

He smiled. "I'm not sorry I did it. I wanted to very badly, and truthfully, I hardly tried at all to talk myself out of it. I hope you're okay with it."

She smirked, leaned over a dresser to stare into a mirror. "I don't know. It depends. How was it for you?"

She caught his grin in the glass. "It was great."

"Then I guess I'll let you get away with your behavior this time."

"Good. Because if it weren't for the picture pusher downstairs, I'd probably be doing it again."

Nearly every instinct in Helen's body urged her to do whatever it took to make Ethan forget that Missy was in the lobby, but common sense and self-preservation took over. Helen had given in to her own impulses too many times in her life where men were concerned, and for what? To be left alone and pregnant and cursing the memory of every irresponsible bum who'd drifted in and out of her life. "Maybe it's good that Missy came when she did." Definitely, she said to herself. Missy Hutchinson was Helen's cavalry, riding in at the nick of time.

Ethan walked up behind her, close enough to touch. "Not from where I'm standing. Come downstairs with me. You know this Missy person. You can run interference for me."

Helen stared at the too-familiar face of her weak alter ego, the live-for-today woman who was a few seconds of increased petting away from being tempted onto that 1960s paisley bedspread. "No way. My face is flushed."

He studied her reflection in the mirror. "I see that, and I'm going to interpret it as a personal compliment to me."

He placed his hand on her waist. She spun around, pressed her palms against his chest. *Sorry, Princeton. I'm not facing Missy right now even if you're not a bum.* "You're on your own," she said. "If I go down with you, and Missy notices these pink cheeks and puffy lips, I'll have no choice but to tell her you slapped me. Is that the reputation you want in this town?"

"No, but you're the infamous can thrower. She'd more likely believe it of you."

"She already does. Most of the women in this town are scared to death of me. Come to think of it, quite a few of the men are, too."

"Doesn't surprise me."

She stepped behind him and pushed him to the door. "So you go on down by yourself, and either wow her with your charm or intimidate her with your powers of sales resistance. Either way, you'll do better than having Helen Sweeney as your wingman."

"Won't she know you're here, anyway? Your truck's out front."

"Tell her you hired me to fix the plumbing. She'll believe you."

"Okay. But you won't sneak out the back door, will you?"

"Until Missy leaves, I won't sneak anywhere."

Helen waited until Ethan had descended the stairs. Then she went down, crossed through the kitchen and entered the dining room where she could eavesdrop on his conversation. She hadn't been completely honest with Ethan because she didn't want to launch into a detailed and humiliating explanation about how Missy was the one woman in town who rubbed Helen the wrong way by just breathing. Missy somehow managed to make Helen feel inferior with just a sharp look from those beady gold eyes peering down the slope of her pointed, aristocratic nose.

No matter what Missy actually said to her, which wasn't much, Helen always imagined the woman's nasal voice questioning, "Are you ever going to amount to anything, Helen?" The truth was, Helen was never going to attain the social and economic plateaus of the Missy Hutchinsons of the world. She was never going to snag an educated, responsible husband, even if he was as boring as Floyd Hutchinson. And even if she had the Bean, her kid would never be as perfect as the gentleman and scholar of Missy and Floyd's loins, dear Bernard.

So it was better to let the similarly armed Ethan handle Missy. Heron Point Nobility meets Manhattan Mogul. It would be a clash of the Titans Helen would enjoy witnessing from the safety of the Dolphin Run dining room.

"I just know you're going to want several Missy Hutchinson originals in your inn," Missy said.

Helen peeked through the swinging door that separated her from the lobby and watched as Missy flipped through a stack of framed photographs she'd carted from her showroom. The photos were probably nice enough, but Helen always wondered how many snapshots of a sunset and a lighthouse one woman could sell. Luckily for Missy, she didn't have to sell any to maintain her lifestyle.

To his credit, as he sat on an overstuffed chair with his ankle crossed over his knee, Ethan murmured complimentary phrases as Missy gushed about shoreline images. In the end, he bought four of the photographs, a modest number in light of Missy's pressure tactics. He went to a desk and took out a checkbook.

Soon after, Helen expected to hear the brisk clip of Missy's designer mules on the plank floor as she began carrying unsold stock to her car. Instead, there was only the hiss of a zipper when she deposited the check in her purse.

"If there's nothing else, I'll have one of my men carry these samples to your car," Ethan said after a moment.

"How considerate," Missy said, "but actually I was wondering about something."

"Oh?"

"I couldn't help seeing Helen Sweeney's vehicle outside. Helen and I are old friends, of course, and since she's obviously here I thought I'd say hi."

Helen grimaced. Right. Old friends. Like two barracuda with a hapless blue crab in their sights.

"Helen's occupied right now," Ethan said. Helen held her breath. "The truth is, I've asked her to come up with decorating ideas for the inn. You know how we men are about furniture. If we can eat off it or nap on it, we don't care how it looks. I definitely need a woman's touch in this place."

Missy tried unsuccessfully to stifle a bark of laughter. "You need Helen's touch?"

"Who better? She's lived here all her life. She's in tune with the island. In fact, she's upstairs right now evaluating fabric swatches for new curtains."

Helen widened the crack in the door and saw Missy blink rapidly several times. She could only imagine Ethan's smile, since his back was to her.

"Our Helen is choosing curtain fabric?" Missy repeated in a slightly high-pitched voice.

"You bet. I should have consulted with her before buying your photographs. I hope you have a return policy. I wouldn't want to stop payment on that check if Helen disapproves."

Missy's eyes rounded. "She'll love them. Helen has always been a staunch advocate of my work."

"Good. Then there won't be any problem." He went to the door, called one of the guards and the two of them carried Missy's art to her car.

Helen leaned against the door frame and enjoyed the huge grin that spread across her face. Despite his financier persona, Ethan couldn't hide the fact that he was a nice guy. And a terrific kisser. And Helen absolutely had to stop thinking that way.

WITH FOUR PHOTOGRAPHS OF Heron Point sunsets stacked against a lobby wall, Ethan closed the door on the most persistent salesperson he'd ever encountered. He turned around, headed toward the dining room and hollered. "Helen, she's go…"

Helen popped through the door. "I know. I heard."

"You've been standing there the whole time?"

She shrugged. "I had to do something to pass the time."

"Great. So you could have walked in here minutes ago and frightened off this woman who, you claim, is scared to death of you."

"I was having too much fun listening to you compare me to Martha Stewart. Besides, I didn't want to interrupt your chance to get to know one of our local artists."

Ethan chuckled. "Like I believe that." He held up his checkbook. "Four hundred and twenty-five dollars." He pointed to the sunsets. "For something I could see for free by walking out the front door of this inn."

She studied the photos. "Come on, Princeton. You can't put a price on goodwill."

He tossed the checkbook on the desk, sank into the nearest chair and refocused his attention where he really wanted it—on all the things about Helen that had attracted him before Missy showed up. It was all he could do to keep from yanking her into the chair with him. Suddenly the photographs didn't matter. Missy Hutchinson didn't matter. Having Helen on his lap and following through on his promise to kiss her again did.

What he'd started to tell her upstairs was true. He wasn't particularly impulsive. At Anderson Enterprises, he was considered the calm, logical one, the go-to guy who could be counted on for deliberate decision making and good judgment. He examined both sides of a question and didn't spend a dollar of company money without believing it was a dollar well spent.

And yet all he'd been able to think about since Helen walked in the door today was, well, Helen. For the last two hours he'd been subtly comparing her to every sophisticated Manhattan woman he'd dated in the last ten years and finding Helen much more fascinating. He liked listening to her talk, letting her make him smile. And he'd more than liked kissing her and imagining himself doing a lot more than that. This woman who'd run him down on the road and tried to make him think it was his fault had grabbed his attention and fired his libido. So what was he going to do about it?

Start listening to what she was saying, for starters.

"…not so bad. She could have talked you into a photograph for every guest room."

He blinked his mind into focus. "Not so. You were listening to our conversation, so you know I've passed decorative decisions to your shoulders."

She nodded at the checkbook. "Hey, it's still your money, boss."

He laughed. "Boss? That's a good one. Does that mean you're going to work with me here at the inn?"

She crossed her arms over her chest. The flimsy little blouse strained against her breasts. Ethan swallowed. "I suppose I'll have to," she said. "Otherwise you'll let every huckster in Heron Point take advantage of you."

"Good. Let's start now."

"Can't. Gotta go."

The disappointment he felt was beyond what was reasonable. "Why? You have a charter tomorrow?"

"No, but I'm going fishing. My mate and I go out on off days for grouper and snapper and sell the catch to the local restaurants. A girl's got to make a living."

"What about your father? Doesn't he go out?"

She gave him an odd little smile. "That's right. You've never met Finn. He'll answer that himself on Thursday at Claire's Thanksgiving dinner."

"I'm not going to see you until then?"

"Who knows. It's a small town." After searching the desk for a piece of paper and pen, she jotted down her phone number and handed it to him. "That's the number to our cottage. Call me if you get any urges to buy painted coconut faces and I'll stage an intervention."

"What's your cell number?"

"Don't have one. I figure as long as everybody else has cell phones, what do I need one for? This town has two thousand people and probably five hundred cell phones. I can usually find one to use."

Thanksgiving suddenly seemed like a long way off. "I guess I'll see you on Thursday, then. I'm looking forward to that cranberry-orange relish you're going to bring."

She released a sputter of laughter. "Right. I've got to make that stuff, don't I?" She opened the door but looked once more around the lobby before leaving. "Thanks for the tour. There's a lot about this place that shows potential."

HELEN CLOSED THE DOOR and hurried to her truck. Her face was burning with a sudden spike in her internal thermometer. She was trembling. She was smiling. She was scared. "You dodged a bullet that time, didn't you, Helen?" she said as she climbed into the truck. "Okay, so maybe he likes you a little, but watch yourself. What good will it do you and Finn and the Bean if you go all crazy and end up liking him more?"

ON MONDAY AFTERNOON, HELEN sat in a chair on the other side of a large mahogany desk and waited for Dr. Tucker. When he came into his office, he carried a file folder that held a record of Helen's medical history since her bout with chicken pox twenty-five years ago.

He walked around the desk and set the file on top before sitting in a comfy chair and tenting his fingers. "It's positive, Helen. Congratulations."

She refrained from answering with one of her trademark sarcastic comments. "Gee, thanks."

"So, generally, how are you feeling?"

Helen looked into the doc's kind gray eyes and fought tears. She'd known what the result of this visit would be, but hearing Dr. Tucker congratulate her made her predicament seem even more dire. And celebrating the life-altering news didn't seem appropriate. "Fine. At this point I wouldn't even know I'm pregnant."

He smiled as he opened Helen's file and tapped a pencil

on the latest entry. "The test doesn't lie, Helen. You are indeed pregnant."

"Right."

"Does Finn know?"

"Heavens, no! No one knows except for Maddie and now you, and I want to keep it that way."

He nodded. "So what are you going to do?"

"I'm still weighing my options."

"May I ask what those options are?"

A number of smart answers popped into her head. Everything from, "Gee, I thought I'd move into a Paris loft until the baby's born," to "I'm deciding on what dress to buy for my wedding ceremony." But this was Doc Tucker. He cared about her answer, and besides, he wasn't known for his sense of humor.

Instead she said, "I suppose you know what they are."

He passed his hand over a crown of coarse white hair. "Do you want this baby, Helen?"

That was the million-dollar question. And lately, the answer had been, *more than anything.*

"Because if you do, you should start considering some lifestyle changes."

Tell me something I haven't agonized over for the last five days.

"I wouldn't advise running your charters during the last trimester."

She slumped in her chair. "I'll take that into consideration."

He sat forward, resting his elbows on her file. "I know you must be thinking of abortion, but Helen, there is another option if you don't want the responsibility of this child." He paused, perhaps waiting for her to deny the possibility of ending the pregnancy. When she remained silent, he said, "You could put the baby up for adoption."

Let someone else cultivate her Bean? It would probably be best for the kid. A nice home, two parents, an education like Helen never had herself and probably couldn't afford to give her deprived offspring. She clenched her hands in her lap and stared at them. The sacrifices she'd made in her life came flooding back, not so she'd feel sorry for herself, but so she'd consider what she'd given up when deciding what was best for the Bean. But she'd become selfish in the last days, and she didn't know if she could give this up, too.

Dr. Tucker stood. "Well, this doesn't have to be decided today. You have a little time. If you decide on aborting, I can't perform that procedure for you, but I can suggest a facility that would. If you decide on adoption, I can help you with placement." He gave her his warmest smile, indicating that his true preference for her situation was still to come. "If you decide to have the baby, then, God willing, I'll be here to help him into the world."

She rose from her chair. "How much do I owe you for this visit?"

"The test is twenty dollars. The advice is free."

"Thanks."

He wrote something on his prescription pad, tore it off and handed it to her. "You need to start prenatal vitamins now. And as time progresses, you'll have to see me once a month, more often if necessary."

She took the prescription, which meant that to avoid gossip, she'd have to drive into Micopee to have it filled.

"Okay." She headed for the door. Dr. Tucker stopped her with his steady, soft voice.

"Remember, Helen, I'm here. If you're determined to deal with this on your own, you might need someone to talk to. You come in anytime."

Her eyes welled up. She turned around and looked into his kind face. And she did something the prepregnant Helen would never have done. She crossed the room, went around his desk and hugged him. Then she left the office and mumbled under her breath, "Damn stupid emotions."

She supposed that hug was a defining moment in her life. By the time she reached the Suburban, she knew she was going to have this baby.

HELEN DIDN'T WANT TO go home and clean up the *Finn Catcher* after her trip into the Gulf that morning. She didn't want to drive into Micopee right now, either. She needed to accept her decision and steady her nerves. Cruising the narrow two-lane road to the county seat wasn't the way to do that. There were always too many drivers on the thirty-mile stretch who weren't any better at operating an automobile than she was.

She stood on the sidewalk and looked across the street. The door to Claire's shop opened, and a customer came out carrying a sack. Claire held the door and waved to the tourist as she walked to her car. Then, spotting Helen, Claire motioned her over.

Yes, visiting Claire for a few minutes would be good. Helen wouldn't have to think about the Bean, wouldn't have to weigh the consequences of her decision until later. She entered Claire's store and found her friend behind the counter sliding two cups into the microwave. "Want some tea?" Claire asked.

"Sure. Thanks."

"Sit down. Talk. Tell me how it went yesterday."

"You really want to know?"

Claire put a fist on her hip and just stared.

"Okay, then. It was awful."

"What? I can't believe it. Ethan didn't think you looked terrific?"

"He did, actually."

"Then what's the problem?"

The microwave beeped. Helen waited for Claire to take out the mugs and drop in tea bags. "Well?" Claire prompted.

"You made me look too good. Ethan kissed me."

"He kissed you?" Claire slid a cup across the counter to Helen. "That's wonderful."

"No, it isn't."

"Why not? He obviously likes you. Isn't that what you wanted?"

"Well, yes and no. I wanted him to like me enough to send customers to the *Finn Catcher*. But I certainly didn't plan on liking him."

Claire pretended that taking her tea bag from the mug was the most important thing on her mind, but her subtle grin said otherwise. "Oh, honey, this is just too good."

"It's not good at all, Claire." Helen dropped her tea bag into a wastebasket. "What the hell is wrong with me, anyway?"

"What do you mean?"

"It seems like I fall for every new guy that comes into town. Why haven't I learned from my miserable track record? Last year there was that sleazy developer who wanted to establish a permanent carnival at Point Park."

Claire waved off Helen's guilt with a flick of her manicured hand. "You never slept with him, so it doesn't count."

"Thanks for that, anyway. But what about the year before? I went crazy for that insurance salesman who bugged the hell out of everyone for two weeks."

"Well, that's understandable. He was a slick con artist and you couldn't help yourself. And besides, you gave him the boot before anything developed."

"And then, of course, there's Donny, the worst of the lot."

Claire sipped her tea and set her mug on the counter. "Yeah, well, I admit that he was a serious breach in judgment. Jack and I always knew he wasn't good enough for you. But he's gone and no harm done."

Those words, spoken so innocently, sliced a pain right into Helen's heart. "But don't you see? I can't do this anymore. I've got to act more responsibly. And that means I can't get my hopes up over a man who's either a loser—"

"Ethan is certainly no loser."

"Okay, but—" Helen held up a finger to silence her friend "—or another in a series of guys who's just hanging around until his work is done or he tires of this place, and me, and takes off."

Claire reached over the counter and covered Helen's hand with her own. Helen felt the comforting touch all the way to her toes. "I know it's scary to let yourself love again, Helen. Believe me, I know. I wish I could give you a guarantee about Ethan. But I can't. All I can say is that he wouldn't be the first Manhattan transplant to decide to stay in Heron Point. Look at Jack."

Helen tried to smile. Everything had worked out so well for Claire. Jack was one in a million. And Claire was gorgeous, smart, wealthy in her own right and a completely decent human being who would never be careless enough to get caught in a situation like Helen's. What man wouldn't give up his job, his Manhattan apartment, his lifestyle for her?

"Sure," she said, determined not to let her problems ruin Claire's efforts to cheer her. "You're right. Anything can happen. But you're not going to blame me if I play this one a little more cautiously, are you?"

"No, honey, of course not. You do what you have to do to protect that big heart of yours."

Helen drank her tea, letting its warmth settle in her stomach and nurture the Bean. *If you only knew how close my heart is to breaking, Claire.*

For the second time in an hour, Helen was close to tears. *You're losing it, Sweeney,* she said to herself. *Just when you can't afford to.*

CHAPTER SEVEN

ON THURSDAY AFTERNOON at one o'clock Helen pulled in front of Tansy Hill Cottage, the century-old yellow bungalow Claire had purchased and restored when she came to Heron Point over three years ago. Like many of the original settlers' houses, this place was known to everyone in town, including the postal workers, by a name rather than an address. "Tansy" was derived from the many herbs that had been growing behind the cottage for decades. The garden was still maintained by Pet, who lived in separate quarters behind the main house.

Helen loved Claire's little home—its prettiness, its charm, its complete, unabashed femaleness, which shouldn't have suited Helen at all, but did. In fact, she'd already decided she wasn't going to like the changes Claire would probably make to her sweetly scented, fussy cottage once the incredibly male Jack Hogan became the king of this castle.

Besides Tansy Hill, Helen also had a great fondness for Thanksgiving, which was odd, too, since Helen hardly ever cooked and never paid much attention to what she ate. But Thanksgiving came in autumn, and no season was more splendid than autumn in Heron Point. So she'd made up her mind to put her problems to rest for today, at least, and just enjoy the food and the cozy surroundings—and Ethan Anderson, if he showed up.

She got out of the truck, came around to the passenger side and pulled the wheelchair lift from under the chassis so Finn could activate the electric mechanism. He opened the door, waited for the ramp to reach the level of the floorboard, and rolled his chair into place. The lift brought him down to street level and he maneuvered himself onto the pavement.

"Don't forget to let Andy out," Finn said before proceeding up the sidewalk to the cottage.

"I won't forget him." Helen reached in the window and patted the Labrador's head. "But it's only polite to wait for an invitation." She knew one would be forthcoming. Andy was always invited into Tansy Hill on holidays.

Following the wheelchair, Helen leaned over her father's shoulder. "You behave yourself today. No comments about Anderson Enterprises in front of Jack and Ethan."

He grunted. "I will, for your sake."

"Not just for mine," she said. "For Claire's, since this is her house, and she's worked all day to prepare this dinner. And for Pet's, as well, since she's got the biggest heart of any woman in Heron Point to have put up with you all these years." Helen noticed the colorful cutouts taped on Claire's windows. There were turkeys and pumpkins and smiling scarecrows. A bunch of Indian corn tied with a giant gold bow hung at the front door. "And for Jane, because—"

"You've made your point," Finn grumbled. "All you women are saints, and we men are the trials you have to put up with."

Helen smiled. She hadn't exactly thought of it that way, but she wasn't about to argue. "Not all men," she said, testing the wooden ramp over the porch steps that miraculously appeared whenever Finn was due to arrive. She went behind the chair to guide it. "But there's certainly one I can think of."

Jack opened the door and helped bring the wheelchair over the threshold. Jane ran out to the porch to intercept Helen. "Where's Andy?" she asked.

"He's waiting in the truck. You know he can't come in unless you get your mother's permission."

Jane looked in the house at her mother, who'd just set a bowl of snacks on the coffee table. "Mom? Can he, please?"

"Of course. It's Thanksgiving. We can't leave Andy to fend for himself."

Jane slipped her hand into Helen's. "Come on. Let's get him."

As she headed back to the truck, Helen glanced down at her once-a-year skirt, the swirly velvet one printed with autumn leaves. She'd bought a gold silk blouse to wear with it this year, a purchase she couldn't resist when she'd seen it in the window of the dress shop next to the drugstore in Micopee. She supposed both garments would be covered with dog hair once she hauled Andy down from the truck. She opened the door to the cargo area and Andy trotted over as best he could. When he saw Jane, he wiggled his entire back end. "Let's go, big guy," Helen said, preparing to lift his bulky weight.

Her task was interrupted when a red Chevrolet pulled up behind the truck and Ethan got out. "Can you ladies use a hand?" he asked.

Helen's knees went weak as she immediately recalled why Ethan was on her list of reasons this Thanksgiving would be memorable. She looked at Andy. She looked back at Ethan, and realized that if anyone should avoid dog hair it was this man. Dressed in charcoal slacks, a dove-gray shirt and black sports jacket, he was a magnet for any furry beast that wasn't especially well-groomed. Besides that, Ethan made a usually sane woman oblivious to the continued licking from a sandpapery canine tongue.

"You trying to lift him out?" Ethan said, accurately summing up the situation.

Helen jerked her hand back to let it air-dry until she found soap and a towel. "Yes. He's got arthritis, so the spirit is willing, but…you know how that goes."

Ethan reached around her and stroked Andy's head. "Here, I'll get him out."

"He sheds," she said.

"I brush off." As if he'd lifted eighty pounds of squirming weight before, Ethan wrapped one arm under Andy's neck and the other under his hindquarters and lowered him to the ground. Once out of the truck, Andy forgot his rescuers and loped up the sidewalk after Jane.

Ethan closed the door to the Suburban, took Helen's arm and turned her toward the house. "Happy Thanksgiving."

"You, too."

He sniffed the air. "It smells good out here."

"Claire's cooking."

"I don't know. I was kind of thinking it was you."

She smiled up at him. "I'm so pleased you noticed. I took a bath in chicken broth. It's a Thanksgiving tradition at our house."

"You really know all the tricks to drive a man crazy, don't you, Miss Sweeney?"

Mostly I know the ones to drive him away.

When they reached the porch, Ethan plucked Andy's fur off his jacket before going inside. A cool fall wind mussed his hair, and for the first time Helen noticed sunlightened streaks running through the light brown waves curling over his collar. Already a trace of Heron Point kicking back was infiltrating that manicured Manhattan sophistication. A little more island adapting, and he'd be just about perfect.

And since she certainly couldn't think about how nearly perfect he was already, she said, "Just wait till you taste that cranberry-orange relish."

THREE HOURS LATER, THE meal was over, the cook had received enough compliments to almost make the job worth it and Helen had confessed that she wouldn't know what to do with a cranberry if someone gave her a bushel of them. Jack and Finn nursed cups of coffee while they watched a football game. And Jane had fallen asleep on the floor with her head on Andy's full stomach.

Ethan came into the kitchen where Helen and Claire had just finished overloading the dishwasher. "What do you say to a walk?" he asked Helen.

She glanced at Claire, who immediately said, "Go. There's nothing more to do here, anyway."

"Walk into the herb garden," Pet said. "I've planted some marigolds and asters around the gazebo. It really is lovely out there."

As she and Ethan went out the back door, Helen heard Pet

whisper to Claire. "There's something different about Helen today. I can't put my finger on it, but her aura has changed."

Oh, great. Just what Helen had feared. Pet's psychic baby radar might be zeroing in on her secret. She began walking briskly to get away from the bungalow and hoped Ethan hadn't heard the observation, too.

"What do you suppose Pet meant by that?" Ethan said, keeping pace with her. "What's different about you today?"

Among his other attributes, the man obviously had annoyingly good hearing. Helen tried to laugh off the question, and kept her gaze focused straight ahead on the gazebo. "It's this silly skirt," she said. "No one ever gets used to me wearing it, even though it comes out of the closet once a year like clockwork."

Ethan held her elbow as she climbed the steps to the wood-planked deck. "The skirt's nice, but I don't think that's what she meant. You do seem different today. You're mellower, somehow. More relaxed than I've seen you."

Relaxed, ha! Thank goodness the man couldn't tell her heart had been hammering like crazy since he'd suggested they take a walk. "Of course I'm relaxed," she lied, trying to prove it by perching on a bench. "It's Thanksgiving. All that tryptophan in the turkey would mellow out King Kong."

He smiled, sat beside her. "I was hoping I might have had something to do with it."

"You?"

"Sure. When I met you, you were barreling around a corner like the devil was on your rear bumper. A day later you were hurling cans at a sailboat. But Sunday and today, you've been more…"

"Normal?"

"Whatever *normal* is," Ethan said. "But I like that I don't have to duck anymore when I'm around you." He angled his body so he could see into her eyes. "I know about that guy, the singer, the one that left town."

"You and everybody else."

"I figure he's the reason you were so angry."

"He had a lot to do with it."

"Did he hurt you that much? Did you love him?"

She looked closely at him, searching his features for a reason to be indignant at the personal nature of his question. But all she saw in his eyes, in the slight furrowing of his brow, was that honest-to-goodness sincerity she'd come to associate with him. And since he had kissed her, and said he'd wanted to again, maybe she should answer his question.

"I cared about him," she said. "I thought we might have a future, actually. We'd made some plans, impractical ones, but plans nevertheless."

"I understand. It can be rough when you prepare for something and it never materializes."

Or when you're not prepared at all for something and it happens, anyway.

"I might have thought I loved him," she admitted. "But I know now that I didn't. At least I don't anymore. I could never love anyone who wouldn't take responsibility for…" She clamped her lips together. *Good grief, Helen, what are you about to say?* "…who would take off like he did." She exhaled a breathy little laugh. "But, hey, I should thank him. He taught me a valuable lesson."

"And that is?"

"A girl has to be careful, safeguard her heart. Donny taught me to be more cautious in my relationships."

Ethan gave her sympathetic smile. "So that's the difference in you? This increased caution where men are concerned?"

"Yes. Maybe. I'm trying."

He looked away, focused on the deck as if he were counting the nails that held it together, and said, "Too much caution can be a bad thing, Helen. It can smother you, keep you from taking any chances at all. Keep you from living."

"That sounds like the voice of experience."

"It is. Caution, like anything in excess, can cripple a person."

Helen thought of the guards surrounding Dolphin Run, Jack's nearly obsessive concern for Ethan's welfare, Claire's references to Ethan needing protection. She realized she probably should exercise a bit of caution right now and keep her mouth shut. But that had never been her way. "You're talking about that security team, aren't you? Those guys your father sent to watch over the inn."

"That's one way of stating it," he said. "But the truth is, they're here to watch over me."

She touched his arm below his rolled-up shirtsleeve. He looked into her eyes and she smiled. "Tough break, Princeton. Too bad you weren't born poor like me, then nobody would worry about you."

"Right. Some people have all the luck."

She curled her fingers over his arm. "So, something must have happened to you, Ethan, something that made your father want to surround you with high-priced muscle. I'm a changed woman, remember? We just heard that from Heron Point's resident psychic. The old can-hurling Helen Sweeney might not have cared about someone else's problems, but I'm the new, hopefully improved version today."

"So what are you saying? You want to hear my sob story?"

"Why not? Besides being the most sensitive, sympathetic woman you've ever met, I'm also nosy, so I'm the perfect one to unload on. I'll listen to every word you tell me, and, lucky for you, the only other living being who ever listens to me is Andy, so your secret's safe."

"It's not very good dinner conversation."

"I stopped eating an hour ago."

"I've never told a woman…."

"Look, Ethan, you can waste all your breath talking yourself out of talking, or you can just start at the beginning. Either way, I'm not going anywhere till you run out of steam."

HE WANTED TO TELL HER, not the most unpleasant details of his captivity, but at least a condensed version of the worst two weeks of his life. For twenty years he'd wanted to tell someone about what happened to him, someone who wasn't a family member and would cry at the first mention of the ordeal. And someone who wasn't a paid medical professional who specialized in treating traumatized children. He simply wanted to tell his story to a person who would listen without overreacting and perhaps connect without pitying. And it would be nice if the someone he picked cared a little about him.

Of course, he couldn't be sure Helen cared about him at all. She'd just hinted that maybe she did, but did he really know Helen well enough to determine if she was telling the truth? He tested her sincerity by saying, "So, this is mostly about you just being nosy?"

She kept her hand on his arm. "No. I'm not nosy in general, and not about everybody. Ask anyone in town and they'll tell you that Helen Sweeney is mostly apathetic. But for some reason I'm nosy about you, and that, my friend, translates to genuine concern."

There, she'd almost said it again, and for now it was enough. What was he afraid of, anyway? He'd tell her about the reason for the guards, and she'd either stay or run. He'd either see her again or he wouldn't. She'd either look at him the same way, or he'd recognize the familiar, god-awful pity in her eyes. Whatever her reaction, he hoped it wasn't that, because he didn't pity himself and didn't want anyone else to, either. What happened to him was over long ago, and he could talk about it with a detachment he'd learned years before.

No matter how she responded, he'd still do his job. He'd still leave when it was finished. And what had he and Helen shared so far that was too much to risk? A couple of conversations, a piece of chocolate cake, one kiss. That wasn't a lot, especially if he didn't consider that the kiss had kept him tossing in bed the last three nights anticipating this Thanksgiving dinner as if he were a starving man.

"Ethan? You still here?"

Her voice brought him back from his private debate. "Okay. Here's the reason for the muscle," he began. "Do you remember when you were ten years old, Helen?"

She gave him the Helen smirk. "I try not to. It's the year my bike was stolen and I bought my first bra."

"Right. Normal things, good and bad, happen to ten-year-olds. That's the way it should be. In fact, at ten, even though we're the center of our own universes, we don't think of ourselves as especially important to the rest of the world. We play, we complain, we do our homework and never consider that anyone views us as any different from the ten-year-old kid at the next desk or next in line in the batter's box."

She nodded. "I suppose that's true, for kids who aren't the ten-year-old sons of Archie Anderson."

"But at that age, I didn't know my father was anybody special. To me he was like the other dads in the bleachers who never missed a Little League game. The day I hit a line drive triple that brought in a ninth-inning winning run, I saw him cheering, accepting the congratulations of the other parents. And I saw the guy waving to me from beside the dugout, the one who was smiling and holding his hand up in a high five. I slapped a lot of hands in that triumphant minute of my life, but when I slapped his, it was my biggest mistake."

"Why? Who was he?"

"His name was Alonzo Vincetti, but I didn't learn that until weeks later. For the next two weeks I only knew him as the man who dragged me behind a van, stuffed me into a bag and threw me into the cargo area. The next time I saw him was in a courtroom."

Her voice trembled as much as the hand she pressed against her chest. On a whisper of choked breath she said, "You were kidnapped."

"Yep. Alonzo brought me in, but it was his two brothers who kept me entertained for the next fourteen days."

"Oh, my God, Ethan. Did they hurt you?"

He stared at the thin, strong fingers that curled gently over his forearm and remembered those other hands, sinister, cruel ones, and realized how far he'd come. Those professionals had helped. For a while after his rescue, he'd recoiled from the touch of another human being. Today, he found strength and compassion in Helen's touch. "Let's just say that the brothers weren't too concerned with my complaints about the accommodations."

"I can't even imagine something so horrible. How did you survive?"

That was a question he'd asked himself many times. And the answer still wasn't clear. Physically he'd survived on bits of food and swallows of water stingily provided by his captors. Mentally he'd survived by not being in the basement, not hearing their voices, not giving in to the cold, sick knot of fear always in his belly, not feeling what they did to him. Not feeling...anything.

But to Helen he said, "I just did. And then one day it was over. There was a lot of noise, loud footsteps above my head, shouting. The police came to get me. It happened so fast. One minute I was in that basement. The next, my dad was reaching for me with tears streaming down his face."

Helen drew her lower lip between her teeth and blinked hard. "How did they find you? Did your father pay a ransom?"

"In the end it was damn good detective work. The funny thing was, the kidnapping wasn't just about the money. The Vincetti brothers asked for a ridiculous amount, but mostly they wanted revenge. They made my father wait, sweat it out. One of them had worked for my dad, and they had a disagreement. Dad fired him, and I guess it ticked him off."

"And you paid the ultimate price."

"I suppose, but I learned an important lesson. I learned

that life for a ten-year-old isn't always about driving in the winning run."

Helen raised her hand to his cheek. Her palm was slightly rough, like a worn blanket, and warm. "But it should be, Ethan."

"Yeah, it should be. And while I criticize my father for still overreacting after more than two decades, I can't imagine that I would be much different. In fact, knowing what my folks went through, I've pretty much decided that having kids of my own just isn't in my future."

Her cheeks flushed. Her lips trembled when she said, "I think you'd be a great father."

"I don't know. When something bad happens, there can be such heartache." He stared into the distance, lost in private thoughts. "But if I ever do have a child," he finally said, "I'll definitely remember that when he reaches thirty, it's time to cut him some slack." He laughed. It came out as a low, rumbling sound that felt good in his chest. "I'd let him go on dates without a pair of two-hundred-fifty-pound macho men backing him up."

Helen looked over her shoulder. "There's nobody here now." She narrowed her eyes. "You don't have one of those GPS tracking chips implanted in your skull, do you?"

"No. I told the boys that I would be with Jack today and they should feast on turkey at the Heron Point Hotel. It was easier than ducking out a back door or leaving Dolphin Run in a disguise."

Helen tucked her legs under her skirt and leaned against the wall of the gazebo. "I'm glad you felt like you could tell me about what happened to you. I've never met your father but I feel like I understand him."

"You're the only Sweeney who does, apparently."

"True. But maybe if Finn knew this story, he'd feel differently. After all, they are both fathers. What about your mother? How did your ordeal affect her?"

"That was the worst part. When I was freed, my dad took me to see her in the hospital. She'd been there for eight days. The anxiety and worry nearly killed her, and doctors kept her sedated. She knew who I was when I came in her room, though, and she nearly collapsed with relief. I felt terrible for putting her through all that pain."

Ethan paused, reflected on the confession he'd just made. It was the first time he'd ever verbalized that emotion. The first time he'd ever admitted to feeling guilty for what his kidnapping had done to his mother. It hadn't been his fault, of course. He knew that on a rational level, but guilt wraps its claws around a person in strange ways and can make the victim feel like the perpetrator. Never before had Ethan recognized his own misplaced culpability in his mother's decline. The realization was both sad and liberating at the same time. Maybe now that he'd said it, he could put it to rest.

"So she was all right after you came home?"

"In a way. She was released from the hospital, and we were a family again. But she was never strong after that. She developed some dependency issues. But underneath all that she was probably the kindest woman I ever knew. She died two years ago. She was only sixty-five." As an afterthought, he added, "My dad still grieves for her. He always will."

Helen folded her hands in her lap and looked out over the wild varieties of growing things and Pet's hand-printed signs that identified their type and purpose. "My mother left when I was four. I hardly remember anything about her, just pieces of images, like a fast-moving slide show."

"She left you?"

"Actually, she left Heron Point. Leaving Finn and me was a by-product of that. She'd fallen for a man she called a cavalier in a wheelchair, but she needed the world to survive, not just this little corner of it. She was a reporter."

"Was?"

"She died covering a story in the Middle East."

"Wow. How did a woman who needed that kind of adventure in her life end up in Heron Point in the first place?"

"My father was a story. She heard about this fishing guide who nearly drowned when he was a young man and suffered a permanent back injury. Despite the infirmity, he became a pretty colorful character. He still is. Anyway, she came here to interview him and fell in love. They married, she got pregnant and, to her credit, stuck it out for four more years."

Ethan thought of his own mother and couldn't help resenting the woman who had given birth to Helen. When a woman decides to have a kid, she should know it's a lifetime commitment, not a four-year test of her ability to adapt to a new environment. He kept quiet, though. It wasn't his place to disparage Helen's mother.

"So that's how Finn ended up in the wheelchair?" he asked. "The near-drowning accident?"

"Yes. It seems ironic now, but it happened at Dolphin Run, probably near the end of the inn's operation. He was pinned between the hull of a boat and the dock, causing irreparable damage to his spinal cord. A Christopher Reeve injury, though not as severe."

"He hasn't walked since?"

"Nope. A few years ago he gave up going out on the boat, too. Left the operation to me with the help of a mate."

So, he'd been right. Helen did most of the work on the charters. Ethan hadn't known until today that Finn was confined to a wheelchair, so he hadn't mentioned the disability to his father. He wondered now if Archie knew about the accident.

Helen sighed. "It looks like our families have had their share of tragedies."

"It sure does." He reached over and picked up Helen's hand. "I don't know about you, but I think it's time we got to the bottom of this mystery about our fathers and find out what connects these two men."

"I agree, and if they won't tell us, I know who will."

Ethan arched his brows in question.

"Pet. She knows what's going on, and I can get it out of her." She frowned. "Unfortunately, Pet often knows too much, so I have to be careful not to reveal more information than I receive."

Ethan chuckled. "You have secrets, Helen?"

"We all have secrets. You know that."

"I don't. Not anymore. I just told you mine."

"You just told me one." She stood up, smoothed her skirt and looked into his eyes. "And I'm glad you did."

"Me, too."

"So, should we go back and see what the score is in that football game?"

"Sure. Right after you say you'll drive to Gainesville with me tomorrow. We can go to the store you told me about."

"I have a charter in the morning, but I'm free in the afternoon."

"Great. I'll count on it."

She started to walk toward the steps that led from the gazebo, and Ethan, who truly hadn't been kidding when he'd told her three days ago that he wasn't an impulsive man, acted purely on instinct once again. He'd started something with this walk today, and he was determined to finish it. He grabbed her wrist and tugged her back to him.

She stared up at him with luminous blue eyes. "What? Did we forget something?"

"You bet we did. We forgot what we came out here for." He pulled her into his arms and kissed her. She emitted a little squeal of surprise, a slight tug of resistance until her body melted into his, and every rounded, womanly part of her pressed against him. He deepened the kiss, moving his mouth over hers until her arms came around his neck, her mouth opened, and she invited him to explore each warm, soft crevice inside.

His hand splayed across her back, massaging her spine as his palm rasped along the silky fabric of her blouse. She arched her neck and allowed him access to her throat. She smelled spicy and fresh like the garden around them. When he returned to her mouth for one more tasty exploration, she was waiting, breathless and eager.

When one of them ended the kiss, he didn't know who for sure, she kept her hands on his chest and smiled up at him. "I knew there was a reason we came out here," she said.

"Right. We told each other a lot of stories today. Each one deserves a happy ending, and this was it."

He took her hand and led her down the steps, and felt in his heart he was glad they'd come this far.

CHAPTER EIGHT

ETHAN LEFT TANSY HILL after pumpkin pie was served. He asked Helen for directions to her house and said he'd pick her up at one o'clock the next day. She hoped her four-hour charter customers would arrive promptly at seven-thirty when she'd told them to. This was one occasion when she wanted ample time to wash off the reminders of a fishing trip. Especially since she hoped to initiate a conversation about a business relationship between Dolphin Run and her charter operation.

The sun was setting as the red Chevy pulled away from Claire's house. Helen waved to Ethan and went back inside. Finn looked up at her and yawned. "Guess that was our sign to leave, too," he said. "I'm about to nod off from all this good cooking."

"In a minute, Pop," she said. "I want to have a word with Pet." Aware that Claire and Jane were on the front porch and Jack was still glued to the football game, Helen followed Pet and a stack of empty pie plates into the kitchen. When they were alone at the sink, Helen took the plates and began rinsing them.

"Thanks," Pet said. "If I look at another dirty dish I'm going to start throwing them in the trash."

Helen pulled out a chair at Claire's kitchen table. "Sit down. You must be exhausted."

"Not too bad," Pet said, though she did settle heavily into the plump cushion. "It was a lovely day, wasn't it?"

"Oh, absolutely."

"Did you have a nice time on your walk with Ethan?"

Helen stacked the rinsed plates in the dish drainer since the dishwasher was still full. "A very nice time."

Pet chuckled. "I didn't really have to ask that question. I could tell just by looking at you. Something is different about you today. You've got this rosy flush about you. And your eyes—"

"You're just imagining that," Helen interrupted, reminding herself once more that Pet had the ability to see things others did not. "I thought it was strange earlier when I heard you mention that I looked different."

Pet feigned innocence. "What, me? When did I say that?"

"Never mind. Besides, I didn't come into the kitchen to talk about me."

"I thought you came out here to wash the dishes."

Helen scowled over her shoulder. "Right. You know how domestic I am."

"Okay. So what do you want to talk about?"

"I'm getting the truth out of Finn tonight, one way or the other, and I thought I should warn you. I found some bamboo plants in the herb garden and broke off a few shoots so I could stick them under his fingernails."

"You mean the truth about him and Archie Anderson?"

"Of course. So now is your chance to prepare me for what I'm going to hear. Is it something really awful?"

Pet stared at the top of the table as if studying the

patterns in its wood grain. "How would I know? I told you, I don't have any idea—"

"Cut it out, Pet. I don't claim to have ESP like you do, but I know darned well Pop told you about what happened between him and Archie."

Pet blew out a long breath. "All right. You win. He told me. I don't know if he told me everything, but it was a start. And yes, it's significant."

"Significant?"

"Weighty. Important. A little shocking."

Helen draped the dishcloth over a rod above the sink and turned to face Pet who was staring at her intently. "Why are you looking at me like that?" she asked. "Does this big secret have anything to do with me?"

Pet squinted, leaned forward, stared harder. "No. It's just that you brought up the subject of ESP, and I'm having a flash of something right now. You really do look different, Helen. Almost like Claire did about eight months before…"

She paused and Helen held her breath.

"That reminds me," Pet continued. "Where is Jane?"

Helen swallowed, looked away. "She's on the front porch with Claire."

"Oh. Well, as I was saying, you have that same look about you, like Claire when she first found out…"

"Don't say it, Pet," Helen warned. "I mean it."

Pet's features split with a wide grin. "Oh, Jehovah, it's true. Helen, you're pregnant!"

Knowing it was futile to get Pet to retract that statement, Helen exhaled the breath she'd been holding and grabbed Pet's hands. "You can't tell anyone. Not Finn, not Claire. No one."

Pet jerked back from the intensity of Helen's reaction. "Why? What are you going to do? You're not thinking of…?"

"No. So I guess I'm going to plan on having a baby."

Pet sighed with relief. "You'll have to tell everyone soon. You'll need help."

"I don't need any now, so there's no point upsetting Pop."

Pet turned her hands inside Helen's and gripped fiercely. "Oh, honey, you can't do this alone."

"I've got time to tell the people who matter to me, Pet. Just promise you'll keep this secret for now. Give me your word."

"Okay, you've got it."

Helen extracted her hands, pressed one of them to her forehead to ward off a headache. "Thanks. I'm going to go home. Finn's waiting."

Pet followed her to the door. As they were leaving the kitchen, she whispered in Helen's ear, "Do you want to know what sex it is? Because if you do, all I need is a needle and thread, and to see if your feet are cold."

"Pet!"

HELEN BEGAN DRUMMING her fingers on the steering wheel the minute she pulled away from Tansy Hill.

"What's the matter with you?" Finn asked. "You're making me as nervous as a fish in a barrel with a twenty-two aimed between my eyes."

She stilled her hand. "My tapping bothers you?"

"Yes."

She snapped on the radio and continued her nervous habit. Finn glowered at her. "Big help."

Helen let her mind wander. Maybe it was a good thing that Pet had guessed her condition. This day had been a welcome break from her worries, but it was time to face reality again, especially since tomorrow would present the perfect opportunity for her to investigate the chance for a future for her and the Bean.

Ethan already liked her. Helen knew that. A man didn't hold a woman that way, kiss her like that if he wasn't interested in taking the relationship a step further. But Helen also knew his infatuation was only temporary, and she should concentrate on what the next step would be for her purposes. Maybe she could take Ethan on a tour of the *Finn Catcher*. She'd tell him about its safety record, technical features, seaworthiness, and then later convince him that her charter company and his inn should strike up a partnership. Her mind raced with the exciting potential. Charters every day of the week, enough money to hire extra help so she could devote needed time to the Bean. There was no doubt. Ethan's fat guest register translated to security for Helen.

This all sounded good, but what about her heart? She was starting to enjoy Ethan's kisses too much. She was wearing skirts and fancy blouses and blow-drying her hair and dabbing Pet's secret potions behind her ears. Was that all so she could ensure a safe and happy future for her family?

"Damn well better be," she muttered underneath the strains of a country song Finn had found on the radio. "That and nothing else."

"What'd you say?" Finn asked.

"Nothing."

Helen knew Ethan would never be interested in her once he knew she was carrying the Bean. He'd just confessed to her that he didn't want kids of his own. Besides, Ethan had so much blue blood in him, he probably leaked Windex when he got a cut. So he surely wouldn't want to raise the offspring of a jerk like Donny Jax.

Bottom line, Helen just had to remember that any future this baby had was up to her logical pursuit of her goal, not a foolish notion of a happily-ever-after with Ethan Anderson. But was it so bad if she used their mutual attraction to accomplish her plan? Forgetting for a moment that Finn was in the truck, she said aloud, "All I have to do is forget about how great he…"

"What's that?" Finn said.

She bit down on her lip. "Nothing." *How great he kisses.*

"Slow down. You're about to go right past the driveway."

Helen swung a hard right. Finn grabbed the wheel of his chair to keep from catapulting forward. She heard Andy's toenails clicking for purchase in the back. "Sorry fellas. I must have been daydreaming."

She stopped next to the house and turned off the engine.

Finn stared at her. "If you've got something on your mind, let's hear it, Helen, before you get us all killed."

Finn was right. Ethan was tomorrow's goal. Finn was tonight's. "That's a fine idea, Pop. I'll brew a pot of coffee and we'll have a little chat, just you and me."

She got out and walked around the front of the truck. As she adjusted the chair lift, she heard him mumble, "I don't like the sound of this, Andy. Not one bit."

HELEN'S PLAN TO SERVE coffee on the back porch was a good one. The evening was cool and dry, perfect Florida fall weather. And she knew Finn was happiest when he could sit in his chair and look out over his little empire—

the moonstruck Gulf, the lights shimmering on the rustic pine dock, the gleaming *Finn Catcher,* rocking gently at her berth, waiting for sunrise.

She handed him a warm mug and settled into the cushions of a wicker love seat. She pulled an old Florida Gators blanket over her bare legs and waited for him to take a long swallow. "It's time, Pop," she said, getting right to the point. "What happened between you and Archie Anderson?"

He stared straight ahead. "Have you ever considered that one reason I've never told you is because I don't like talking about it?"

"I've considered it, yes."

"And, reason number two, until now, the Andersons never had any bearing on our lives."

"True enough."

He spared a quick glance at her. "But apparently neither of those good reasons is going to get me out of this, now."

"Nope. The time for talking is here, and so are the Andersons, which suddenly makes them extremely relevant."

He scowled down at the mug cradled between his hands, and Helen prepared herself to hear the second confession of the day. Two very different men from different worlds. Two stories. Who would have thought that a connection could exist between them? She reached over and lightly stroked the worn flannel covering Finn's arm. "I'm not going to judge you, Pop. You know that, don't you?"

His eyes narrowed. "It's not me you'll be judging, Helen. It's Archie. Darn it, girl, I don't know why you always assume I'm the troublemaker."

She smiled. "Sorry, Pop. Force of habit."

"I've known Archie Anderson since the early fifties when his family came down here every summer to vacation."

"And they stayed at Dolphin Run?"

"They did. It was quite a place in those days. Live entertainment, lots of Northerners spending gobs of money. Good-looking girls. I met Archie in…let's see." He paused to reflect. "It was 1954, and Dolphin Run was a paradise for a couple of randy bucks like me and him."

Finn chuckled and Helen was relieved. At least not all of this memory was bad.

"I could barely keep my mind on my job once the Andersons got here every June. I ran a bait shop at the end of the dock during the summers. It was a little ol' building made of cedar and spit. Doesn't exist anymore. Blew over in the storm of 1960. Archie was a year older than me and smart as a whip—that private school education, I guess."

Helen caught a glimmer of something warm and pleasant in Finn's eyes.

"Archie worked right along beside me in the bait shop for no pay. 'Course he didn't need any. His folks had plenty of money, though you couldn't tell it by the way he acted. He was bold and brassy. Got into trouble more often than not. Not bad trouble, just things boys'll do when the reins are loosened."

Helen refilled Finn's mug from the pot she'd brought to the porch. "Sounds like those were good times."

"They were. And there weren't any better friends in the world than me and Archie. We hated to see Labor Day come because we knew we wouldn't see each other for nine whole months. Seemed like an eternity. 'Course we didn't have computers or e-mail in those days. Even if we did, we probably wouldn't have stayed in touch. Boys don't do that kind of thing. But we both knew that when June rolled around, nothing would have changed. We'd meet up and be the same old Finn and Archie."

Helen drank in every detail of Finn's description of his relationship with Archie. It was Tom Sawyer and Huck Finn, boyhood and adventure, long summer days of sun and sand and azure Gulf water. And yet tension clenched in her stomach because she knew this portrayal of idyllic innocence was going to take a drastic turn.

"Everything changed in the summer of 1960," he said with a gravelly edge to his voice. "That's the summer the Cheswicks came to Dolphin Run. They were Boston people, not country New Englanders like the Andersons. They were proud, dignified, some would say haughty." Finn closed his eyes, sipped his coffee and waited, as if searching for the right words. "But not Lottie Cheswick. There wasn't a haughty bone in her body." He expelled a long breath. "And Archie and I fell in love with her the day she carried her suitcase into the lobby."

Helen touched his arm. "You loved someone before Mom? You never told me."

Finn smiled, a sad, tentative upturning of his lips. "I've loved lots of women, Helen, but never the way I loved Lottie. She was the moon in the sky, the sparkle on the water, the beat of my heart."

Helen smiled to herself at Finn, the poet. She was certain she'd never heard the name Lottie before. "Why haven't you mentioned her to me?"

"I suppose I thought you'd blame me for your mama leaving. And maybe I was to blame. Carol knew about her.

Lottie was part of the story she came here to write that time. Lottie will always be a part of my story."

"What happened to her?" Helen asked. "What happened to Lottie?"

"She became the third link in the chain that summer. It was the three of us. Archie was twenty-two, just out of college. I was twenty-one, and Lottie had just turned twenty. We were like the sand and the sea and the tide, one not functioning without the other two. And Lottie knew we both loved her. Hell, a blind man could have seen our devotion to her. But she never played one against the other. She treated us both the same—the prince and the fisherman."

"Did Lottie love either one of you the way you both loved her?"

Finn chuckled, wiped a handkerchief under his nose. "If I had to guess the truth of it, I'd say she loved us both." He held up his thumb and finger, leaving an inch gap of space between them. "But maybe me a little more than Archie. At least that's what I've always chosen to believe." He paused, looked out toward the *Finn Catcher.* "I might have got up the courage to ask her to marry me if it hadn't been for the storm."

"What storm, Pop?"

"Labor Day weekend, 1960. A gale-force wind blew up from the Yucatán faster than anybody'd ever seen before. There wasn't but a few hours' warning till it hit. The adults hunkered down in Dolphin Run, shuttered the windows, boarded the doors. Told us young ones to stay inside."

Nineteen-sixty? Helen recognized the reference. "That was the year you had the accident, wasn't it? When you had the spinal injury?"

Finn nodded.

Helen guessed where the story was headed now because she knew Finn so well. "Obviously you didn't stay inside, did you, Pop?"

He gave her a sad sort of smile. "We thought we were invincible. The Three Musketeers of Dolphin Run. We went out to spit in the eye of the gale with a lantern, a radio and a six-pack of beer. Me, Archie and Lottie with the wind nearly knocking us on our fannies, the rain pelting our faces, and the waves rolling over the dock to our knees. We held on to each other and mocked the threat till the force of the gale stole our breath. And till we realized that Lottie's little brother had followed us out."

Helen's heart hitched. She saw the tension in the subtle change in Finn's face. His jaw tightened. His eyes closed, perhaps seeing again what had happened nearly five decades ago. "What about Lottie's brother?" she whispered.

"He was only twelve, a skinny mite, sickly. We heard him holler above the wind just before we saw him swept away. The wave took him like the wind takes the last leaf of autumn. He was there one minute, and the next he disappeared over the side of the dock."

Helen didn't speak. She knew the worst was coming and just waited for Finn to tell it.

"Lottie screamed and called out for us to help him. She looked to Archie, probably because he was the tallest and strongest, and begged him to save the boy. I never saw such fear in a person's face as I saw in Archie's that night. He clung to a piling and bent down, swiping his hand uselessly at the water pounding the seawall. Then Lottie cried to me, pleading, terrified, her heart breaking. And I saw the kid...I saw Hunter, bobbing in the churning surf, his face twisted with a silent scream, his arms flailing about for anything solid."

"And you went in?"

"I dived, but I couldn't find him. It was so dark, the water so powerful. I went under time after time, coming up with my arms empty. And then I grasped something, a slip of fabric, and I pulled it up with me. It was Hunter. I got him to the seawall, and Lottie and Archie dragged him onto the dock. Archie ran for the inn to get help."

Helen's hands clenched into fists. Her fingernails dug into her palms. "What about you, Pop? What happened to you?" But she knew. After all these years of hearing vague stories, half-truths, she knew.

"I couldn't get out. I reached for a piling, but my hands slipped off. And then something hard slammed into my spine, and I don't remember anything until there was a blur of activity. Me shivering on the floor of the lobby with folks standing by, pressing my chest, urging me up from a place so black I didn't think I'd ever see sunlight again. I couldn't feel anything but the cold."

"And you couldn't feel your legs," Helen said. "That's how it happened, when a boat pinned you to the dock?"

"That's what they told me."

Helen covered Finn's hand with hers. "And the others?"

"Archie and Lottie were all right."

"And her brother?"

"The adults struggled over him for a long time, but I expect he was gone when we hauled him out of the water. The next morning the Cheswicks left Dolphin Run. Took the body back to Boston. Never came back."

"And what of Lottie?"

"I never spoke to her after that. I wrote her a letter some weeks later. She answered it, but that's the last I ever heard from her."

Helen wanted to ask what was in the letter, but sensed there were aspects of Finn's tale that no one had a right to know.

"The Andersons never returned, either," he said. "They left the day after the Cheswicks did. That morning Archie came to the hospital in Micopee to see me. Said he was sorry he hadn't jumped in instead of me. Said he should have, because he loved Lottie more, because she asked him first."

Helen didn't know when she'd started crying, but she was thankful the tears rolled silently down her cheeks. Finn had never been good at dealing with overt sentimentality. In a choked voice she said, "So now I know why you bear a grudge against Archie Anderson."

Finn nodded. "It's more than just the fact that he has two good legs, and I never took a step after that day. It's that when it happened, we weren't boys any longer. We were men, and he should have done something. He was my friend, my best friend, and all he did was cling to that piling. I've tried to forgive him, Helen, but that night, what he did, what he didn't do, it wasn't enough."

Finn stopped talking. It was as if the words just dried up, leaving a yawning gap of sadness between them. Sensing he needed to be alone, Helen patted his hand and left him on the back porch while she went into the house. Andy followed her inside, and she paused in the kitchen, looking for something to do for the old dog. His water bowl was full. There were treats beside the plumped pillow he never slept on. He didn't need her right now, and if he did, it was in a way she couldn't help.

She went into the living room, sat on the sofa, picked up the television remote, set it back down again. Suddenly weary, she laid her head back and closed her eyes. For some reason most kids don't think of their parents as troubled, as people who have loved and suffered and lost, whose hearts have been broken. Perhaps because parents don't let their children see this wounded side of them.

"Thank heavens for Pet," she said aloud, knowing her father's companion and lover could reach inside his soul better than anyone else. Finn loved Pet deeply. And while Helen knew that, she also realized now that no one would ever take the place of Lottie in his heart. And maybe that's the way it should be. Emotions ebb and flow like the tides. Love enters a life and leaves it. But that first love, the greatest, perhaps, the one that shapes our lives more than any other—that is the one that should forever remain as the apex of our experience, alone, revered, perhaps altered by time and memory, but never replaced.

And yet Finn's confession tonight had left her restless, uncertain of the man she'd lived with for thirty years. She understood his resentment of Archie, the "why-me-and-not-him" gut reaction that is so very human. But she also recognized Finn's basic nobility well enough to know that if given the chance to change places that night, he probably wouldn't have. If, in the middle of that terrifying ordeal, the fates had suddenly decreed that he could have switched places with Archie—that he could have clung to the piling and Archie would have lost the use of his legs, would Finn have taken the deal?

No. Helen was certain of it. Finn would never wish his own misfortune on another human being to save himself, especially one as dear to him as Archie Anderson. And maybe that was the source of the greatest pain. That night Archie had that chance. Lottie had asked him first, and he let Finn take the risk.

Now that Helen knew the story and felt she'd almost lived through those terrifying moments with Finn, she still couldn't shake the feeling that he had left something out. There was something he hadn't revealed. She thought of tomorrow, the trip to Gainesville with Ethan. Perhaps he could fill in the gap Helen was certain existed in this sad tale.

ETHAN ARRIVED PROMPTLY AT one o'clock the next afternoon. He parked his car in front of Helen's cottage and walked to the door. She resisted the inclination to go outside and meet him as she had done countless times in the past with other "dates." Ethan was a gentleman. He liked to do things the right way, the old-fashioned way. And while Helen had always considered such gallantries obsolete, it was kind of nice to play along.

He took her elbow and guided her down the cracked sidewalk. "You look nice," he said.

She supposed maybe she did. She was becoming more comfortable with the procedures Claire had taught her. She now blow-dried her hair in a smooth, manageable style in under ten minutes. She applied her scant makeup with growing confidence. She had pulled her white denims out of the closet with a flicker of genuine concern for keeping them stain-free. And she had buttoned a loose-fitting, light blue rayon blouse that showed off her figure without scolding herself for trying to be someone she obviously was not.

"Thanks." Another first. She'd accepted a compliment without a smart comeback.

After she slid into the spotless vehicle, Ethan went around to the driver's side. Before starting the engine, he smiled over at her. "This is our first official attempt at combining business with pleasure," he said.

She remembered the previous Sunday. "Unless you count the day you first asked me to help you with Dolphin Run. As I recall, there was some pleasure involved then."

He pulled away from the curb. "You're right. There definitely was." He reached over, curved his hand over her thigh for a moment and then returned it to the steering wheel. "And since then I've been thinking of little more than our next opportunity to conclude a business discussion."

She'd been thinking of the same thing, and she reminded herself to keep her goals foremost in her mind. But then she looked over at him, at his finely chiseled profile, his slightly mussed, sandy-colored hair, which was now a bit long for a boardroom, his casual knit shirt stretched over toned upper arms, and found it difficult to remember her plan. She laid a hand over her stomach and wished things were different. Not that Ethan would ever choose her for a permanent relationship even if the Bean weren't in her future, but if circumstances were different, then dreaming might seem slightly less futile.

"So how did your charter go this morning?"

His question brought her back from a place she had no right to be. "Okay. Rusty and I took four overstuffed Thanksgiving celebrators on an exciting adventure."

"They caught fish?"

"Mostly they drank beer and sang old college songs."

He laughed. "And what else have you been doing?"

He'd asked the perfect question. "I talked to Finn last night," she said.

"Really? About the mystery?"

"Yes."

He gave her a quick, intense look. "Did you find anything out?"

"A little. Have you ever heard of the Cheswicks from Boston? They came to Dolphin Run in 1960. There was a daughter named Lottie."

Ethan smiled, spared her another glance. "I haven't heard her called by that name in years. Charlotte Cheswick was my mother."

CHAPTER NINE

HIS MOTHER! HELEN BIT HER LIP to keep from expressing her shock at the information Ethan had so casually offered. Finn had left out a very important element of his story, the fact that Lottie Cheswick had not only left Heron Point forever, but she had married his rival, Archie Anderson.

Helen believed she knew what was in that one and only letter Finn received from Lottie. It had to have been an announcement of her intent to wed Archie, as well as her final goodbye to a man who'd sacrificed dearly to earn her devotion.

Now Helen truly understood why Finn hated Archie. The wealthier, privileged man had not only stood by and watched as the poor fisherman risked his life for the woman they both loved, he'd stolen that woman, leaving Finn a broken man both physically and emotionally.

Helen's mind raced with the possible implications of this outcome. Had Lottie loved Archie, or had she truly loved Finn more, as Finn believed? Perhaps her heart urged her to choose Finn, but her strict, Bostonian family persuaded her to pick the more suitable Archie. Perhaps the horrific death of her brother and the family's decision to leave Heron Point and never return had forced her into a decision she never would have made otherwise. Or had she chosen Archie because he was whole and Finn was not?

Helen longed to ask her father these questions, to get to the bottom of a decades-old tragedy whose end seemed destined to come full circle in Heron Point in a matter of days. But how could she ask? Finn had lived with the bittersweet consequences of that summer practically his whole life. What right did she have to bring up memories he'd kept locked away? But what would happen when Archie arrived in Heron Point?

She barely heard Ethan when he spoke, but when he lightly touched her shoulder, she was brought back from her thoughts. He smiled at her. "Helen? Did you hear what I said?"

"Yes, of course. Charlotte Cheswick was married to your father."

"I told you about her yesterday. She died two years ago."

Did Finn know she was dead? Helen focused on Ethan's profile. "When is your father coming to Heron Point?"

"This Thursday. I'm picking him up at the Tampa airport."

"Has he said anything to you about seeing Finn?"

"Not specifically, no. He did mention something about having some fences to mend where your father is concerned."

Mending fences? This situation was more like fixing the Great Wall of China!

Ethan's brow creased with concern. "What is it, Helen? What did you learn about our fathers and my mother?"

How much should she tell him? At what point in the retelling of the story would she violate Finn's confidence? And yet, Finn hadn't asked her to keep the past a secret, so why should she hide the facts that were certain to come to light on Thursday, if not before. These were facts that Ethan had a right to know so he could prepare to deal with a potentially volatile confrontation between Archie and Finn.

Keeping her conjectures about Lottie's motives to herself, Helen revealed a little of what she'd learned. "They were all connected that summer of 1960, before your mother and father were married. It was the three of them, Archie, Finn and Lottie for those three months. Finn and Archie had been friends for years, but apparently when Lottie arrived that summer, the friendship was changed forever."

He remained silent, thoughtful. "I think I see where this is going. It was a love triangle, wasn't it? They both loved her."

Helen nodded. "And, according to Finn, she loved them both."

"She loved two men?"

If Ethan was surprised, he didn't show it. Instead, his lips curled into a grin. "If you'd known her, Helen, you would believe that she could truly have loved them both. My mother's capacity for love was boundless. She only saw the good in everyone, until…"

Until you were kidnapped, Helen thought. "But she chose Archie."

"I suppose."

"When were they married?" Helen asked. "How long after the drowning?"

His eyes left the road to spear her with a penetrating glance. The car's right tires ground on the rough gravel of the shoulder. He quickly corrected. "What drowning?"

"Your mother's brother." She saw the confusion in his expression, in the rapid pulse at his temple. And she felt his shock in her own pounding heartbeat. "You didn't know?"

He shook his head.

"Oh, Ethan, I'm so sorry. Your mother's younger brother was swept off the dock at Dolphin Run in a storm. His body was recovered, but…"

"No one ever told me. In fact, I never knew my mother had a brother." He remained silent. Helen gave him a moment to absorb the news. When he spoke again, his voice was low, somehow tentative. "If I'd known, maybe I would have understood her breakdown better. Maybe I could have helped."

"Your father knew," she said. "I'm sure he tried to give her the support she needed."

"He treated her like a porcelain doll, like she would break. Even long after the kidnapping, when she fell apart, he coddled her, forgave her all her lapses into her fantasy world. He worshipped her, Helen, despite everything." His hands gripped the steering wheel so tightly his knuckles blanched. "Maybe he thought she would actually break. Maybe she did, and that's why she made the wrong choices with her life after what happened to me."

And maybe she made the wrong choice over forty-seven years ago when she married Archie, Helen thought. No one would ever know now.

Having reached the end of the thirty-mile stretch of two-lane road that led from Heron Point to the county seat, Ethan turned onto the four-lane that would take them to Gainesville. He flexed the muscles in his shoulders, extended and stretched his fingers. When he spoke again, his voice was calm, controlled. "Was anyone else hurt, in the storm, I mean?"

She nodded, and he asked her to explain.

"Finn jumped in to save the boy. That was the hurricane I told you about on Thanksgiving. The one when Finn lost the use of his legs."

"Finn jumped in? Not my father?"

Since that was the way she'd heard the story, Helen nodded.

"My God, Helen, no wonder there are bad feelings between our fathers."

Bad feelings? Helen resisted pointing out that such a mild description did not begin to identify the undercurrent of animosity that Finn felt toward Archie.

"Do you know what this means?" Ethan asked.

"It means that if Jimmy Carter were to suddenly appear in Heron Point as a mediator, he would have a hard time negotiating a peace between these two men."

THE OWNER OF In The Groove Furniture Store was practically giggling out loud when Helen and Ethan left the shop at closing. Four complete bedroom sets would be delivered to Dolphin Run on Monday, along with retro-style lamps, 1960s poster art, colorful dishes and chrome kitchenette accessories.

"I couldn't have done it without you," Ethan said as he and Helen walked back to his car.

"Thanks, but you probably could have. All I did was point and pick."

"Yeah, but you got her down ten percent on the price."

"Well, okay, maybe you needed me for that. I have years of haggling experience that you probably lack."

He shut the passenger door and walked around to the

driver's side. "Where to for dinner?" he asked after starting the engine.

"Are you up for a little adventure?"

"Sure. Name the place."

"We'll go to Gator Burgers for takeout and then eat in The Swamp."

He laughed. "I hope this is the kind of swamp that's surrounded by bleachers and seats eighty thousand people."

"There's no fooling you, Princeton. You know your sports stadiums."

An hour later, they sat in the third row at the fifty-yard line looking directly onto the grassy field of the University of Florida's football arena, known to the school's ardent fans as The Swamp. Helen took a foil-wrapped sandwich from a bright orange takeout sack and handed it to Ethan.

"It's not really made of gator, is it?"

She passed him a large order of fries and a chocolate milkshake. "No, but gator meat is probably better for you than whatever beef parts and additives are in this meal." She unwrapped her own deluxe burger. "But, heck, there's no better artery-clogging hamburger in the state, in my opinion."

Helen took a big bite and wiped special gator sauce from the corner of her lip. "Just imagine," she said, "tomorrow afternoon this stadium will be filled with screaming, excited fans." She cupped her hand around her ear. "Can't you almost hear it already?"

His slow gaze swept over one hundred yards of brightly chalked greenness and then settled on two runners who churned their way around the running track. Those two, plus a maintenance crew, were the only people in The Swamp now. Except for the two of them, of course.

He popped a fry into his mouth. "I don't think my imagination is as good as yours, but okay, I'll admit I can hear something. Maybe it's just the huffing and puffing of those joggers."

He turned toward her, looked into her eyes which must have reflected a rapt expression, and said, "You're quite a Gators fan, aren't you?"

"Born and raised."

"Have you ever been to a game?"

"Oh, sure. The first was when I was a senior at Micopee High School. A busload of us came over for a university visitation trip."

"Really? You said you never went to college."

She took a sip of her milkshake, then set the cup down beside her. "That's right. I didn't. But I applied here and was accepted. At one time I had this idea that I wanted to be a teacher."

"But you never came here to get your education?"

"No. It never worked out." When he just stared at her, she added, "Things happen, Ethan. Plans change." *Dreams die and responsibility takes over.* She remembered the day she sent her regrets to the administration office. *Helen Sweeney will not be attending the University of Florida. Please refund my deposit on a dorm room and cancel my attendance at freshman orientation.* She cried when she stuck the stamp to the envelope and slid it into the mailbox. And then she got on with what she had to do.

Ethan was still looking at her with those soul-searching brown eyes. "What changed for you, Helen? Why didn't you go to college?"

"Bad karma, I guess. Just about the time I was thinking

about dorm room accessories, Finn realized he could no longer manage the charters, and he turned the business over to me. I was finished with high school, and I'd been working the water for as long as I could remember."

"Did he know what you were giving up?"

"I never told him." Helen sighed, realizing now that while she and Finn had been closer than many fathers and daughters, they had kept some secrets from each other. "When my acceptance letter came, I hid it in my dresser drawer. I knew it would be hard enough to leave him when the time came. So I kept quiet, and squirreled away every spare dime and studied the course catalog in private." She shrugged, pretending it didn't matter, as she'd always done, until it almost seemed she wasn't pretending any longer. "It just wasn't meant to be."

And now, twelve years later, the charter business was no better off than it had been then. She was still running three or four charters a week, still struggling with payments on the *Finn Catcher,* still waiting for life to get easier and close to accepting that it never would.

She glanced at Ethan, whose expression had turned somber. Maybe his arrival in Heron Point could turn things around for her, but if so, she still had to deal with the dilemma in her belly. If Ethan and the Andersons could save her business, that would be a great start toward building a future. They couldn't turn back time to before Donny Jax came to town, or so she could pursue that college education. But a smart person should be grateful for a savior, no matter when he showed up.

She gathered up the dinner wrappings and stuffed them in the sack. "Hey, quit looking so glum," she said to Ethan. "We've had a good afternoon, a super meal on the sidelines of hallowed ground, and on Monday, four rooms in Dolphin Run are going to look like the set from *Happy Days.*"

And as soon as we're back in the car, I'm going to talk to you about your inn and my business. In her mind, Helen had already designed the flashy brochure she was going to put in the lobby of Dolphin Run. Any guest who had the least desire to catch a fish was going to want to do so on the *Finn Catcher.* She climbed the stadium steps to a trash can and dropped in their garbage. With Ethan close behind her, she looked down at her belly. It just might work out for us, Bean, she thought. This man can make it work.

He took her hand as they headed to an exit. It was as natural a gesture as she could remember any man extending in a long time. She couldn't recall Donny Jax ever holding her hand. "I need to talk to you about something, Ethan," she said.

"Good, because I need to talk to you. Can I go first?"

"Well, okay."

"I want you to take me out on the *Finn Catcher* as soon as you can."

Was he reading her mind? He'd just given her the perfect opening. Of course he'd want to go out with her, check her skills, test her ability to navigate and find the schools of fish that would reward his guests' efforts and payments. Ethan was a businessman. He would want to know that the charter service he recommended to his customers was a competent one.

"That's a great idea," she said. "I have a charter in the

morning, but I'm free in the afternoon. Can you go out to-morrow?"

"Sure. It'll be a first for me. I've never been fishing the way you do it. I've never been with a guide before, or on a charter boat."

She smiled up at him. "Well, then, Princeton, you've chosen the best."

"I've already figured that out. And I'll need every tip you can give me. You and I are going to make Heron Point the fishing destination of Florida's west coast."

She sent him a narrowed gaze. "We are?"

"You bet. I've decided to open a charter fishing operation at Dolphin Run."

SHE NEARLY STUMBLED, WOULD have if he hadn't grabbed her elbow. Ethan steadied her and looked back at the path they'd just taken. "Was there something on the sidewalk?"

She rubbed her ankle. "Must have been." She stared straight ahead and walked as if her legs were made of pins and sticks. Had she heard him correctly? The statement came from so far out in left field, it deserved a second listen. "What did you just say?"

"That I'm going to start a charter fishing service at Dolphin Run."

Yes, she'd heard every unbelievable word. How could he say that without thinking what this announcement would do to her? To her future? To the Bean? Well, he didn't know about the Bean, but still... She stammered in an effort to gain control of her emotions. "Wh-what made you come up with this idea?"

He smiled, all innocence, pretended or real. She didn't

know. Was Ethan Anderson, whom she'd referred to many times as a genuine *good man,* too good to be true? Hell, that was just her luck. They were all either too good to be true or not nearly good enough.

He raised his hand in a placating gesture. "Don't get angry. Just hear me out. The truth is, you made me think of it."

"Me? I never suggested you should start your own charter business."

"No, not in so many words, but you and I have gotten close, right?"

He expected an answer, and she was tempted to give him the one that burned on the tip of her tongue—that right now she felt as if an ocean stood between them. But she remained silent, waiting to see what kind of game he was playing.

"Anyway," he continued, "I've got the capital to do this, and you have experience. I understand business principles, but I don't know anything about fishing, so that's where you come in. You can advise me on the kind of boat to buy, the equipment to use, the best places in the Gulf to fish."

Almost numb from the direction this conversation was taking, Helen got into his car.

"And believe me, Helen, the rewards for you will be great," he said as he slid into the driver's seat. He inserted his key into the ignition. Everything he'd done since announcing his plan had been irritatingly normal.

Rewards for me? She crossed her arms over her chest, looked at him and said in her sharpest tone, "Believe *me,* Ethan, you and I are definitely *not* on the same wavelength about this."

He smiled! Couldn't he sense the tension in the air, feel

it crackling around the interior of the automobile? Good grief, she was seething with it, and he was acting as though he'd reinvented the wheel!

He started the car, pulled into heavy Friday afternoon traffic. "Look, Helen, it should be obvious by now. I like you. I respect you. You're different from any of the women I've…"

He paused.

The women you've *dated?* she filled in for him in her mind. Come on, Princeton, can't you say the word, or have you suddenly realized that under normal circumstances, in your *real* life, you wouldn't be dating me on a bet? And you wouldn't be asking me to teach you to fish.

"…been with," he finally said. "You've lived a different life, done amazing things. And what you know, what you've experienced…it's very impressive."

Now he was using flattery? *What I've experienced? Baiting hooks? Sanding a sailboat? Getting repeatedly tromped on by inconsiderate jerks? Yeah, this is quite a life.*

"You and I are going to make a crackerjack team. Besides learning the ropes from the best fishing guide in the area, I get to spend time with you." He looked over at her, confidence and sincerity in his features. "Right now it's a win/win situation." His eyes practically sparkled. "I get to be with you, soaking up all that information, and your profits will increase more than you can imagine."

No, they won't! You'll end up stealing all the customers from me! Helen couldn't believe the play of emotions on Ethan's face. Excitement, enthusiasm, and yes, even blissful ignorance. All while he rambled on about the possible ruination of her life! She wasn't interested in sharing. She wanted *all* the customers, just as she'd always had. That was the whole purpose of this relationship. She and Ethan were supposed to partner up, yes, but not like this, not so he could be the first inconsiderate jerk to tromp on her business!

They had left the city boundaries of Gainesville and turned onto the four-lane. Apparently Ethan had run out of conversational steam because the silence was getting ominous.

"Why haven't you said anything?" he finally asked.

Restrain yourself, Helen. This is not the time to blow your top. "Ethan…" His name rolled off her tongue calmly, without any indication of her simmering temper. A good start.

"Yes?"

"Since you're obviously aware of how I support myself and Finn, I'm a little curious as to why you might think I would help you start up an identical business a mile away from mine." She mentally patted herself on the back. She'd managed to ask the question without inserting a single swearword.

He glanced at her, then back at the road. His brow wrinkled. He tapped his index finger on the steering wheel just as she did when she was struggling to figure something out. And then he said, "Helen, I hope you're not worried about competition."

Her jaw dropped. She stared at him a moment before saying, "Honestly, Ethan? Yes, I am. And I can't believe you asked me to help you set up a competitive operation. How naive do you think I am?"

"I don't think you're naive at all. But I am starting to get that you're angry."

"Hell, yes, I'm angry."

"Helen, competition is the most basic of economic principles. Competition is healthy, life-supporting, industry-growing. You know that."

"Maybe for shoe stores, but…"

"For any business," he said. "Trust me on this, whenever two businesses go up within the same block, on the same street, both benefit. Why do you suppose auto dealerships spring up within blocks of each other, sometimes existing on opposite corners of the same intersection? It's because competition gets the juices flowing, brings customers to the area, and therefore increases profits. It's a proven business tactic."

"Heron Point isn't Madison Avenue," she pointed out.

"It doesn't matter. You've been the only charter operator here for how many years?"

"A lot."

"Yes, and what has it gotten you? I've done a little checking. Ten years ago, you ran three or four charters a week, on a good week. How many do you do now?"

She mumbled the answer, which he darned well knew without making her say it.

"That's my point. You're stagnant. You need growth. Competition builds growth. And that's not even taking into account the greater number of people who will be visiting this island once the inn is opened. With the right advertising and marketing plan, Heron Point can definitely support six or eight charters a week, double what you're doing now."

Maybe so, but I wanted them all to be mine! I need them to be mine. She glanced down at her stomach. *We need them.* While she wanted to scream her desperation at him, she somehow said calmly, "Ethan, I've done some checking myself. Dolphin Run only has twenty-four rooms. That hardly accommodates this tidal wave of paying customers you're expecting."

"But it's a start. Tomorrow twenty-four rooms, next year, who knows? With you and Dolphin Run working the only charters, we'll have a lock on fishing trips for years to come. And once Anderson Enterprises is firmly entrenched in this town, real progress can be made for all the businesses here."

But, damn it, I can't wait for some arbitrary time in the future. I need my charter company to grow now!

The sun began to set, and Ethan's car breezed along the narrow two-lane road to Heron Point as if a volcano of emotions weren't threatening to blow inside the vehicle. He looked over at her, smiled, patted her shoulder. "Give this some thought, Helen. I've studied business growth and profit potential for years. I know what I'm talking about. Once the word gets out, and believe me, I'll make sure it does, that there are now two charter companies in Heron Point, there will be ample customers for both of us. I'm right about this. You'll see."

He paused, obviously waiting for her to comment. She didn't. Finally he said, "You're not still mad, are you?"

Silence. *Don't say it, Helen.*

He smiled again. She wished she were growing tired of his smile because he'd sure used it a lot in the last half hour. But each one seemed more genuine than the last. And each one made her grow soft inside and want to believe him.

"Don't tell me you're going to renege on taking me out on the *Finn Catcher*," he said. "I suppose I could learn about fishing from another source, but the idea of you and me as a team is awfully appealing, and not just for business reasons."

Helen had her faults, but going back on her word wasn't one of them. "No, of course not. We'll go."

They rode without speaking until they passed groves of cedar trees and the old Indian mounds. In a few miles they would be back in Heron Point. Helen looked out the window at darkness descending over the sacred burial ground. Heron Point old-timers talked about the ghost of a young woman who wandered the mounds with her large dog at her heels. A few folks claimed to have seen her. Some claimed the ghost of a young boy haunted Dolphin Run, too. Helen had never believed it, but now, after hearing about Lottie Cheswick's brother, she wondered.

She continued thinking about Dolphin Run, its legends of good times and bad, its potential to be the answer to the town's troubled financial future, while at the same time causing the demise of her own, and she had an idea. She was the one smiling when they pulled into town. By this time tomorrow Ethan might not be so positive about his plan to open a second charter company. Helen had come up with the perfect antidote to his optimism. All she had to do was talk to Finn….

Ethan broke her concentration. "It's still early. Would you like to come back to the inn with me?"

She looked at him, raised her eyebrows in an unspoken question.

"We can decide where all that furniture is going," he added.

There was that optimism again. That glimmer in his eyes. That incredibly natural and heart-stopping smile. He didn't fool her for a minute, but she had to give him credit. Planning furniture arrangements was the most original euphemism for sex she'd heard in a long time. "Gee, that sounds swell," she said. "But, like I told you, I have an early charter in the morning. Maybe some other time."

"Are you sure?" He seemed truly disappointed.

"Yeah, it's for the best."

"Okay. Home, then?"

She nodded, secure in her decision that it was the right thing to do. She couldn't very well scheme in the morning against the same man she'd made love with the night before. A girl, even a desperate one, had principles.

But as they drove past those big iron gates, Helen's emotions betrayed her. Maybe Ethan was disappointed, but she was miserable. It didn't seem to matter how angry she was at him. She most definitely wished she were going to the second floor of Dolphin Run to talk about where dressers should go.

CHAPTER TEN

HELEN GOT OUT OF THE CAR as soon as Ethan pulled up to the front of her cottage.

"Wait," he said. "I'll walk you to…"

She was halfway up the sidewalk when she turned around and said, "I'm fine. See you tomorrow afternoon."

He leaned over and peered out the car window. "Should I bring anything?"

"No. I'll furnish everything we need." *Including the seasick pills.*

"Okay, then. I'll be over about one o'clock."

She waved as she got to the door. "Perfect." Waiting until he'd driven off, she went inside.

Finn was in the living room. He looked at her, for the moment ignoring the football game on TV. "Back already?"

"Yeah. It didn't take me long to spend a couple thousand of Ethan's money."

"Sounds like fun. Was it?"

"Yes. No. I don't know."

He squinted at her. "What kind of an answer is that?"

She plopped down on the sofa. "What's the weather going to be tomorrow afternoon?"

Wisely refusing to comment that her question failed to

answer his question, Finn said, "Weather Channel reports we're due for storms late in the day. I wasn't worried because your charter is in the morning."

She smiled. She could depend on his answer because Finn had always watched the forecasts as if he were still captaining the *Finn Catcher.* "That's good."

He returned his attention to the TV. "Yep. No worries."

"No, I mean it's good because I'm going to be out in the middle of it."

He hit the mute button. "What are you talking about? You know better than to be out in rough waters."

"Normally, yes. But sometimes it's necessary." She sat forward, rested her elbows on her knees. "Are you ready for this one?" When Finn's face showed appropriate attentiveness, she said, "Ethan just told me he's going to start a charter company at Dolphin Run."

"What?"

"And that's not all. He wants me to take him out tomorrow afternoon and show him the ropes. He wants the whole fishing experience."

Finn's cheekbones crested with scarlet. "You mean he wants you to teach him how to take the business right out from under us?"

"Well, yes, but he doesn't look at it that way. He acts like I'll be doing both of us a favor. He says competition is healthy and will help our businesses grow."

Finn's hands tightened on the arms of his chair. "Isn't that just like an Anderson? They want what they have and what everybody else has, too." He faced Helen with a scowl pulling at his moustache. "I'm not surprised. Not one bit.

I could have told you Ethan was a low-down snake, just like his father. The apple doesn't fall far from the tree."

Helen wouldn't go that far. She'd seen Ethan's sincerity, knew he believed all that textbook lingo about marketing practices even if she wouldn't put a penny's worth of faith in it. "Look, Pop, don't blow a gasket. I've come up with a plan that I think might discourage him."

"Well, what is it?"

She gave him a coy smile. "Just because we go out deep-sea fishing doesn't mean we'll catch anything. And if the wind kicks up, it doesn't mean I have to steer away from it. At least not at first."

Finn's eyes crinkled at the corners. He was starting to follow her line of thinking. "You're absolutely right, Helen. Take him bottom fishing and rig the lines with spoons and skirts." He thought a moment and then grinned. "Take some cut bait out of the freezer tonight so it'll be good and spoiled by the afternoon." Finally he laughed out loud. "And for good measure, cut up some of that leftover turkey Claire gave us. There's not a fish in the Gulf that would take a liking to poultry. Mix it in with the cut bait. Once it all starts smelling the same, that New Yorker won't know the difference."

Helen raised her eyebrows at him. "You know something, Pop? You've got a conniving streak in you."

"Don't I know it. You might mix in a couple drops of kerosene, too, just to make extra sure you won't get a bite. But, Helen, don't get caught in a bad blow tomorrow. Teaching the city boy a lesson isn't worth you putting yourself or the *Finn Catcher* in danger."

She reached over and squeezed his hand. "Don't worry, Pop. I'll just give him a little taste of Gulf Coast rock 'n' roll." She walked to the kitchen to get herself a glass of milk. As she poured, she rubbed her hand over her belly. "I'm counting on you, Bean. If it gets a little smelly and rough out there tomorrow, I don't want you turning the tables on me and making my gills turn green."

She took the milk and went onto the back porch. A few hours still stretched ahead of her before bedtime. She wished she had something to do, something that would make her forget how she could have been spending these hours with Ethan at Dolphin Run. Knowing these thoughts were counterproductive, she set down the glass of milk and rubbed her arms briskly. There was only a slight chill in the air so she couldn't blame the tingle up and down her extremities on the temperature.

Why did Ethan have to be such a nice guy one minute and such a jerk the next? Why did he have to be so different from the men in Heron Point? His very uniqueness made it impossible for her to imagine ever settling down with one of them. Why did she have to meet someone who treated her like a lady all the time and had her believing she could be more like Claire—all soft and feminine? Why did he seem so perfect for her when she allowed herself to dream, and so completely her opposite in reality?

She stood up and walked off the porch toward the *Finn Catcher*. Why did Ethan have to occupy her mind nearly every minute of every day, lately? Even when she was plotting to thwart his plans, she couldn't stop picturing his smile, eager and kind, hearing his voice, deep and cultured, feeling his hand, gentle and sure on her elbow.

Helen stared at the *Finn Catcher*, remembered the eighteen more months of payments she had to meet before she got the title and forced her mind to focus on what she had to do. She didn't like playing this prank on Ethan, but a girl had to take care of her own. Ethan didn't need a charter business to survive. He would move on to the next project in the next town and meet the next woman. That was the sad reality she had to think about now. She would always be stuck right here, scrabbling to make a living the only way she knew how. Even the nicest guy in the world couldn't blame her for resorting to desperate measures to protect her future—as pitiful as it was—and the people destined to live it with her.

But, oh, my, those soft brown eyes that said "trust me" even when she knew she shouldn't. That special smile that seemed capable of taking every little problem she had and tossing it into the clouds. She kicked at a piece of driftwood and headed back to the porch and the glass of warm milk. Damn. She'd sure rather be having a beer.

ETHAN STOPPED AT THE gate of Dolphin Run and spoke to the guard on duty. "Hey, Joel, anything going on?"

"Not much, Ethan." He pointed to a box on the ground. "I just had a pizza delivered and ate the whole thing, so I guess some heartburn is about all the excitement I can expect tonight."

Ethan sympathized with the guards. They had boring jobs. And unnecessary ones. "I keep trying to tell Dad that you're not needed here," he said. "Have you had any luck convincing him?"

The big man tugged his shirtsleeve away from his impressive biceps. "I don't mind it. I'm getting a tan."

Ethan drove up the pathway to the front entrance.

Another of Archie's staff left his position at the front door and came to the car window. "How you doing, Ethan?"

"Pretty good, Wayne," Ethan lied. His evening hours didn't look any more promising than Wayne's or Joel's did. Even less. These two guys would be relieved of duty in a couple of hours and they would go into town to mingle with the weekend tourists. And Ethan, who'd imagined an extremely satisfying conclusion to his afternoon with Helen, would end up watching whatever TV programs were available on the recently installed satellite dish.

While maintaining a casual conversation with the guard, Ethan kept thinking about his backfired plans with Helen. He'd thought tonight would be a celebration. He and Helen had bought the first furnishings for the inn. He'd come up with a sensible plan to bring new fishing customers to Heron Point. And, most important of all, he'd believed that he and Helen were ready to take their relationship to the next level. He'd figured they would come back to the inn, have that bottle of wine he'd left in the refrigerator and maybe light the logs he'd stacked in the fireplace.

Not that he'd expected to sweep Helen up the stairs and into his bed. But at least he'd hoped to progress to more than hand-holding and a few passionate kisses. He was ready for that, and he'd thought Helen was, too.

So what had happened? Was she more upset about their fathers' troubled history than she'd let on? If that was the case, then so was he, and he had a few choice words he was saving up for Archie. Like, why had he kept his son in the dark all these years about what had happened in 1960? Why hadn't Charlotte or Archie told him about the tragedy? Was his father ashamed of his reaction the night of the storm?

Or was Helen really angry about his announcement to start a charter operation at Dolphin Run? He hadn't expected that. Any more than he'd expected that his only choice for company for the next couple of hours would be New York superjock, Wayne Bertoli. Oh, well, a guy had to make the best of a situation.

Ethan got out of the car. "Say, Wayne, it's obviously pretty quiet around here tonight."

"Yep. Like every night. Never hear anything but the owls hooting."

"How'd you like to go out on the dock and have a beer with me?"

"I don't know. Your dad…"

"…would be having a beer with us if he were here, which he will be in just a few days. Come on. I'd really like the company."

Wayne thought a moment and then rolled one beefy shoulder. "A beer sounds good, Ethan."

"Great. I'm going upstairs to change and then I'll meet you outside. I'll bring the beer."

Ethan climbed the stairs to the second floor and went into the room he'd appropriated as his own while he was renovating. The front window looked out on the Gulf and the northern end of Dolphin Run property. The boathouse was illuminated in new pole lights recently wired by the electrician. Shingles on the new roof shone golden brown in the soft amber light. The place was coming around. His father would be pleased, especially with Ethan's attempts to keep the original casual atmosphere intact.

Ethan tossed his button-down shirt on the bed and slipped a long-sleeved T-shirt over his head. He'd just pulled on a pair of jeans when his cell phone rang. He picked it up from his dresser, recognized the number and connected. "Hey, Cam, how's everything?"

His sister's voice was cheerful as always. "Hello, little brother. Where'd I catch you? At a five-star restaurant or front center at a live concert?"

Ethan looked out his window at the waves rolling endlessly to shore. "Very funny, Camille. I've just finished a gator burger, of all things, and I'm about to join Dad's storm trooper, Wayne, for a Budweiser and a concert of crickets down by the boathouse."

Camille laughed. "Don't feel bad. I'm three blocks off Park Avenue on a crisp, clear fall night, and I just finished eating Chinese takeout and watching Alex and two of his friends play a video wrestling game."

Ethan wasn't surprised that Camille was home on a Friday night. Though an accomplished businesswoman who'd made her mark on Manhattan according to her own terms, she was first of all a mother. And she was a good one, even though she'd become pregnant at twenty and hadn't had any training for the job.

"Sounds like we both have an exciting evening ahead of us," he said.

"Yeah, well, my social life is about as stimulating as watching chickens roost, but things aren't quite as hopeless for you. I called to tell you I ran into Trish Howard today at Bloomingdale's."

An image of the willowy redhead he'd recently dated a few times popped into Ethan's mind. Funny, while he'd found her attractive and enjoyed her overt flirting, he'd barely given her a thought since he'd left for Heron Point.

"In the shoe department, I would guess," he said. Trish had told him she had more than a hundred pairs of shoes. He didn't know why he remembered that fact tonight.

"Gloves. Kid leather," Cam said. "It's chilly here."

"Oh. If you see her again, give her my regards."

"You're going to have to do better than that, Ethan. She grilled me unmercifully to find out why you haven't called her."

"I did call her."

"Right. The day after you got to Heron Point, you called. She told me about that, and then she told me she's called you twice since then."

"I suppose she has."

Camille snickered. "I might be wrong, but I got the distinct impression that Trish has pinned her hopes on a future with you that goes beyond a Jets game and tickets to the Lincoln Center."

Ethan felt the need to defend himself. His sister could be a tough critic when it came to his relationships with women. "I never gave her any reason to think that we were more than friends," he said.

"*Any* reason?"

Okay, there had been a couple of semipassionate episodes, but nothing he wanted to confess to his sister. "I'll call her," he finally said.

"Hey, do what you think is right. But while we're on the subject, is there any explanation for why your interest in Trish has cooled? Like, maybe you've met a tropical beauty down there?"

Helen? A tropical beauty? Ethan couldn't honestly say she was. Trish was sophisticated, chic, educated. She turned heads wherever she went. Even Camille, with her down-to-earth practicality and her strong drive to succeed, was, in the ways that counted, a typical Manhattan woman. She always displayed a confidence to the world that Ethan suspected she used to bluff her way through life. But she did it well.

No, Helen was practically the antithesis of classic womanly grace and beauty. Her hair was mostly styled by the sea breeze and shone with natural highlights from the sun. Her skin was golden bronze, about as far from porcelain perfection as cotton was from silk. Her body was toned and even sinewy, sculpted by hard work and meals that took ten minutes to eat, not two hours. And yet he'd spent quite a bit of time imagining those lean, muscled legs wrapped around him, thinking about those unpainted full lips pressed against his, remembering the special scents of sea, air and something fresh and floral that floated behind her wherever she walked.

And so he found himself saying to his sister, "Yes, actually, I have met someone."

Camille squealed. "Ethan, really? Who is she? What does she do? How long…"

"Now, hold on, Cam. I've only been here a little over a week. It's a bit early for you to plan a wedding."

She laughed. "Well, you know, darling, that if I can't plan one for myself, you'd be my next choice."

He smiled sadly. Here they were, the children of two parents who'd stayed devoted to each other for over four decades, and neither one of their hapless kids had been involved in a truly meaningful relationship. When she'd become pregnant, Cam had tried the marriage thing. Unfortunately she'd done all the trying while her husband had done all the avoiding. The marriage ended before Alex was born.

Ethan thought about the way he'd left Helen just a few minutes ago. Right about now, another wedding in the Anderson family seemed a very remote possibility, not that he'd seriously considered it before his little tiff with Helen. He found her interesting, unpredictable, sexy as hell and even cute when she wasn't ticked off at somebody. She was someone he'd definitely like to get to know better. But a wife? No, that thought hadn't entered his mind. Only, now here it was, challenging him to ignore its presence.

"It looks like we're doomed, Cam," he said. "I can picture a couple of old rockers on the porch of some cabin in the Poconos one day, and they're going to belong to you and me. We'll be sitting there night after night waiting for Alex to call."

"Not me, brother. I'll be on a chaise lounge on a rooftop in downtown Manhattan still looking at this skyline."

"I suppose."

"So, will Dad like her?"

Ethan flinched. "I don't know. You ever hear of Finn Sweeney?"

Camille paused a moment before answering. "I've heard the name. I think I remember Mom and Dad talking about someone named Finn. Why?"

"The woman I've met, Helen, is Finn's daughter. He and Dad go back a long way, and there are bad feelings between them."

"About what?"

"It's a long story. And the ending is anything but certain

right now." He looked out at the boathouse and dock. Wayne was there, sitting on a bench, staring at the water. "Can I fill you in on the details some other time? Like I told you, I've got big plans for tonight."

"Right. Can't keep Wayne waiting. Tell him I said hi. And, Ethan, you owe me that story."

"I'm sure you'll hear about it, one way or another. Give Alex a hug for me, will you?"

"I'll try. But he's fifteen years old. Hugging is out for now, even if I tell him it's coming from you and not me."

"Right. I remember what it's like to be fifteen. Talk to you later, Cam."

"One more thing. I don't guess you're going to call Trish, are you?"

He exhaled a long breath. "You never know."

AT TEN MINUTES TILL one Helen was on board the *Finn Catcher* applying the finishing touches to the lines she'd rigged for the outing with Ethan. She looked up from clipping a silvery metal disc to a leader and saw her fishing partner walk across the lawn toward the dock.

"He's even early," she said to herself, and tried once again to push any guilty feelings into a remote area of her mind where she could forget about them for the rest of the day. She'd convinced herself over and over that she had to do this. And the fact that he looked so rugged and un-Ethan-like in shorts that showed off his lean, muscular legs shouldn't allow her to veer off course. It didn't help that he also wore a knit shirt printed with coconuts that molded to his chest quite admirably and a spanking new

Heron Point ball cap that gave his otherwise brawny appearance an endearing boyish quality.

He waved to her and sprinted to the dock. Before boarding, he looked up at the sky. "Do you think we'll get some bad weather?"

"No, it's supposed to blow over."

He jumped gingerly from the dock to the stern deck and set a small cooler on the bench seat. "I know you said not to bring anything. It's just water and a couple of sandwiches from the convenience store in town. I didn't know if you would have had time to eat between your charter and this trip."

There he was, being so nice again. She yanked on the string she was tying with a force that nearly cut her finger. "Can't hurt to have a little food just in case."

He frowned at the sky. "In case what?"

She grinned at his worried expression. "In case one of us gets hungry."

"Oh." He looked around the *Finn Catcher,* bent over to see into the small galley, stared up at the bridge. "Nice boat."

"Thanks. Look, Ethan, before we get started, I owe you an apology."

He gave her a funny look, as if he couldn't believe what she'd said. "Should I get a tape recorder?"

She laughed. "No, I'm willing to admit I was wrong. I condemned your idea about starting your own fishing operation without thinking."

"Don't worry about it."

"No, I want to be fair. After all, you're the one with all the business experience. I should be grateful for your advice."

His eyes narrowed suspiciously. Maybe she was laying

it on a bit too thick. Ethan was a smart man. "Besides, Finn thinks having two charters in town is a good idea, too."

"Oh? Finn thinks so?"

"Yes. And who am I to argue with both of you?" She set the rod she'd been rigging on the deck floor and stuck out her hand. "So, no hard feelings?"

He clasped her hand in both of his. "Of course not." While she readied the boat, he leaned against the railing and watched. "Tell me about the *Finn Catcher*," he said.

Helen breathed easier. He'd accepted her apology. "This is a thirty-four-foot Sportfisherman. She's powered by a pair of two hundred horse diesel engines." She pointed to the chrome outriggers mounted to the deck rail. "The boat's fitted for both trolling and bottom fishing."

"And today we're bottom fishing?"

"Yep."

He pointed to the silver disc she'd been tying to a line. "What's that?"

"It's called a spoon. When it moves in the water the fish are attracted to it."

That would be true if they were going to be trolling on the surface, which they weren't. A stationary spoon definitely didn't attract anything on the bottom.

"And what are those things with the fringes?" He indicated the other rods, propped up against the cabin entrance. Each was rigged with colorful plastic lures.

"They're called skirts. They work on the same principle as the spoon. When a fish sees them, it thinks a bait fish is in the area, and goes for it." True again, if they were trolling.

"What are we going to use for bait?" Ethan asked.

Knowing the proper bait for spoons and skirts was ballyhoo and squid, Helen opened the lid to the bait box to show Ethan the specially prepared contents. "Have a look. We're using cut mullet." *Tainted with leftover turkey and a few drops of kerosene and left out overnight to get good and ripe.*

He peered inside and immediately jumped back. "Whew, that stinks."

She grinned up at him and slammed the box shut. The smell was almost more than she could stand. "Not to a fish it doesn't."

"So, how do you think we'll do today? Did you catch anything this morning?"

"I'm sorry to say we didn't," she said, thankful that the rule of the *Finn Catcher* was that catches had to be released back into the water. There was no evidence of the successful trip she'd had this morning. She tried to sound casual when she added, "The truth is, Ethan, it's getting harder and harder to find decent schools these days."

"Why is that?"

"Waters get fished out. Sometimes it's only temporary. Sometimes it lasts for years."

"What causes that?"

"Too much commercial fishing. A change in environmental conditions. New algae growth. Any number of factors. Here in Heron Point, we've been in kind of a dry spell." She smiled up at him as she unwound the heavy mooring line from the dock. "Of course, we don't advertise that fact to our customers."

"So, you're saying we might not catch anything?"

She shrugged, not wanting to appear overly negative.

"It's possible." She pointed to the chair bolted next to the captain's position. "Have a seat. We're ready to go."

He adjusted the bill on his cap and looked into the horizon. "Those clouds…you really think they'll blow over?"

"Oh, sure. Nothing to worry about."

She kicked the storage bin under his seat with the toe of her sneaker. "But just so you know, your life jacket's in there." She laughed when his gaze snapped to hers. "It's required by law, Princeton. We've never had to use them."

She started the powerful engines, feeling the vibrations of the restrained force of twin Mercury motors. Then she thrust the throttle forward and the *Finn Catcher* shot into the pearl-gray water of the Gulf. With most rookie fishermen, she would have started out slowly, built up to the *Finn Catcher's* potential. But not with this rookie.

She looked at Ethan. His eyes were wide. He gripped the edge of his seat and said, "Wow."

Wow is right. Hang on, Princeton. It's going to be a bumpy ride.

CHAPTER ELEVEN

HELEN SKIRTED AROUND THE SMALL ISLAND where the 1850 Heron Point lighthouse sat proudly, guarding the entrance to Heron Bay.

A group of Saturday tourists had boarded the ferry to head back to town. The weekend educational visits were a highlight of Heron Point activities, and the retired naval commander who lived at the lighthouse did a great job explaining the details of the beacon's operation.

Helen slowed the boat's speed so she wouldn't swamp the shore of Lighthouse Key, but once past the docking area she sped up again. "Have you been to the lighthouse yet?" she asked Ethan, who still looked as if he were a long way from acquiring his sea legs.

"No. It's on my list, though." He flinched as the bow came out of the water, rode a five-foot wave and slapped the surface again.

From out of nowhere, Helen had an image of herself in her junior year at Micopee High School. She was in Home Economics class, straining over an apple appliqué she was required to stitch on the pocket of an apron she'd made the week before. The teacher came up behind her, looked over her shoulder and said, "My, Helen, you take to sewing just like a lobster takes to roller skates."

If Helen hadn't adored old Mrs. Feldman, who'd been a fixture at the school for forty years, she might have truly been hurt and lashed back with a few choice words. As it was, she merely smiled up at the teacher's smug grin and said, "I see you've been out to Heron Point, Mrs. F. The crustacean roller derby is one of our biggest tourist attractions."

The two had had a good laugh, and Helen had proceeded to insult her gingham apron with the biggest, most grotesque stitches anyone had ever sewn.

At this moment, Ethan reminded her of that lobster on roller skates. That's how uncomfortable he looked sitting stiff-backed in his chair, his eyes fixed on the gathering clouds, his hands glued to the arms of the chair. He was probably wondering how he could get into the storage bin under his seat to get to that life jacket without being hurtled into the Gulf.

"Relax, Princeton," she said. "Everything's fine." It was. Helen knew that, and Ethan was obviously struggling to believe her. She had to give him credit. He was trying to prove himself an apt sailor. He'd asked lots of questions about the boat's gauges and equipment, the wind direction, the *Finn Catcher*'s speed and, as the shoreline disappeared behind them, how she knew the way back. He'd listened most intently to that last answer.

Helen slowed when they were a few miles offshore. She carefully checked the depth finder to be certain there were no schools of fish in their vicinity when she released the electric anchor, which would keep the boat from drifting into a more fertile area.

Ethan stood up, spread his legs to balance himself in the rough surf and arched his back. "We're here?"

"Yeah, this looks as good as any place." She gestured to the depth finder screen. "See those blips?"

He studied the monitor, focusing on the dots of undersea activity which were probably only a school of tiny bait fish, sardines or even floating seaweed. Certainly not anything with gills worth hooking. "I guess so."

She chose a rod and reel for him, the one with the silvery spoon, and opened the box loaded with her specially prepared bait. She couldn't be so cruel as to make him bait his own hook, not with the disgusting mess she and Finn had created out of rotting fish, turkey and kerosene. "I'll set this one up for you and get you started."

Grateful to close the lid on the box again, Helen quickly slipped a mushy glob on the hook, tossed it over the side of the boat and lowered it into the water. She then handed Ethan the rod and showed him how to release enough line to lower the hook forty feet to the Gulf floor.

"Now what do I do?" he asked.

"Now you wait. If something down there finds the menu attractive, you'll know it."

"What about those clouds? Aren't they getting close?"

They were, but Helen only shrugged. "That storm's miles away yet. We've got plenty of time. Besides, we can outrun it."

Ethan leaned against the deck rail to steady himself against the increasing waves that rocked the *Finn Catcher*. He stared at his line where it disappeared into the murky water. Helen sat in a chair, leaned back and lowered her cap onto her forehead. It was a good time for a rest.

After a few minutes he said, "Shouldn't I be doing something?"

Helen raised her cap bill, opened one eye and said, "Jiggle it a little. Can't hurt."

After a half hour he said, "Helen, nothing's happening. I should be feeling tugs on the line, shouldn't I?"

She stood up and walked over to the railing. "If there were fish, yes." She glanced at the depth finder which still showed insignificant radar blips. "Oh, they've moved," she said in her most convincing voice. "So should we."

She raised the anchor, moved the boat a few hundred yards, dropped anchor, changed his bait and handed him the rod again. "Maybe this is a good spot."

Thirty more minutes went by. The only change in their situation was an increase in the intensity of the waves. The boat pitched with each pounding of the whitecaps against her hull. The water was almost as gray as the sky. In the distance, lightning zigzagged across the horizon.

Ethan's face paled. "Guys really like doing this?"

Helen smiled to herself. "Everyone I take out has high hopes when we start into the Gulf. But, like I told you, fishing has been pretty bad lately."

He pressed a hand over his stomach and trapped a burp in his throat. "Shouldn't we be getting back? It's a little rough."

"Getting squeamish?" she asked.

"No. I'm fine."

Right. She took a small aluminum square out of her pocket, broke open the seal and handed him a tiny pill. "Here, chew this. It'll calm your stomach."

He didn't argue. "Maybe we should change the bait," he suggested after another few minutes.

"Probably a good idea," Helen said as a clap of thunder

rolled over their heads. Ethan cringed and she was suddenly convinced it was time to leave. "Never mind," she said. "Reel up. We're going back."

He worked furiously to bring up the hook. Helen thought she heard him murmur, "Thank God."

Feeling the effects of the waves herself, Helen held on to boat fixtures to return to the captain's position. She sat down and turned the key in the ignition. The motor rumbled to life. And Ethan, who had stopped reeling, was coming to life himself.

He called from the side of the boat. "Helen! I've got something!"

What? Impossible. She looked over and sure enough, he was hanging on for dear life to a rod that was arcing at a nearly ninety-degree angle. "Don't leave yet!" he said. "I can't believe it. I caught something." He shot her a frantic look over his shoulder. "What do I do now?"

Well, damn. She couldn't help herself. Her fishing instincts took over and she rushed to his side. She pretended the rod and reel were in her own hands. "Do this," she shouted above the thunder. She arched her back, pulled upwards and then used her right hand to illustrate a reeling motion. "Pull the rod up with a steady motion. When you let it down again, reel. Keep the tip pointed at the water. When you feel another tug, yank up again!"

He followed her instruction. "Oh, my God, I feel it." He glanced at her for a second before turning his attention back to the task. "This is a good-size fish, isn't it?"

Unbelievably, it seemed to be. "Looks like a ten-pounder, at least," she said.

He pulled up with a steady pressure and reeled. "This

is so great, Helen," he laughed. "Much better than just standing here counting lightning bolts."

But it wasn't supposed to happen! Helen continued coaxing him, feeling the fight of the fish in her own arms, in the pit of her stomach. And she realized that this board-room executive was experiencing the thrill of a big catch as if he'd been born to it. And despite her plan to keep him from snagging anything, she was happy for him.

After another minute of fighting the fish, Ethan looked over at her, the excitement of the moment glowing in his eyes, fixed in his wide grin. His gaze held hers and grew intense. "I need both hands to do this, right?" he said.

"Of course. Don't let go."

He handed the rod to her. "Then hold this a second. There's something I need to do."

She took the rod without thinking, her instinct to continue the action automatic. She spared a quick glance at the water and then looked at Ethan. He was so close she could feel the heat from his skin, smell the combination of sea air and pine-scented aftershave. In one swift movement he reached around her, cupped the back of her head and lowered his mouth to hers. The kiss was hard, hungry, charged with energy, and the pull of the line equaled the pull deep inside her.

Her grip on the rod loosened as her knees grew weak. And then he raised his head and grinned at her. "I just had to do that," he said. She blinked, drew her lips between her teeth, still tasting him. He grabbed the rod handle and went back to work. Thunder clapped. The boat rolled. Helen swayed and grabbed the deck rail. This was the most exciting time she'd ever known on the water.

She was still feeling the effects when she realized that whatever was on the end of Ethan's line wasn't a fish.

"Looks like I've tired him out," Ethan said when the pull on the rod lessened and the reeling became continuous and effortless.

Helen leaned over the rail. "That can happen, but…"

She was the first to see rippling plastic break the surface of the choppy water. With her arms crossed on the rail, she looked up into Ethan's eyes. Her elaborate plans to keep him from catching a fish had proved successful. And she felt terrible about it.

"What is it?" he asked, staring at her as if sensing her disappointment in her features. He had no idea that all he was dragging to the boat was a clear plastic bag.

"Sorry, Princeton. Looks like a false alarm," she said.

He looked down as the bag, weighted with a couple of pounds of seaweed, rose above the water. The words Clear Cubes of Tampa were still visible in blue ink. He gave the rod one final tug and the bag, now empty of ten pounds of water, flew over his head and landed on the deck of the *Finn Catcher* with a disheartening soggy plop.

His face fell. He set down the rod and said, "It's an ice bag."

"Yeah, it is." Helen tried to smile, to make light of the situation, but it wasn't easy. "Look on the bright side," she said. "It's a ten-pound size, an impressive haul for a bag catch. And besides, think about what you've done for the environment today."

He didn't look mollified. "Oh? What's that?"

"Some ignorant fisherman probably threw this bag into the Gulf not knowing, or not caring, that this stuff is almost indestructible. It takes years for plastic to decompose in the water, and in the meantime, fish and other sea creatures can get caught in it and die."

He picked up the slippery mess, held it over the side and squeezed it, letting water dribble back into the Gulf. "Glad I could help." Then, tossing the limp bag into the cooler, he said, "So, after two hours, this is all we have to show for our effort."

She raised her palms, a gesture of commiseration. "Don't say I didn't warn you."

A streak of lightning followed her words. The storm was definitely too close for comfort. "And don't say I didn't warn *you*," Ethan said.

"You're right." She went to her seat as fast as conditions allowed. "Sit down, Ethan, and hold on. It's time we got out of here."

She pulled up anchor, turned the boat around and raced in the direction of shore. When she'd put a safe distance between the *Finn Catcher* and the threatening sky, she glanced at Ethan and shouted above the roar of the powerful diesel engines. "It wasn't a total waste of time." When he merely raised his eyebrows, she touched her fingers to her lips. "I liked the way you expressed your excitement."

It was maybe the first time all afternoon she hadn't been lying.

WHEN SHE PULLED THE *Finn Catcher* alongside the dock at nearly five o'clock, Helen realized she was exhausted. Fishing, guiding the boat through a storm and being down-right deceitful to a guy she really liked was wearing her out.

She recalled Doc Tucker telling her that she could

expect to feel tired quite often during the first trimester of her pregnancy. Of course, when he'd said that, Helen had dismissed it as nonsense. She'd worked long hours her whole life. She was used to it. Now she understood that being accustomed to hard work was not the same as being accustomed to pregnancy. Or maybe guilt had exhausted her. It wasn't so easy to rationalize cheating someone out of what could have been a truly memorable experience.

Ethan climbed onto the dock, taking his cooler with him. "You want one of these sandwiches?" he asked.

Food was the last thing on her mind. "No, I'll pass."

"Thanks for taking me out," he said.

This guy really knows how to twist the knife, Helen thought, conscious of the fact that he was innocently thanking her for conniving against him. She dropped the dock bumpers over the side of the boat, the last step in securing the *Finn Catcher*. "Sure. Anytime."

"You want to get together later? Maybe dinner at the Tail and Claw?"

This was too much. He was even willing to take her on a date. "I'm kind of tired," she said.

"Okay. Why don't you have a rest. I'll call you in a couple of hours to see if you're up for it."

"How 'bout if I call you? I'm not sure if Pop needs me for anything."

He stroked his thumb and finger across his jawline as if pondering her suggestion. "You're really going to call?"

"Of course." That was true. She'd call him, but her guilty conscience probably wouldn't allow her to accept his offer of a dinner out, at least not tonight. "I'll definitely call."

"Talk to you later, then."

He walked off, leaving her to sort through her mixed feelings. Yesterday she'd been absolutely certain that a wild fish chase was exactly what Ethan deserved. But today, as she retrieved a garbage bag from the *Catcher*'s small galley, and dumped the stinking mess of altered bait into it, she wondered if she wasn't getting what *she* deserved. She wrinkled her nose and fought a wave of nausea. "I hope you can't smell any of this, Bean. You shouldn't suffer for the stupid stuff your mother does."

She tied the bag and dropped it into the garbage pail on the way to the cottage. Twenty minutes later she'd relayed the ice bag story to Finn, taken a shower and climbed between clean sheets. As she drifted to sleep, she let the mountain fresh scent of laundry detergent erase the foul reminders of how she'd spent the last four hours.

BY SEVEN-THIRTY ETHAN was starved and convinced that Helen wasn't going to call him, despite her promise to do so. Plus, he was no longer confident about his plan to start his own charter fishing business at Dolphin Run. If Helen was right, then the waters around Heron Point no longer yielded enough game fish to make the enterprise worth the expense. He'd witnessed the accuracy of her evaluation himself, and decided he should consider giving up his idea.

But was he willing to give up Helen? Lately, she'd been sending him mixed signals. Last night she'd declined his offer to spend time with him at Dolphin Run. But just today she'd responded to his kiss with the passion he'd come to enjoy from her. She'd turned down his dinner invitation but promised to call him. But she hadn't, and he wasn't about to spend another night surfing channels in the lobby of Dolphin Run. So what else should he do? Bother Jack and Claire? No. Mingle with the tourists who no doubt still clogged the main artery into town? Possibly, but not his first choice.

Left with no appealing alternative, Ethan once again sought out Wayne Bertoli. He found the guard in the kitchen slicing a twelve-inch submarine roll. "Is that what you're having for dinner?" Ethan asked. "A sandwich?"

"Yeah. I bought some salami at the deli today."

Maybe Helen turned down his invitation to dinner, but Ethan knew the Anderson Enterprises security guards wouldn't. "Call Joel at the gate," he said. "We're going into town to eat. My treat."

This time the guard didn't hesitate. Ethan figured Wayne had become as convinced as he was that kidnappers were no longer interested in Archie's son.

Assuming the guards had gotten around more than he had and knew the best places to eat, Ethan asked, "Where would you like to go?"

"There's a little dive over by the marina," Wayne said. "It caters to the locals and has the best chicken wings in town. And the cheapest beer."

"Sounds good to me," Ethan said. Five minutes later the three men were headed around Gulfview Road to the town's only marina. Neon signs directed Ethan to the roadside restaurant next to the public docks, and he parked between a pair of old pickup trucks. The beer was cold and the service was good. Maybe the night wouldn't be a total loss.

Ethan was devouring his twelfth wing when he took the time to notice the decor of the old restaurant. Nautical items covered the grease-spattered walls and even hung from ceiling hooks. Photographs of local residents caught his eye and he scanned the various pictures to see if he recognized anyone. Jack or Claire, perhaps.

Or Helen Sweeney.

Once he saw the first picture of Helen, he noticed quickly that she appeared in many of the photos. And in every one of them, there was also a fisherman or two proudly displaying his catch. To Ethan's unpracticed eye, the fish in the pictures were admirable specimens ranging from five to possibly almost a hundred pounds. And in each photo, Helen was smiling as if she'd personally contributed to the successful outing.

Ethan stopped his waiter as he walked by. "Those shots on the wall of Helen Sweeney…"

The waiter took a quick look, scanning the nearest photos. "Yeah?"

"Those must have been taken a long time ago."

"Why do you say that?"

"I was fishing with Helen today," Ethan explained. "She told me that the waters around Heron Point are fished out. Have been for a while, now."

The waiter laughed. "You gotta be kidding." He pointed to a nearby photo. "That one was taken yesterday morning. The tourist who caught that twenty-pound grouper stopped on his way out of town and gave us the picture. Said it's the only reminder that he'd bagged such a good catch since Helen makes everybody release their fish."

"Yesterday?" Ethan pushed his chair away from the table and gestured around the room. "What about the others? Are any other pictures recent?"

"Oh, sure." The waiter pointed out several examples.

"Each one is dated on the back," he said, "so you can check for yourself. But I don't think any of these shots go back more than a couple of months." He shook his head. "And as for the Gulf being fished out, I don't know what kind of line Helen was feeding you, but it sure isn't so."

The vein in Ethan's temple began to throb. He slid his plate to the middle of the table. Suddenly, the smell of spicy wing sauce was as unappetizing as the news he was hearing. "Is Helen a good fishing guide?" he asked.

The waiter didn't even need a second to think about his answer. "The best. A couple other fishermen around here will take customers out on private trips, but Helen's the one who does the charters. And she should. She knows these waters like the back of her hand."

Ethan squeezed the bridge of his nose. He knew the answer to his next question but asked it anyway. "Tell me something, would you use a spoon or a skirt to bottom fish?"

The waiter laughed. "To bottom fish? A spoon? No way. That's for trolling, for going after sailfish or marlin. Your bottom fish, like groupers or snapper, would ignore a line rigged like that."

"Why, that little—" Ethan stopped when an appropriate ending to his sentence eluded him. Right now he couldn't think of anything to accurately describe Helen.

"Anything else?" the waiter asked.

"No, that ought to do it," Ethan said.

Wayne leaned over the table. "What's the matter, Ethan? You look like your puppy just died."

Ethan took his cell phone out of his pocket. "If it's okay with you two, I'm going to call Jack to take you back to the inn. I've got an errand to run."

"That's okay, but we're supposed to be there whenever you are."

"Don't worry. I'm not going to Dolphin Run. You guys stay here as long as you want."

He made the arrangements with Jack, paid the tab and went to his car. He rolled the window down as he headed toward Helen's cottage, but even the chill in the night air didn't cool him off.

CHAPTER TWELVE

HE'D LIED TO THE GUARDS. Ethan definitely intended to take Helen to Dolphin Run where he could confront her about her deceit on *his* turf for once. He would get her away from her cantankerous father and any other hometown cronies who might interfere, and sit her down in the lobby where she couldn't run away. He wasn't sure how he was going to convince her to come with him, but one way or another, he was determined to prevail.

The Suburban was in the driveway. Lights were on in Helen's cottage. Ethan strode up the sidewalk and pounded on the front door. After a minute, Finn opened it. When he saw Ethan, he scowled. "What are you doing here?"

"Hello, Finn. Where's Helen?"

"Sleeping."

"Would you please wake her up?"

"No. You can come back another time. Or better yet, call."

Tightly controlled civility masked both men's voices. "Sorry, but I need to see her now."

Finn blocked the entrance with his wheelchair. "Too bad. I already told you…"

"I know what you told me…"

From the hallway, a door creaked open. Helen walked

into the living room rubbing her finger over one eye. She wore a pair of jersey boxer shorts and a Green Door Café T-shirt. "Pop, who's here?" When she saw Ethan, she dropped her hand to her side and her eyes widened. "What's going on?"

He stepped over the threshold, forcing Finn to retreat. "I've come to have a word with you, Helen. I'm sure it doesn't come as a big surprise."

She stared at him a moment as if judging how seriously to take his commanding attitude, or, typical of her, figuring out how much she could get away with. "Actually, it does. I told you I'd call you."

He glanced at his watch. "It's almost nine. When were you planning to call?"

She attempted a casual shrug, but the flush in her cheeks indicated she felt anything but casual. "About nine…or so."

"Well, good. Then my timing is just about right."

One hip jutted out when she placed her fist on it. The hem of her boxers rode up the other thigh, displaying even more of a slender, tanned leg. Ethan swallowed hard, focused his gaze above her neck where her hair stuck out in the craziest way, as if she'd been tossing in bed. He dropped his attention to her chest. No help there. Her breasts thrust against the thin fabric of her shirt, the nipples erect. Ethan silently cursed himself when his mind took a dangerous detour. He didn't want to think of devious Helen as sexy and desirable.

"So, what do you want?" she said.

"I'd like you to come with me so we can talk privately."

She looked at Finn. He pointedly cleared his throat and shook his head. "It's late, Ethan," she said. "Maybe tomorrow, or…"

She wasn't putting him off. Not after what she'd done this afternoon. Not after the way his body was reacting to her tonight. Ethan struggled to shove those reactions to the back burner of his brain. Unfortunately, *burning,* in more ways than one, was exactly how he felt. "I'm not *asking* you, Helen."

She released a long sigh. "Well, then, I guess I'll go with you. Give me a second."

She headed toward the kitchen. Ethan positioned himself so he could see the back door. She wasn't going to escape. Finn followed behind her, talking as if he'd forgotten Ethan was in the room. "You don't have to go with him, Helen. I'll send him packing. He can't bully you...."

She raised her hand in a placating gesture as she opened the refrigerator door. "It's okay, Pop." She mumbled something about slipping up somehow, and Ethan knew she realized her little plan had been discovered.

She came back into the living room with a bottle of ginger ale in her hand. "Want one?" she asked.

"No."

"Okay. Let's go."

The wheelchair squeaked as Finn trailed them to the door. "Don't you lay a hand on her, young man. If you do..."

Ethan spun around. "For Pete's sake, Finn. I'm not going to hurt her. Even if I were that kind of a guy, which I'm not, I'd be afraid she'd rip my head off."

Finn's chest puffed out in an exaggerated expression of pride. "She could, you know."

And from halfway down the sidewalk, Helen sputtered a chuckle as she wiped ginger ale from her lips with the back of her hand.

"WHERE ARE WE GOING?" she asked when they were in the car. She looked down at her attire. "Usually I don't worry about this sort of thing, but even I know I'm not dressed for the Tail and Claw." She seemed to find something fascinating about his profile. "And from that throbbing in your temple, I'm pretty sure this isn't a real date, anyway."

"We're going to Dolphin Run."

"You have any food there?"

Obviously she wasn't the least bit concerned about being alone with him. He remembered the deli fixings Wayne had put back into the refrigerator. "I can make a sandwich."

She nodded, accepting his offer.

Neither spoke during the mile-long trip. Helen sipped her ginger ale, stared into the darkness out her window. At the gate, Ethan got out and opened the lock. He drove through overhanging trees and parked in front of the inn. Helen got out and walked to the door, waiting for him. When they went inside, Ethan turned on a lamp by a sofa nearest the fireplace. The logs were still there, stacked neatly, waiting for someone to light them. Ethan mentally chastised himself for the romantic notions he'd had the night before. And for the regret he was feeling at not being able to light the same fire now.

"Have a seat," he said. "I'll get your sandwich." He put the car keys in his pocket, but still stopped midway to the dining room. "Do you know how to hot-wire a car?"

"Of course." She settled into the sofa. "But don't worry. I won't."

He went into the kitchen and fixed the sub. When he brought it to her, she dropped a magazine she'd been reading on the coffee table. "This *Saturday Evening Post* is over forty years old," she said. "You could probably sell it on eBay."

He smirked. "Great idea, Helen. I see you never tire of giving me the benefit of your knowledge."

No doubt pretending to miss the point of his jibe, she took a big bite of the sub and leisurely chewed and swallowed. After taking another sip of her drink, she finally said, "Okay, Ethan, let's hear it. How'd you put it together?"

He sat in a chair on the other side of the coffee table. "It wasn't hard. I went to the Marina Tavern tonight. Your picture is plastered all over the walls—yours and several gigantic fish which you personally helped customers catch."

She paused with the sandwich partway to her mouth and stared at him. "You went to the Marina Tavern?"

Sensing an undercurrent of amusement in the question, he said, "What's so strange about that?"

Her gaze traveled from the top of his head to his leather boat shoes. "Oh, come on, Princeton. It's a local place. I sure never figured the Marina Tavern would be my undoing. Only our burping, beer-bellied male population goes there. You're definitely the Tail and Claw type—all spit and polish, and city-bred poise…."

Her words obliterated any remaining thoughts about the fireplace, their utter aloneness, the sheen of her softly curling hair, the outline of her breasts. He was that angry, and determined to let her see it. "Will you cut the crap for once, Helen?"

She dropped the sandwich to her lap. Her eyes were suddenly as round as the salami he'd just layered into the bread. "What did you say?" The question was indignant, self-righteous.

"All this Princeton nonsense. The name-calling, the unfounded assumptions about what I'm like, the condescending attitude that I'm not up to your standards."

Her breath came out in a bark of laughter. "My standards? Hell, I don't even have any standards! You're the one with the college education, the rich father, the perfect manners."

"Yeah, and for some reason you love pointing out to me that I don't fit here. That I don't fit you. I'm tired of it, Helen. I'm well aware there's a lot I don't know. You had a grand time pointing that out to me today. Well, congratulations. You successfully put me in my place—again. You humiliated me and pointed out my shortcomings. And since you obviously haven't figured this out on your own, let me tell you—what you did was low and conniving and dishonest. And beneath you!"

She huffed. "Beneath me? No, it isn't. It's all I know how to do. I can't fight your ridiculous threat to open your own charter company with money. I don't have any. I can't fight it with logic. I don't have your debate-team savvy. After living here all my life, I don't even have your power, which you just gained by coming here as the answer to all our financial woes. You've got the upper hand. All I can do is fight dirty."

"Oh, please. This 'poor little me' act of yours doesn't impress me, any more than your underhanded plots and deceitful maneuvering."

She breathed heavily, the air escaping her lungs in short, frantic bursts. She slammed her plate on the coffee table. "What exactly do you want from me, Ethan? Do you expect me to apologize for protecting my business, my future, my—" She stopped short, pursed her lips.

He waited a moment and then said, "It would be a start, yes!"

HELEN WAS SEETHING. If she hadn't seen for herself that the sky had been gray and threatening all afternoon, she would have sworn this man had been out in the sun too long. She leaned forward on the sofa and fixed him with a glare that had made many men before him back off. Unfortunately, in the last few minutes, she'd begun to understand that she had underestimated this particular *GQ* specimen. "So, you're just going to sit there and wait for me to apologize?"

He folded his arms over his chest. "Yes, I am."

"What would I be apologizing for, exactly?"

He held up his hand and began counting off on his fingers. "Wrecking my rental car and running off leaving me with a false phone number." He narrowed his eyes. "I still don't know if you have auto insurance, by the way." He bent the second finger. "Risking both of our lives by heading hell-bent into a thunderstorm just so I would be miserable on the open water…"

"We weren't in any danger. I know what I'm doing out there—"

He threatened her into silence with a piercing stare. "I'm not done." Third finger. "Making a fool of me, not just this afternoon with your little fish game, but many times."

"Oh, for heaven's sake. When have I ever made a fool of you?"

"You've done it by being the most frustrating woman I have ever met. One minute you're coming on to me. The next you're too tired, you're too busy. For all I know, you're comparing me to your louse of an ex-boyfriend, and I'm coming up loser."

Her mouth dropped open. He was accusing her of coming on to him? That hadn't been her plan, but it was sort of cool to hear he'd thought she was. "I've never come on to you," she said, her voice reflecting the awe of discovering that she may have used a few feminine tricks she didn't even know she possessed.

"Oh, yes you have. You pull my chain about as easily as I turned on that lamp a few minutes ago."

"That's ridiculous. I do not."

He shook his head. "Don't play dumb. You're not, and we both know it."

She threaded her fingers together and stuffed her hands into her lap. For some idiotic reason, she felt like smiling, but didn't think Ethan would appreciate it. She'd considered that he was interested in her, in a fling sort of way. But other than one brief consultation with Claire, fixing up her hair and buying a new blouse, she hadn't done anything to make him think she was chasing him—not with any sexual intent. She wasn't trying to get him into bed, though of course that thought had entered her mind. He was gorgeous, and she was human, after all.

Still, her intentions toward Ethan had always been single-minded. She wanted his cooperation for the *Finn Catcher.* For the Bean. She wanted his contacts, his influence, his *help.* But she was never foolhardy enough to think she could actually have *him.* They were as opposite as any two people could be. Nor was she trying to trap him into marrying her or assuming any responsibility for the Bean. He'd stated very plainly that he didn't want children, and even if he hadn't made that fact perfectly clear, she didn't play *that* dirty. Or that stupidly. Ethan Anderson was Manhattan. He looked it, acted it, good grief, even smelled it. He would never stoop so low as to settle for Heron Point.

So, who was pulling the chains at this moment? As far as Helen could tell, Ethan was yanking the guilt chain with a vengeance. Sure, he was angry, maybe he even had a right to be, but he wasn't going to get away with making her the only villain in this situation. Until a minute ago, Helen was convinced that she didn't have the skills to come on to a man like Ethan. But as she stared into his eyes at this moment, she decided that he was about as desperate for an apology and a mending of his fractured ego as any man she'd ever seen. Imagine—Helen Sweeney had somehow wounded the self-esteem of Ethan Anderson. It was almost preposterous.

"So, where do we stand on this?" he said after moments of uncomfortable silence.

Quite casually, so much that she mentally applauded her ability to remain cool in the face of pressure, Helen took a small bite of sandwich, prayed it wouldn't stick in her throat, and said, "I think I've made myself quite clear about where I stand. I want you to give up the idea of competing with my business."

"That's ridiculous."

She lifted her chin, not to be haughty, but to give the appearance of being in control. "Not to me it isn't."

He stood up, rolled his shoulders and began to pace. "Let me get this straight," he said. "I'm supposed to overlook everything you've done, ignore sound business principles, give up my obvious right to an apology and say, 'Sure, Helen, whatever you want'?"

She swallowed, took a sip of ginger ale. "That would

be nice. But I would also like you to send your Dolphin Run customers interested in fishing to me."

The shoulders he'd just rolled suddenly squared as he nearly choked on his astonishment. "I'm sure you would. And what do I get?"

She leaned back on the sofa and gave him a smirk. It was a dangerous thing to do, but sometimes her mouth acted without apparent guidance from her brain. "I'll give up my idea of going to the town council to establish a moratorium on new businesses in Heron Point."

He stopped pacing, fisted his hands and placed them on his hips. "What? You could do that? You *would* do that?"

"And I promise to stop torturing you with all these womanly wiles I've somehow managed to acquire in the last week and a half." She stood up with the intention of escaping his incensed glare by taking her plate into the kitchen. Just the coffee table separated them.

He leaned slightly forward. "You think this is a joke, don't you?"

"No. I think it's a pitiful attempt to get what you want, which is what I have."

"You think I've admitted how you get under my skin just so I can convince you that I should start my own fishing charter? You think I'm that manipulative? That deceitful?" He shook a finger at her over the coffee table. "Oh, no, Miss Almighty Righteous. That's your game. That's how you play."

"Oh, come on, Ethan. Look at me." She raked her fingers through her sleep-tousled hair, gave a self-deprecating sweep of her body, taking in the stretched-tight T-shirt, the skimpy boxers, her bare feet. "I'm not buying

your story about how I tempt you for a New York minute."
She reached across the table and grabbed his wrist. "So you
can just point that finger where it rightly belongs…"

A sound came from his throat which was almost a
growl. With one smooth move, he twisted his hand so that
he now held her wrist. He raised his foot, slammed it
against edge of the coffee table and sent the piece of furniture skidding across the room. "You're driving me crazy,
Helen, and I can only think of one thing to do about it."

She didn't have time to ask what that one thing was. He
pulled her to him with such force she collided against his
chest, which she noted again was surprisingly solid for a
bonafide member of the Executive Washroom Club. And
nicely rippled, and pounding with a rhythm that was as
rapid as her own. Were they both so fired with the adren-
aline of their anger that their hearts were about to burst out
of their rib cages?

His mouth covered hers, parted her lips and made way
for his tongue. His probing kiss instantly stirred emotional
embers that had been simmering right along with her
temper for the last half hour. Maybe they were angry at
each other, but there was something else going on that was
even more potent, and she was powerless to deny it. He
looped his arms around her waist, and the palms of his
hands cupped her fanny. She reached up and threaded her
fingers at his nape. And in typical Helen Sweeney style,
she gave as good as she got.

When he finally drew back, his eyes were glazed with
a passion that had nothing to do with wild-fish chases or
battle tactics. She thought about speaking, but was afraid
only a rusty little squeak might come from her throat. He

stared at her a moment, narrowed his eyes as if trying to evaluate what was happening between them with some semblance of logic and then hissed through clenched teeth, "Damn it all, Helen."

He scooped her up into his arms and headed for the wide staircase. She held on, clinging to his neck, dizzy with the sensations coursing through her limbs and the taste of him still on her lips. "Where are we going?" she whispered in a hoarse voice.

He gave her an indulgent sort of cockeyed grin as his arms tightened around her body. His fingertips pressed the side of her breast through the thin jersey. Her breath hitched.

"From this level, the stairs only go one way," he said.

She curved her mouth into an oval of surprise and stared at him wide-eyed. "Why, Ethan Anderson, this isn't you. You don't pick women up and carry them off to your bedroom."

He paused, holding her over a plush easy chair. "You want me to drop you right here? Would that make you feel better about who you think I am?"

"No. I kind of like experiencing this side of you. I'd like to see how far you're going to take this."

"Good. Then we're going up." He hit the first step. She felt as if she was floating, weightless in his arms. "I might give you one more chance to back out when we get up there," he said. "And then…"

She chuckled into his ear and pressed little kisses against his skin. "You know me better than that. I'm not a woman who backs down."

AN INTENSE HEAT PENETRATED Helen's clothes everywhere Ethan's hands touched. Even when he carried her into the bedroom and the breeze from the open window rushed over her, she still felt the liquid warmth seeping through her body. Maybe it was the hot flush of mortification over what she'd done to him that day. Possibly the fire of her anger fed the emotions building inside her. But, most definitely flames of passion stoked her senses and warmed her to her toes.

She thought she might explode from the combustible yearning swirling inside her. She wanted to free herself of her scanty clothes, feel the cool wash of wind against the smoldering slickness of his skin on hers. She'd never experienced a need quite like this one—not with any other man. Stone-cold sober, her wits threatened only by desire, she was keenly aware that she needed Ethan against her, inside her, part of her.

He set her down on the floor and she immediately reached for the bottom of his T-shirt. She yanked the garment over his head and dropped it to the floor. Her fingers sought the fastening of his jeans and she worked it free. She went down on her knees in front of him, jerking the jeans and his underwear to his ankles. He stepped free of his clothing and shoes as he grabbed the material of her shirt in his fists and pulled the jersey over her head.

She stood, her breasts bared to his eyes. He slipped his hands inside her shorts, flattening his palms against her hips. With one motion, he drew the shorts to the floor, his hands sliding along her thighs, her calves, scooping under each foot to rid her of the last piece of clothing that kept him from exploring every fevered inch of her.

He clasped her face between his hands and bent to kiss her. "Are you coming on to me now, Helen?" he said. "Because it's definitely working."

She smiled. "Yes, now I am."

His lips crushed hers, almost stopped her breathing. She wrapped her arms around his neck and urged them toward the bed. They fell in a tangle of arms and legs, groans and throaty laughter. Her fingers frantically searched for body parts she'd only imagined until now. She raked her nails over his shoulders, down his chest, to where the fine mat of hair pointed downward.

His erection pressed between her legs, throbbed against her opening where need ached desperately, almost beyond reason. He thrust his tongue inside her mouth, circling, probing, riding the ridge of her teeth. He cupped her breasts, kneading them until the tips puckered in rhythm with the tightening between her legs. He curled one hand over her where her need burned most fiercely, slipped his finger inside and out, again and again, bringing her to a quick, intense orgasm. She shuddered, bit her lips and twisted her fingers through his hair. "Ethan, now…"

He reached out, yanked open a nightstand drawer and slapped at the interior. Pulling his mouth from hers, he leaned over, growled, "Damn, where is that thing?"

Her breath came in sharp gasps she almost didn't recognize as her own. She mumbled incoherently against his ear before finally pleading, "For Pete's sake, will you find it, *puh-leeze!*"

"I'm looking!" After a frustratingly long moment during which she thought she might scream with the anticipation of wanting him inside her, he released a moan of satisfaction. She heard the subtle tear of plastic. A second later he entered her, full, hard, throbbing. She climaxed again almost instantly, and again when his body jerked and shuddered as his breath warmed her neck and his cry blended with hers.

He collapsed on top of her before rolling to his side and covering his forehead with his arm. His breathing was shallow, ragged. She turned toward him and watched his chest rise and fall. "Ethan?"

He blew out a long puff of air. "Good grief, Helen. That was…"

"I know."

He lowered his arm, slid it under her head and pulled her next to him. "That was quick."

"I know."

"Intense."

"Yes."

"I can do better."

"I don't see how."

He laughed softly. "Give me a few minutes. I'll show you."

She swallowed. Her nerve endings quivered at the myriad delightful tingles racing along her skin where his fingers caressed her. "Okay. A few minutes."

The phone beside his bed rang. "I'm going to ignore that."

She nodded. "I think you should."

It stopped and immediately started again. "What about now?" he asked.

"Ignore it."

It rang a third time. "Now?"

She sighed. "Answer it. It might be Pop."

He picked up the receiver, tucked it between his chin and shoulder. "Hello." After a pause, he said, "Yes, she's here." He held out the phone to her. "It's for you. Stan from the Lionheart Pub."

"Really? For me?" She propped herself up on one elbow and took the phone. "Stan?"

"Yeah, Helen, it's me. Finn gave me this number. Said you might be there."

"What's going on?"

"You told me to tell you if anybody ever came for Donny's boat. Well, they're out there now hitching it up to a truck."

She sat up a little straighter, read the clock on Ethan's bedside table. "No kidding. This late on a Saturday night?"

"Maybe they work kind of like repo guys, under the cloak of darkness."

That would be like Donny, Helen thought. Sneaking the boat away in the middle of the night so she couldn't find out where it was going.

"You coming over?" Stan asked. "I'll try to keep them here a while longer to give you time. I'm not promising anything, you understand, but I'll do my best."

She looked down at Ethan. He curled his hand over her shoulder and gave her a smile that threatened to melt her heart. Oh, hell, she thought. Maybe her Bean would never have a father, but that would be better than asking Donny for anything. "Never mind," she said to Stan. "Let it go. I've decided that the louse doesn't deserve what he left behind, anyway."

"Okay, Helen. Whatever you say."

"Thanks, Stan."

She handed the phone back to Ethan and he replaced it on the cradle. "Trouble?" he asked.

"No. Somebody I used to know was just leaving town for good. Stan thought I might want to say goodbye."

"But you don't?"

"I already did." She snuggled next to him. "Now, what were you saying?"

He slipped his finger under her chin, tilted her face up and kissed her deeply. She didn't think of Donny Jax again.

CHAPTER THIRTEEN

PET PADDED ON BARE FEET into the Sweeneys' kitchen and opened the refrigerator door to get the water jug. As she reached to take down a glass from the cupboard, she saw her reflection in the side of the old chrome toaster. Her face was flushed with the pinkish glow of sexual satisfaction. She smiled, touched her fingers lightly to her cheek. "You still love it, don't you, Petula?" she said. "And you love that ornery old man in the bedroom."

It was an apt description, since Finn had been especially ornery tonight. He was worried. Pet glanced at the wall clock. Almost twelve-thirty, not late for a young person like Helen to be out on a Saturday night, but Finn had spent the last half hour listening for the front door to open. Pet twisted off the cap of a pill bottle and shook one capsule into her palm. She walked back to the bedroom and handed the glass of water and pill to Finn. "Take this," she said while plumping his pillow. "I can tell you need it tonight."

He stared at the pill. "I don't know if I should. This medicine always makes me sleepy, and I want to stay alert as long as Helen is out with that Anderson fella."

"Now, Finn, don't jump to conclusions...."

"You didn't see him. That boy was really angry." He

frowned, closed his fist over the pill. "I suppose I should confess something to you."

Pet released a sigh. "What did you do now?"

"Helen and I sort of conspired against Ethan today."

Pet pulled a chair next to the bed and sat. "You were sneaky? Why, Finn, I can hardly believe such a thing."

He dismissed her sarcasm with a wave. "We had no choice. That fool is thinking of starting his own charter company at Dolphin Run. He wants to put us out of business. Helen and I were just protecting what we've taken years to build."

Pet covered her ears with both hands. "I don't want to know what you two did. That way, I can't be accused of aiding and abetting."

"Now who's jumping to conclusions? It's not like we broke the law or anything."

She dropped her hands to her lap. "I'm happy to know that. But I still suspect you might have broken a moral law, if nothing else."

Finn scowled at her. "Anyway, I suppose Anderson discovered what we did, and when he and Helen left the house tonight, he didn't look any too pleased."

"I don't guess he was." She placed her hand on Finn's arm. "But you don't have to worry about Ethan. From everything I can tell, he's a gentleman."

"You've heard of a wolf in sheep's clothing, haven't you, Pet?"

"Of course, but even a wolf would be in for the fight of its life if it tangled with Helen. She can take care of herself." She smiled. "If you want to know the truth, my sympathies right now are with Ethan."

She'd meant only to calm Finn's fears, but as she joked about Helen's prowess, she realized an underlying truth that maybe even Helen couldn't handle everything that life had thrown at her recently. "Except for…" Pet paused, aware that she'd been about to break a confidence.

"Except for what?" Finn prodded. "What are you thinking?"

"Nothing." When he returned a doubting look, she decided to confess to a little of what concerned her. It was time for Finn to step in and support his daughter, considering the overwhelming responsibility she might be facing in eight months and her growing attachment to a man who wasn't the baby's father. Without violating her promise to Helen, Pet said, "There is a way I think Helen could be hurt by Ethan."

"That's what I've been telling you," Finn said. "Helen's strong, but Ethan could crush her and our business with his power and his money and his high-handed ways…."

Pet raised a placating hand. "No, Finn. If anything, Helen could be crushed by his goodness."

Finn stared at her. "What are you talking about?"

How could she explain that Helen could be wounded by Ethan's decency, by subconsciously setting her hopes on a man whose honor, no matter how strong, wouldn't be able to stand up to the ultimate test she'd give him? She sighed, leaned over the bed. "Talk to Helen. Try to get her to open up to you. She needs you right now, maybe more than she ever has."

He narrowed his eyes. "What do you know? Is your ESP working overtime again?"

"This isn't ESP. I'm talking about facts, a situation in your daughter's life that needs addressing. You're her

father. You need to let her know that you're here support-
ing her every step of the way."

He looked down as if studying the patchwork design of
his blanket and slowly shook his head. "I hate when you
talk in riddles, Pet. Especially when you know I'm no
good at this female stuff, all this emotion, and…"

Pet shushed him by placing a finger at her lips. "Listen.
I think I hear a car pulling up out front." She hurried to the
door and returned a moment later. "She's back. Ethan's
dropping her off now."

"Thank goodness. Stay for a while. Can you?"

She sensed the insecurity in his voice, but she couldn't
help him. She'd given her word to Helen, and she'd
probably said too much already. Now it was up to Finn to
be the parent Helen needed. "I've got to work in the morning," she said, and curled her hand over Finn's arm. "You'll
be fine." She brushed his forehead with her lips and headed
for the bedroom door.

He stopped her before she could leave. "Petula?"

She turned back to him, waited.

"I don't know what I'd do without you sometimes."

She smiled. "You'd survive. There are a dozen women
in this town just waiting to fill my shoes."

"But none of them could. It's your footsteps I've gotten
used to, as well as every other part of you."

She felt the first hint of tears burning the backs of her
eyes. A spurt of warmth seeped through her body. After all
these years, was she finally close to getting what she
wanted? Once, not so long ago, she'd vowed never to get
married again. She'd tried it three times, and each union
had ended in disaster. But then she'd come to Heron Point

and met Finn, and she'd never been so much in love. She sniffled, ran a finger under her nose. "Finn Sweeney, you're a sentimental old goose."

He chuckled. "Good night, gorgeous."

HELEN COULDN'T SEEM TO make herself get out of the car. She had a charter in the morning, so she needed her rest, but Ethan's hand on her rib cage felt so good, so reassuring. His thumb lightly caressed the side of her breast, reminding her again of what they'd just shared. Though she couldn't see his eyes, she felt his gaze on her face, warm, caring, comforting. And for one of the few times in her life, Helen really needed someone to comfort her.

He drew her to him for one more kiss. "I'll see you tomorrow night, then?" he said. "A real date this time."

"You mean combed hair and clothes suitable for the public?"

He smiled. "When we start out, at least."

The thought of spending another few hours wrapped in the soothing press of his arms made her go soft and mushy inside. The second time he'd made love to her he'd been slow, seductive, agonizingly tender. He'd made every inch of her skin come alive, respond to the trace of his fingers over her energized body until she'd almost begged for him to enter her. Now, thinking back with a mind still numbed by satisfaction, she didn't know which she'd enjoyed more, the quick, intense passion of their first encounter, or the second, deliberate approach to lovemaking that took time, care and infinite pleasuring.

She only knew she wanted more of him, to experience all the ways of giving and taking that this relationship promised. She opened the car door reluctantly. The interior light glowed from under the dashboard, giving her one more look at his face that she could take with her to her bed, along with the realization that this man, this corporate giant from another world, in the span of a few hours, had angered her, thrilled her, ignited her deepest passion. Unfortunately her sudden, profound connection to him scared the living wits out of her, as well.

"I…I have to go," she said.

"I know." He laid his hand on her bare thigh. "I'm just trying to think of a way to keep you in the car."

"Oh? Did you come up with anything?"

"Yeah." His eyes lit with a spark of humor. "I don't think you've apologized yet. Maybe we could sit here until you do."

She touched her fingers to her mouth where the moisture from his lips still lingered. And she chuckled. "Funny, I thought I had. Maybe not in so many words, but in other, nonverbal ways."

He smiled. "Okay. You're off the hook…for now."

She stepped out of the car, closed the door and leaned inside the window. "Maybe you'll dredge up something else I've done that requires an apology, and we'll have to do this all over again."

"I'm already thinking." He waited until she'd made it to the front steps before driving off.

Helen reached for the door to the cottage, and was shocked when it swung open and Pet stepped over the threshold.

"Have fun?" Pet asked with a grin that said she already knew the answer.

Helen smiled uneasily. "Ah, yes, as a matter of fact I did."

Pet placed her hand against Helen's cheek, studied her features. "Finn's been worried that Ethan might try to release some pent-up emotions on you." She smiled again. "I see he did exactly that."

Helen's skin warmed to the roots of her hair. "There was some mutual releasing going on, if you want to know the truth."

"I see. Are you okay?"

"Why wouldn't I be?" Even as she said the words, Helen realized there were only about a thousand answers to the simple question.

"Oh, I don't know. I was just thinking of the current circumstances of your life."

Helen nodded slowly. "I suppose those circumstances could lead to complications."

"So, do you like him?"

"Too much, maybe."

Pet's gaze fell to Helen's tummy. "I'm assuming you haven't told him."

"No."

"What are you going to do?"

A spark of guilty anger ignited inside Helen, and she glared at Pet. "Why do I have to do anything right now? Can't I just enjoy the moment?"

"Oh, sure," Pet said, "but remember, moments turn into hours and days and suddenly you can find yourself mired so deep in deception that there's no easy way out."

Helen dropped onto an old wooden bench beside the door. "There's no easy way out now. This has all become so complicated."

"I thought maybe it had," Pet said. "But complications

can be taken apart, dealt with one at a time. Let's start with the big question. The baby. You haven't changed your mind about having it, raising it?"

Helen layered her hands over her stomach, comfortable at last with the conclusion that had ended the tug of war between her emotions and her logic. The possibility of *not* having the Bean no longer existed. "No, I'm committed to this child."

"Okay, then we start from this point. Now you decide who you're going to tell, what support you'll need. What steps you're going to take." She smiled. "You know that my name is at the top of that support list, now and always. And Finn's should be, as well."

Helen swallowed, feeling the burn all the way down her throat. "I can't tell Pop."

"Well, honey, you're going to have to."

"He'll be so disappointed. I know he gets upset with me sometimes, but basically Finn has this idea that I'm some kind of superwoman...."

Pet had the strangest reaction to Helen's comment. She laughed. "Oh, Helen, you think that man in there hasn't had to face up to his own responsibilities about a million times in his life? You think he hasn't had regrets? Made mistakes? He may be surprised at this secret you're harboring, but I guarantee you one thing. Once he adjusts to this news, he'll stand beside you through that baby's first breath and for years afterward, and neither one of you could hope for a better champion."

Pet's words were comforting, and Helen's mind absorbed them until a frightening thought made her heart skip a beat. She grabbed Pet's arm. "You didn't tell him? You promised...."

"Of course I didn't. But you're going to have to. And I'd say the sooner the better."

Pet took Helen's hand and gave it a squeeze. "In fact, I'm pretty sure he's still awake." After sending Helen a smile of encouragement, Pet headed down the steps to her car. She stopped before getting in. "Remember, honey, you're not alone. You've got a passel of people in this town to back you up."

Helen wanted to believe her. She did have a few friends in Heron Point who would stand behind her decision and think none the less of her for choosing it. Unfortunately, the Bean's father wasn't one of them. And neither was the man with whom she feared she was falling in love—really and truly in love, this time.

HELEN WENT INSIDE THE cottage, closed the front door and crept down the hallway to Finn's room. She peeked inside. The bedside lamp was on, and she watched her father pop his medication into his mouth and swallow it with a gulp of water. He looked up when he became aware that she'd blocked the hall light. "'Bout time you got home," he said.

Smiling at his attempt at a fatherly reprimand, she entered his room. "I met Pet outside, so I know you weren't lonely for me."

"Did Anderson mind his manners?"

She sat on the edge of his bed. "Yes, he did. I'm sorry if I caused you any worry."

He shrugged off her apology. "I wasn't worried. I know you can keep him in his place."

"I saw you take your pill. Are you having some pain tonight?"

"Not bad. Pet just hounded me till I figured I should take the damn thing. For all I know she's standing outside the window checking to see if I do."

"Actually, I watched her drive off. But she's right. The pill will help you sleep." She leaned over and kissed his cheek. "G'night, Pop."

When she reached the door, he said, "Wait a minute. You didn't tell me how it worked out with Ethan. You didn't admit anything, did you?"

"Sorry, but the evidence of our misdeed was a little overwhelming. He had dinner at the Marina Tavern."

Finn whistled through his teeth. "All those pictures told on us, then?"

"Yep."

"Did you talk him out of that fool idea to start his own charter?"

Helen didn't know how to answer that. Once she and Ethan had moved on to more interesting endeavors, neither one of them had mentioned the charter possibility again. "I'd have to say that topic is still up in the air," she said. "But I'm not as worried about it now, for some reason."

She moved to flick the light switch in the hallway. "See you in the morning, Pop."

"Ah, Helen?"

"What is it?"

"Is there something you want to tell me?"

Helen's hand froze on the switch. Maybe Pet hadn't told, but she'd sure as heck hinted. Helen decided to feign ignorance for the moment. "What do you mean?"

"I don't know. You seem kind of distracted lately, like maybe something's bothering you." He shifted in the bed, as if he were suddenly uncomfortable. "I know I'm not much good at this dialogue stuff, but if there's something you want to say…"

Dear Pop. He was in pain, and right now a pill was flowing through his bloodstream that would knock him out in a matter of minutes, and he was trying his best to be the patient, caring father. Tonight wasn't the time. Helen knew that, but she had to give him something to chew on. "Well, there is one thing."

He blinked, already struggling to keep his eyes open. "What's that?"

"Archie Anderson gets here on Thursday. I thought you might want to know that."

"Aw, hell. That's enough to ruin a night's sleep."

Yeah. And enough to keep you from wondering what's going on in my life. "This time we'll meet an Anderson head on," she said. "No tricks up our sleeves."

"You got that right. Archie Anderson is no match for the two of us."

She turned off the light and went to the kitchen. By the time she'd filled Andy's water bowl, taken her prenatal vitamin and headed back down the hall, she heard Finn's even snoring and figured he was imagining that first meeting with Archie in his dreams. And if it was a good dream, he met his old nemesis standing tall, on two sturdy legs.

ETHAN WAS HAVING HIS second cup of coffee when the painters arrived at eight-thirty on Sunday morning. He'd hired them to work seven days a week since his father was arriving on Thursday. They'd finished the first floor and had promised to paint the six upstairs rooms, which would be furnished with the delivery from the Gainesville furniture store on Monday. Luckily, the electrical wiring in the inn had passed inspection, and only smoke detectors and sprinklers were needed to bring the place up to twenty-first-century codes.

With his hand curled around the coffee mug, Ethan stood on the back porch and looked at the boathouse. Before long, pleasure craft would fill the empty berths. New gasoline tanks would be installed to meet the guests' needs for fuel, and maybe a craft large enough to accommodate groups of fishermen would be tied to the seawall. Ethan still had to make up his mind about that possibility.

As natural as the sun rising, thoughts of establishing his own charter business made him switch his musings to Helen. He concentrated on tonight, when he would see her again. He took a sip of coffee, relishing the warmth that had suddenly enveloped his whole body.

And then his cell phone rang, scattering the pleasant images and reminding him that it was time to face the topic that had weighed heavily on his mind since Friday. He pressed the connect button. "Morning, Dad."

"Just a few more days now, Ethan. I'll be checking in to see how things are progressing down there."

He could have told him about the furniture arriving tomorrow, about the painters working overtime, about the good news from the county electrical inspector. Instead, he said, "Why didn't anyone ever tell me that Mom had a brother?"

It was as if the line went dead. For several seconds Ethan heard nothing, and then his father drew a couple of deep breaths. "How did you hear?"

"Does it matter? The point is, why didn't you tell me?"

"You didn't need to know."

"And you decided that? For God's sake, Dad, I'm standing here about two hundred yards from where a kid drowned, my uncle, and for the last thirty-two years you've kept that piece of information from me. You never even thought to mention it when you bought this mausoleum!"

"Ethan, you're overreacting."

"Am I?" Ethan stared up at the floor of the second-story balcony where the voices of the painters filtered down to him on a Gulf breeze. "You want to know what's really crazy, Dad? A couple of the old-timers in town have hinted to me that this inn is haunted. A homeless guy used to stay out here, and he said he saw a vision in the windows—a small, slight figure passing through the upstairs rooms."

Archie gave a nervous chuckle. "You don't believe in ghosts, do you, son?"

"No, I don't, but some people here do, and..."

"That's just a few crackpots who thought up a story to make the place some kind of urban legend."

"Look, Dad, ghosts aside, even one who is supposed to be my uncle, I do believe in karma or bad luck or whatever you want to call it. There's a reason this place never was a success after that summer, a reason why the original owners sold it and why the last owners left it to rot in the sun. There's a sadness about this place that no amount of paint is going to cover."

"How much do you know about that summer, Ethan?"

"Everything but your side of the story."

"Then I'll only ask one thing of you. Reserve judgment until I get down there. No more speculating about Dolphin

Run. If there's a sadness hanging over that inn, it's not the fault of the property. Things need to be made right again, and fixing the old place up is just a beginning. You've got a good start on that, Ethan, but the rest is up to me."

"And how are you going to do that, Dad?"

"By looking Finn Sweeney in the eyes."

"He's in a wheelchair," Ethan said. "Did you know that?"

"I know it."

"And you also know why, don't you?"

"Of course. That's why you're taking me to see Finn first thing after we get to Heron Point."

Ethan disconnected, and his thoughts immediately returned to Helen. They had the next four nights, and if he was going to cement any kind of relationship with her, then he'd better do it before Thursday, because he had a feeling that when Archie and Finn got together, all hell was going to break loose.

CHAPTER FOURTEEN

TUESDAY MORNING HELEN AWOKE slowly, leisurely stretching into an awareness that the sun had risen and that she was more in love than she'd ever thought possible. The night before, Ethan had sent the guards away, and he and Helen had enjoyed dinner and classical music at the boathouse under the glow of pole lights. No one had ever entertained Helen so lavishly, so considerately. And afterward they'd made love on a blanket thrown over the soft new sod which now carpeted the lawn of Dolphin Run.

As thoughts of the last two nights with Ethan drifted in Helen's consciousness, she resisted the niggling of guilt that seemed determined to undermine her inner sense of completion. But doubts haunted her this morning just as they had for the last few days. She still hadn't told Ethan about the baby, and while she'd had good reasons for keeping her secret, she still feared Ethan would view her actions as unforgivable. She rationalized her behavior by telling herself she didn't know if Ethan loved her. She'd sensed they'd come close to saying the words a couple of times, but something had held them back.

Helen's reluctance to confess her true feelings for Ethan

was born of a conscience that gnawed at her constantly. Hiding a pregnancy from a man who didn't want children was the worst kind of deception. Deep inside, Helen almost wished that Ethan didn't love her, that he was merely toying with her, as other men had. Then she could justify her deceit, even tell herself that he deserved it.

But her instincts told her otherwise. His tenderness, his passion, his interest in everything she said and everything she did spoke of a deep emotional attachment—the real thing. She truly believed he loved her, though he had yet to say the words, and that was eating her up inside.

She had to tell him soon, and she would. But not before Archie arrived. She and Ethan had talked for hours about the implications of a meeting between Archie and Finn, about old wounds being opened, old animosity stirred to life. Helen didn't know if her relationship with Ethan would survive the bitterness between their fathers. Would their enmity erode the happiness she and Ethan had experienced the last few days? With such doubts plaguing her, Helen had decided not to tell Ethan about the baby until the matter with their fathers was settled. Maybe the ties of blood and family would be stronger than the ones of passion, and there would be no need to tell him after all.

She threw off the covers and sat on the edge of her bed. Finn's voice carried down the hallway from the kitchen. He was talking to Andy as he often did, two old friends sharing the promise of a new day.

Finn would soon have much more to share with the patient Lab because she planned to tell him about the baby this morning. She'd thought about waiting until Archie arrived to tell Finn, as well, but he knew something was up. He'd questioned her several times, inviting her to open up to him. And so, over coffee in a few minutes, she would. Maybe this information would take his mind off Archie's arrival. Some things were more important in the long run than old resentments. She dressed quickly and went to the kitchen.

Finn looked up from skimming the local newspaper. "Good morning. Sleep well?"

"Fine." She waited for Andy to slowly make his way across the floor to accept her scratch behind his ears before she filled a mug. Sitting down at the table, she said, "We've got to talk, Pop."

He folded the paper and pushed it aside. "I figured as much."

She took a sip. "That's good coffee."

His gaze on her face never wavered. "I suppose."

She set the mug down and took a deep breath. "I have to tell you something, and I don't know how you're going to take it."

He waited. When she didn't immediately offer more information, he finally said, "Do you want me to make this easy for you?"

She stared at him and placed her hand over her belly. "You know what I'm going to say?"

"I expect it's that you're in love with Ethan Anderson."

Relief pushed the breath from her lungs, though she knew she was experiencing only a temporary reprieve. "That's what you think?"

"Well, aren't you?"

She shook her head, a series of short, nervous movements. "I...I don't know. Maybe."

"Does he love you?"

"Again, maybe. We haven't said it in so many words."

"And you want my permission?" Finn frowned. "Good grief, Helen, never in your life have you asked for my permission to do anything. I can't imagine you're asking me now if you can tell Anderson you love him."

"I'm not asking, Pop. It's not Ethan I want to talk about."

"It's not?" He sat forward, threaded his fingers together. He looked almost hopeful. "I'll be darned. I thought I had this one figured out."

She smiled. "Actually, I don't think you've even considered what I'm about to tell you." She covered his hands with both of hers. "I'm pregnant, Pop."

He tugged his hands free and flattened them over his chest. "Did I hear you right?"

"I expect you did."

"You're pregnant?"

She nodded.

His lips twisted as if he had just swallowed something bitter. "Aw, Helen. I never thought…"

"It's not so bad, Pop, not when you get used to the idea."

He ran his hand over his close-cropped beard. "But an Anderson in this family? I can take a lot, but I don't know about that…."

She jerked back in the chair. "What? No! Ethan's not the father. Donny Jax is."

A range of emotions crossed Finn's face, from outrage to disappointment. Was he actually considering that Ethan would be a less-of-a-rat father than Donny? It was possible. He'd never liked the singer, had warned her about him repeatedly.

"Does he know?" Finn said after a moment.

"He knows."

"But he left town."

Helen shrugged her shoulders. "Exactly. But things could be worse. He could still be here and expecting a place in this baby's life."

Finn set his hands on the arms of his wheelchair and pushed down, as though he were trying to stand up. Then he slapped at the padding, attacking a lifelong resentment of his limitation. "That snake. That low-down scum..." The rest of his sentence was a list of unintelligible mutters.

Helen took his cup to the counter, refilled it and brought it back—anything to establish a sense of normalcy to the situation. "There isn't anything you can call Donny that I haven't already called him," she said. "Believe me, a blue streak of swearwords followed him to wherever it is he went."

"So what are you going to do?"

She slid the sugar across the table. "I guess I'm going to start looking at cribs." She attempted a smile, but bit her lip when it started to tremble. "And I suppose we'll have to start thinking of what the baby can call his grandfather."

His lips twitched. "You're thinking we'll manage, then?"

"I'm thinking we'll have to. After the baby comes I'll try to get help to come in on the days I have charters, and..."

Finn's eyes narrowed. "What help? I'll take care of him."

"You, Pop? I don't know."

"Better me than a stranger." Then, as if a thought suddenly occurred to him, he leaned forward. "You haven't told anybody about this, have you? Besides Donny, I mean?"

"Of course, Pet knows."

He waved his hand as if that were a foregone conclusion. "Pet knows everything. Anybody else?"

"Dr. Tucker knows. And Maddie. And now you. That's it. Look, if my pregnancy will embarrass you, I'm sorry. But people will talk, and…"

"Embarrass me?" He pounded a fist on the table. "You know me better than that, Helen. At least, I would hope you do. I don't care what people think. And I care even less about what they say."

Grateful she'd misinterpreted his question, Helen eased back in the chair. "Well, good. But if you're not concerned about what people will say, then why do you care who knows?"

"Because this town's got a population of about two thousand people, and I'd say at least half of them are like that Missy Hutchinson—busybodies. If we're not careful, we'll have 'em coming out of the woodwork to tell us how to raise our baby before the little guy's even born."

Helen cringed a little, thinking of Missy and how she'd talked Ethan into buying her photographs that day. True, Missy was a busybody, and as a fawning mother she was in a class by herself. "We won't have to worry about Missy," she said. "She's got all she can handle to keep little Bernard on his pedestal." She grinned at Finn as a slow, rich warmth seeped through her limbs. "What's that you said about 'our baby,' Pop?"

His cheeks colored above his beard and he looked away. "The wheel's in motion, Helen. Not much we can do to stop it from turning now. Have to accept that the tyke's coming and make the best of it." He sniffed. "Besides, it's not the little guy's fault that his father is the worst kind of scoundrel."

Helen stifled a burst of laughter. "Is that you talking,

Pop? Because you might actually be saying that a man's son shouldn't be held responsible for what his father did, say, forty-some years ago? And if I'm interpreting your words correctly, then you've come a long way in forgiving one certain man I can think of for the circumstances of his birth."

He glared at her. "Don't get ahead of yourself, young lady. And don't be putting words in my mouth." He stared at her while she tried to control the smile that threatened to burst on her face. "Don't you have to service the *Finn Catcher*'s engines today?" he finally said.

She stood up. "I was just going out to do that."

"Fine. Just 'cause you're expecting, you can't let the chores slide."

"Didn't intend to."

She headed to the door and was almost outside when Finn stopped her. "One more thing, Helen…"

"What's that?"

"Poppy. I think that would work just as well as anything for a grandpa name."

"It's a good choice," she said. And she smiled as she went to tackle the engines.

ETHAN TOOK A SWALLOW of beer and signaled for the waiter to come to their table. "I'll have another twelve wings," he said, looking at Helen, Jack and Claire. "Anybody else?"

The three of them gave him an incredulous stare. "I couldn't eat another wing if they were giving them away," Claire said.

"Hey, they practically are." He glanced around the grimy walls of the Marina Tavern, the place he claimed was now his favorite restaurant in town. "We've got nothing like this in Manhattan," he said. "Ten cent wings every Wednesday. It's fantastic."

Helen raised her eyebrows and made a circle at the side of her head with her finger. "Out-of-towners," she moaned. "Finn always said they come to Heron Point sober and leave half-crazed."

"He wouldn't get an argument from me," Jack said. "As chief of police, I've seen a lot of oddball behavior." He turned to Ethan and shook his head. "I've been to this bar more in the last few days than in the whole time I've been on this island. What is it you like so much about it?"

Ethan grinned at Helen. "Oh, here we go again," she said.

He leaned back in his chair and gestured to the pictures on the walls. "I feel a special connection to this place. Mostly I like to bask in the photographic proof of Helen's accomplishments on the water. If she tries to tell you that the fishing's no good here, don't make the same mistake I did. The evidence on these hallowed walls doesn't lie."

Helen tsked. "Don't listen to him. Ethan has become the most despicable sort of person lately—a gloater." She knew Ethan was still reliving his success at catching her in a lie, but that was fine with her. Now that the truth was out, she'd been having a great time intimidating him with her knowledge of deep-sea fishing. As long as she convinced him she had no equal, maybe he'd accept the futility of starting his own company. This new tactic had worked so far.

"I'm not gloating," he said, sitting forward and staring into her eyes. "I'm just proud of you, honey."

Claire shot Jack a look and mouthed the endearment

Ethan had just used. Jack, obviously surprised, as well, stared at Ethan. And Helen's face heated as if she'd just consumed everything spicy-hot on the Marina Tavern menu. It wasn't the first time Ethan had called her that, but this was a public place, and there were two witnesses.

The waiter deposited another mound of chicken in front of Ethan, and he rubbed his hands as if he were Midas, and the wings were gold. He bit off a glistening morsel, spared a glance at Helen and said as casually as if they'd been discussing the subject for days, "So, you'll go with me tomorrow to the airport?"

"What? No. What made you think I'd go to the airport with you?"

Unaffected by her denial, he continued to chew. "I've been planning on it."

She expressed her disbelief in a breathy chuckle. "You don't need me to be with you when you pick up your father."

He dropped a stripped bone onto a plate, picked up a small drumstick and grinned. "Speaking of chicken…"

"What's that supposed to mean?"

"It means you're chicken."

She nearly choked on a sip of Coke. "I am not. That's ridiculous. I'm not afraid to meet your father. It just doesn't make sense for me to tag along…."

Ethan took another gulp of beer and smiled at his old friend. "What do you think, Jack? Is Helen nervous about meeting the old man?"

Clearly trying to stifle a grin, Jack said, "I gotta admit, Helen, this is the first time I've ever seen you back down from a challenge."

"I'm not backing down. I just—"

Ethan interrupted her. "Hard to believe, isn't it, Jack? This is the same woman who reeled in half the fish pictured on these walls. And she's scared of Archie Anderson."

The men were obviously not going to show any mercy. "Yeah, it's a shame," Jack said. "Helen's going soft on us—backing down from Archie, drinking Coke all of a sudden. She's a changed woman." He sighed. "I kind of miss the old Helen who would take on the world and say it wasn't even a fair fight."

Luckily Helen wasn't outnumbered by the males, and Claire came to her defense. "Stop teasing right now," she said. "If Helen doesn't want to go to the airport, that's her choice."

"She's only postponing the inevitable," Ethan said. "If she doesn't meet Archie in Tampa, she'll meet him before the day's up in Heron Point. He's instructed me to bring him to Finn's cottage even before we go to Dolphin Run." He pointed at Helen with a fresh chicken wing. "So why shouldn't I have her company on the ride to the airport?"

"I can understand why Helen wouldn't want to put herself in an uncomfortable situation," Claire said.

Helen flashed her haughtiest expression at both men but spoke to Claire. "Thank you for your support."

"You're welcome."

Ethan raised his hands, palms up. "So that's it? You're not coming with me?"

"'Fraid not. I'll have enough to do to keep Pop from planning an ambush on your father."

Ethan popped a fry in his mouth. "I still say you're chicken."

She narrowed her eyes. "You want to go outside and say that, tough guy?"

He made a great show of shying away from her. "No way."

Jack laughed and stood up. "Come on, Ethan. I'll buy you another beer and beat you at a game of eight ball. Unless you're afraid of me, too."

The men headed for the pool table, and Helen and Claire settled into a few moments of comfortable silence. Finally Claire said, "I thought they'd never leave. Now we can talk."

"Okay. What do you want to talk about?"

Claire leveled a serious gaze on her. "You. I want to know what's really going on with you."

Helen emitted a burst of nervous laughter. "What? Nothing. Everything's great, as a matter of fact."

"I don't believe you. You wanted Ethan to notice you. Well, you've done it. He not only noticed you, he's crazy about you."

"Oh, I don't know about that…."

"So why don't you just relax and be yourself?"

"I am being myself, obnoxious as ever."

"Not quite. I'm all in favor of abstinence, for temperance ladies, but you're not one. You haven't had a drink in two weeks. Why the sudden change?"

Helen hitched one shoulder, dismissing the question as best she could. "I'm just watching what I consume. I was getting a little concerned about my drinking habits, that's all."

"I hope you don't think you have to be Little Miss Perfect for Ethan's sake." Claire reached across the table and covered Helen's hand. "We all love you just the way you are, and I think Ethan does, too. You don't have to pretend in front of him."

"I'm not pretending. Ethan has seen the best and worst of me, I guarantee you that."

"Then what is it? The only times I've seen a woman stop drinking completely, she was either trying to impress somebody or she was…"

Claire stared. She pulled her hand back and placed it over her chest. "Helen, you're not pregnant?"

Helen sputtered a pretense at indignation. When she found her voice, she said, "What a thing to say." She had to resist the urge to pick up a menu and fan her heated cheeks.

Claire continued as if Helen's dramatics hadn't affected her in the least. "You've only known Ethan a couple of weeks. Even if you and he had hooked up right away, you probably wouldn't even know by now." She chewed on a manicured fingernail. "So it's got to be Donny's." She leaned forward, bringing her face within inches of Helen's. "Are you pregnant with Donny Jax's baby?"

Helen hushed her with a sharp look. Even though Claire had voiced her suspicions in a quiet tone, Helen said, "Not so loud. Everyone will hear."

Claire glanced at the pool table. "You mean Ethan will hear." Her eyes widened. "He doesn't know!"

Helen tried not to look guilty. "No, he doesn't. No one knows. Except a couple of people, and now, apparently, you. You and Pet have this way of worming things out of me."

"Aunt Pet knows and didn't tell me?"

"That's hardly the point."

"Okay, never mind." The shock on Claire's face slowly transformed to blissful acceptance. She practically cooed the words, "A baby. Oh, Helen."

Helen frowned. "You can stop planning to knit booties right now, Claire. I'm not exactly ready to celebrate. There are a lot of issues to consider."

Claire glanced at the men again. "One tall, good-looking one, for sure. What are you going to do about Ethan?"

"I don't know. I just figured I'd wait until the first mega complication in his life was worked out before adding another."

"Oh, you mean the Archie-Finn thing?"

"Exactly. And the Dolphin Run thing."

"But you can't wait to tell him until he's finished the renovations on the inn. The man is obviously falling for you in a big way."

"I don't know if that's true. He hasn't said so."

Claire gave her a skeptical look. "Come on, Helen, you know—"

"All right. Our relationship has progressed in the last few days. I think he's stopped looking at me as just an oddity, and now maybe thinks of me as a woman."

"Of course he does. So tell him. It isn't fair not to."

Damn these stupid emotions, Helen thought for what seemed like the hundredth time since Dr. Tucker confirmed the pregnancy. She wiped at her eyes. "Here's the truth of it, Claire. If I tell him, it's goodbye."

"You don't know that. I've gotten to know Ethan pretty well. From my own impression and what Jack has told me, he's a stand-up guy."

"Not about this." Helen swallowed, forced her voice to remain steady and told Claire about the confession Ethan had made on Thanksgiving Day. "So that's it. Because of that kidnapping, he doesn't want children of his own. He saw what the pain and worry did to his mother. He just doesn't think the risk is worth the reward." She sniffed, straightened her spine and said the words that had been haunting her since her feelings for Ethan had spiraled out of control. "And he especially wouldn't want to have anything to do with somebody else's baby, especially if the father is that pathetic weakling, Donny Jax."

Claire laid her hand on Helen's arm. "Oh, honey, I'm so sorry." Her lips curved up into a smile. "But you can't be sure that Ethan will react that way. And I'm still thrilled for you. You're going to be a wonderful mother, and your life will be enriched beyond your wildest dreams."

Helen couldn't help feeling some resentment at Claire's enthusiasm. Claire had tons of money, a smart, beautiful daughter whose father had wanted her, a terrific fiancé now who loved Jane as if she were his own. Helen, on the other hand, had a business that could go bankrupt at any moment. The father of her child was probably a thousand miles away by now. And the man she loved was certain to leave town as soon as she did the right thing and confessed her latest transgression. As hard as it was to admit, Helen had to accept that Ethan was not going to be the answer to her prayers.

A firm hand curved over her shoulder and sent a shiver through her. She whirled around in the chair and looked up into Ethan's teasing gaze.

"What's so serious all the sudden?" he asked, looking from one woman to the other. He bent down and kissed the top of Helen's head. "Are you that upset because Jack wiped the floor with me at eight ball?"

Helen laughed, a small, tinny noise that didn't sound the least bit like her. "No, no. We were just worried that you guys were plotting a way out of paying the check."

He pulled out his chair and sat. "No worries, Sweeney. I'd never renege on a tab on ten-cent wing night."

She stared into her Coke, unable to keep looking into his eyes. Friday. She'd tell him Friday, once the initial meeting between Finn and Archie was over. By then she'd have no more excuses. And soon after, she'd have no more Ethan.

THE PHONE IN THE Sweeney house rang just as the noon news was concluding its broadcast. Helen watched Finn stiffen in his chair as she picked up the receiver. "Hello."

"Hey, Helen, it's me, or should I say 'us'?"

Ethan's voice was chipper, animated. She couldn't tell if the drive from Tampa was truly going well or if he was pretending an enthusiasm he didn't feel, just as she'd been doing all morning with Finn. "Are you almost here?" she asked.

"About another half hour. We're approaching the two-lane road. Dad's getting excited. Says he feels like a kid again."

"Well, good. I'll see you soon, then."

She hung up, looked at her father.

"Right now I hate this damn chair more than I ever have in my life," he said.

"Why's that?"

"Because if I were able to get out of this house and to the *Finn Catcher*, I'd be halfway to Galveston before those two ever got here."

She pulled up a chair and sat close to him. "I've never seen you run from a fight before, Pop, and I don't believe you'd do it now. Don't you think forty-seven years is long enough to avoid Archie Anderson?"

"I don't know if there will ever be enough years between us, Helen."

She reached over and rubbed his bare forearm. "You've got thirty minutes. How much of that anger can you let go in that amount of time?"

"Certainly not forty-seven years' worth," he grumbled.

CHAPTER FIFTEEN

As ETHAN'S CAR APPROACHED the end of the two-lane road to Heron Point, Archie turned off the air conditioner, rolled down his window and propped his elbow on the door. "Feels great, doesn't it, son? Back there by the airport, there was no breeze, but here it's cool and fresh and salty."

Ethan rolled down his window, too, and drew a deep breath. "Yeah. I don't know what it'll be like in the heat of summer, but now it's beautiful."

Archie remained silent for a moment, and then said, "This road sure brings back memories. It's just like it was when my father used to bring us here."

"But they weren't all good memories, Dad."

"No, not at the end. But back before it happened…"

Ethan darted a quick glance at his father's face. His features were hard, unyielding. "So, what do you hope to accomplish at this meeting with Finn?"

Archie scrubbed his hand down his face. "Peace. That's what I want. It's what I need."

Ethan thought of Wayne and Joel, the bodyguards right now positioned at Dolphin Run, the men who kept reminding Ethan that his father was a long way from achieving peace with the past. "I hope you can find it, because frankly, Dad, there are several areas in your life where you need to find acceptance and let the past go."

"You may be right, but unless I make peace with Finn, there won't be any for me or maybe for the rest of us until I die."

Thinking that was probably the most truthful statement he'd ever heard his father make, Ethan said, "Don't you think it's time you told me what happened that summer, about how Mom's brother died? I know that Finn jumped in the water during the storm to save him. And I heard that you could have, but didn't." He stared at Archie's rigid profile. "Is that the way it was?"

A muscle worked in his father's jaw. "It's hard to explain to someone who wasn't there. You can't know what it was like that night."

That was true, but Ethan was aware that his father had not denied the implied accusation. "How are you going to make peace with Finn after all that's happened?" he asked.

Archie pursed his lips, narrowed his eyes. "That's between me and Finn," he said.

"He's not going to welcome you, Dad. There's a whole lot of resentment in that man. Forty-seven years of not walking."

Archie shaded his eyes and leaned out the window. "There's the old Native American burial grounds," he said. "Timeless and spiritual." He chuckled. "Reminds me of when you and I were talking on the phone, all that ghost business. When I came here as a boy, Finn and I used to come out to these mounds and look for a lady ghost the locals said had roamed the hills for years with her old dog. We never did see her, but hell, we believed we would."

"Did you hear what I said, Dad?"

Archie continued staring out the window. "I didn't say it wouldn't be hard, Ethan. Most things worth accomplishing require a great amount of effort. Marriages, relationships, even friendships. But if they're worth having, they're worth fighting for."

Ethan drove over the short bridge that connected Heron Point to the mainland and turned right toward the Sweeneys' cottage. "We're almost there."

His father nodded once. "I know. I remember." He turned toward Ethan. "Maybe you'd better fill me in on just exactly what you and Finn's daughter have going on. You've told me about as much as you ever tell me about your private life, which is pitifully little, but Camille suspects it's more than friendship."

Ethan saw no reason to deny what he'd come to accept as true. "It is more than friendship."

Archie smiled. "All I can say is if that gal's a Sweeney, then she's a corker. What happened to her mother, Finn's wife?"

"Her mother was a well-known journalist who came to Heron Point to write a story about this disabled fisherman. Apparently, she found more to like about Finn than just his tale of heroism."

"I'm not surprised. Finn could turn a girl's head. And he could always make 'em laugh. So where is she now?"

"I understand that she found Heron Point too provincial for her global aspirations. She ran off when Helen was still a girl. She was killed in a conflict in the Middle East some years later." Though his father hadn't asked, Ethan added, "Helen's not like that. She sticks." He thought of the college education she'd given up to stay with her father, and his admiration for her swelled even more.

"I'm not going to let this animosity between you and Finn break us up," he said. "Like you say, good relationships are worth fighting for. And so are good women. Helen's one of them."

He pulled in front of the Sweeney cottage and turned off the engine. "We're here."

Archie looked long and hard at the little house he'd no doubt seen countless times in his youth. As he yanked up on the door handle, he said, "And not a minute too soon."

FROM JUST INSIDE HER front door, Helen watched Ethan's car stop in front of the cottage. She took a deep, steadying breath and stayed in the shadows, so she wouldn't be visible to anyone outside. She needed the advantage of sizing up Archie before he could do the same to her. Maybe Ethan and Jack had been right, after all. Maybe she was a little afraid of the great Archie Anderson.

Ethan got out of the car and came around to meet his father on the sidewalk. Archie stepped to the pavement with slow deliberation, glanced up and down Gulfview Road, and finally crossed his arms over his chest and gazed on the cottage thirty yards ahead of him. Ethan said something to him, patted his back, and Archie nodded.

As the two men approached, Helen couldn't help making a comparison between father and son. They were almost the same height, though even at nearly seventy, Archie had a slight advantage. His back was straight, his shoulders squared and his stride was confident. He was definitely a force to be taken seriously in the boardrooms of Manhattan…and in a small cottage in Heron Point.

Both men had full, thick hair. Ethan's light brown waves

were mussed from the wind. Archie's coarse silver style was swept back from his face, revealing a strong, prominent brow. His face was a mask of determination, prompting Helen to conclude that he was a man who'd come on a mission and was hell-bent on seeing it accomplished.

She opened the door when they reached the porch, and stepped outside. Standing beside his father, Ethan smiled at her, and the churning in her stomach eased. He introduced her to Archie. They shook hands.

"Young lady," Archie said, his granite features finally cracking with a smile, "there is no denying that you're Finn's daughter. No one could miss that hint of the devil in your Irish eyes."

She held the door open. "I'm not so sure that last part is a compliment."

Archie chuckled. "You'd know it was if you'd known your father when I did."

He walked into the living room and froze just over the threshold, a few feet from where Finn had positioned himself like a sentinel protecting the palace gates. Archie stared at him, seeming to take in everything about Finn's appearance with an intensity Helen found unsettling. Did he think her father's ponytail and beard, his worn island attire, were too Bohemian for his tastes? Or was he mesmerized by the sight of his old friend in a wheelchair? Helen searched Archie's face for a sign of disapproval, but what she saw in his eyes was only bittersweet longing.

Neither man so much as blinked for several tense moments. Even Andy, who normally expressed at least a semblance of guarded excitement at a stranger's presence, remained silent but attentive, the hackles on his back standing tall as if he, too, recognized the significance of this occurrence.

After a seemingly interminable silence, Archie said, "You haven't changed, Finn. I'd know you anywhere."

Finn scoffed. "That's not saying much. I don't go anywhere."

Ethan stepped between the two men, put one hand on Archie's arm, and said, "Well, here we are. After all these years."

Neither man spoke. Even Helen, who never was at a loss for words, couldn't think of anything to add to Ethan's bland attempt to defuse the situation.

Finally Finn inched his chair closer to Archie. "Let's get to it," he said. "What are you doing here?"

"I'm reopening Dolphin Run. But I think you already know that."

Finn jerked his thumb in a vague direction that might have pointed somewhere near the old inn. "That's there. I asked what you are doing *here*."

Archie's lips twitched as if he were about to smile, but didn't. "Right to the point, I see. No mincing words."

"We're old men, Archie," Finn shot back. "We don't have time to mince words."

Helen cleared her throat and put her hand on Finn's shoulder. His muscle contracted with tension. "Would anyone like some lemonade?"

"Never mind the pleasantries, Helen," Finn said. "Archie's not staying long enough to get thirsty."

"Pop…"

Archie raised his hand to Helen, his way of saying everything would be all right, before he walked around the wheelchair to the sofa. "May I sit down, Finn? Then I'll answer your question."

"Doesn't make any difference to me whether you sit or stand."

Archie released a long sigh as he sat on the edge of a cushion. "Okay, here's why I've come. As you just pointed out, we're both getting on in years, and I'm trying to make amends in my life, trying to pay back debts. And I owe the biggest one to you."

Finn wheeled around to glare at him. "You don't say?"

Ethan touched Helen's elbow, leaned close to her ear. "Archie's not armed," he whispered. "How about Finn?"

"He's clean, except for the TV remote on his lap. And all he can do is throw it."

"Then I think we should leave them alone."

Though Helen agreed that it was best to let the two men thrash out their problems on their own terms, she didn't want Finn to think she was abandoning him. "Is it all right with you, Pop, if Ethan and I go outside?"

Finn nodded once. "Don't go far. This conversation shouldn't take too long."

Ethan and Helen walked out on the porch, stopped and listened. They both seemed to release a deep breath at the same time. Ethan put his arm around Helen's shoulders and drew her close. "I don't hear any fists pounding or furniture breaking, so do you want to go for a walk? I know your father said this wouldn't take long, but I think once those two get started, it could be a while."

Helen let herself draw support from the solid comfort of his body for a moment. "A walk sounds nice," she said, "but no, I think we ought to stay here. I would feel better about it."

"What you're really saying is that you want to listen in, aren't you?"

She responded with a guilty smile. "We *should* listen in. You have your cell phone, and we might need to dial 911."

He led her to the bench below the open parlor window and gently urged her down beside him. "Is this good? Can you hear everything?"

She listened, heard Archie's comment that Finn had a fine-looking daughter, and Finn's guttural response. "Yeah, I think this will work."

A short silence followed before Archie said, "Aren't you going to ask about Lottie?"

Helen held her breath. Wow. No avoiding the tough issue. She could imagine the pain on Finn's face as he said, "I already know what's important. Helen told me she's gone."

"It's been two long years," Archie said. "I'll never be done grieving."

"If you're looking for sympathy from me, you've come to the wrong place. I've been grieving Lottie for forty-seven years."

Archie exhaled a labored breath. "I know we agree on one thing. Lottie was the best part of both of us that summer. I can't imagine what my life would have been like without her."

"A lot like mine, I guess," Finn said.

Helen covered Ethan's hand where it lay on his thigh and gave it a squeeze. They were talking about his mother, and she knew he must be suffering as much as the other two men who had loved Charlotte Anderson.

"As long as you're imagining things," Finn said, "how

about wondering how our lives would have been different if Hunter hadn't been swept into the Gulf that day."

"Or if I had gone in after him as Lottie asked me to. Isn't that what you really mean?"

Finn grunted his agreement. "That's right. She did ask you to. At least we both remember that detail the same. Unfortunately I was doped up on medication the day you came to see me in the hospital, and I never had the chance to ask you why you didn't jump in for the boy." He paused and finished with, "Well, I'm asking now."

Helen's heart hammered against her ribs when she looked at Ethan. Did he know the full truth about that day, or was he hearing it for the first time now? His face was set as if in stone, and she sensed his anxiety was equal to hers as they waited for Archie's answer.

"I don't know that I would have answered you honestly the day I came to the hospital," Archie said. "I had a story all made up to tell you about how I was protecting Lottie from the force of the wind or some such blatant lie. But I'll tell you the truth now because you know it anyway. I was scared. Plain and simple, scared out of my wits. And the gut-wrenching power of that fear stayed with me long after the storm. Every day for the rest of my life, I've watched that boy going under, only in my mind he always pulls me down with him."

"And you think I wasn't scared? You think you were the only one?"

"No, but I stopped comparing the two of us that day. I learned what I'd always suspected, that you were the better man, and I've never forgotten it." Archie cleared his throat, and Helen had to strain to hear his next words. "And I don't think Lottie ever forgot it, either."

A scornful growl came from deep inside Finn. "If that's true, then where's the justice? You ended up with it all—money, power, two good legs…and Lottie."

"You've got it wrong, Finn. What I really ended up with was the thing I was most afraid of, even more than the thought of diving in that water."

"What's that?"

Helen felt Ethan tense beside her. His chest expanded with a quick intake of breath. Finally Archie said, "That Lottie never really loved me."

Finn's words were razor-sharp when he said, "She married you."

"Right, because enough people told her to. And I tried our whole life together to make her happy. But the best I could give her was contentment, and even that didn't last. I never made her truly happy because while I was the man she chose, I wasn't the man she loved."

The parlor was eerily quiet for a few minutes until Archie continued, "If any woman could love two men equally, Lottie tried, but even she couldn't pull it off. She always loved you more. She was never unfaithful to me, but I know in my heart that every day she wondered how her life would have turned out if she had picked you."

A dull buzzing in her head was the first Helen knew she was crying. She brushed at tears gathering in her eyes—tears for both men, because both had longed for the same woman all their lives. And she cried for Lottie, whose heart had been huge but whose will had been weak.

Finn's voice was soft, the words barely audible when he said, "So why have you told me this now? What do you want from me?"

Hearing the rasp of a velcro fastening, Helen recalled that Archie had carried a small duffel bag when he entered the cottage. She listened to his footsteps as he crossed the room. "Right now I want you to watch this."

Helen recognized the sound of a tape being inserted into the VCR.

"What's that?" Finn asked.

"My kids gave this to me for Father's Day a few years ago. I want you to see it."

Familiar with the subtle click and hum the machine made, Helen knew that the tape was playing. However, there was no sound.

"This was made from some old home movies my parents had," Archie said.

Both men were quiet until Finn remarked, "Remember that old boat?"

"It belonged to that investment banker from Pennsylvania," Archie said, "and was the finest craft on the water every summer. That boat shone like a polished walnut, didn't she?"

Finn chuckled. "That's right, and one night you, me and Lottie *borrowed* it and went all the way to Apalachicola Bay."

Archie laughed. "And the next morning everyone kept wondering who had stolen all the gas out of the motor."

Minutes passed while the men watched the tape and commented about things they'd done and people they'd known. Finally Helen heard the tape being ejected from the machine.

"Okay," Finn said. "We've taken your trip down memory lane, but it only brings me back to my original question. What do you want from me?"

In the pause that followed, Helen heard a series of soft thumps, as if Archie were tapping the tape against his palm. "I want forgiveness for not diving in instead of you," he said. "I know I don't deserve it, but somewhere in my soul I believe the Finn I knew back then, the man on that tape, would have given it to me, if I'd ever had the guts to ask. Maybe he wouldn't have forgiven me right away, but sometime over the last forty-seven years he would have. Now I hope it's not too late." He sighed from deep in his chest. "What do you say, Finn? Can we get past this?"

Ethan locked his gaze on Helen's eyes as if, for that moment, as they waited for Finn to respond, their futures depended on what he would say. Would Finn provide the absolution Archie needed, or would he keep old resentments alive and eating him up inside, as they had for years? Helen tried to prepare for whatever Finn would do. She would support him either way, just as she would expect Ethan to support Archie.

The one reaction she didn't expect, however, was silence. But the click of Andy's toenails on the wooden floor was the only sound that came from the cottage.

Archie's frustration, as profound as Ethan's and Helen's, was revealed in his gruff voice when he said, "Are you going to keep me hanging here for the rest of the day while you decide on an answer?"

"What's your hurry?" Finn said. "You've waited forty-seven years to finally do what's right. A few extra days won't kill you while I think about it."

There was an exaggerated snort of contempt followed by Archie's footsteps as he paced the room. "Damn it, Finn. Can I at least have that lemonade?"

The wheelchair squeaked as Finn rolled it toward the front door. "Helen," he called out. "You want to get these Anderson men something to drink?"

"Sure, Pop." She started to rise from the bench, but Ethan held her arm. He turned her face to his and kissed her quickly and soundly.

"I'll help," he said. "It will be step two in the Anderson-Sweeney Peace Accord."

TWO HOURS LATER, HELEN and Ethan stood on the deck of the *Finn Catcher* watching Archie and Finn head back to the cottage. Pushing the wheelchair, Archie leaned over, whispered in Finn's ear, and Finn nodded. They were sharing an old memory perhaps, one that had transformed into a renewed tie that was working to cement the fractured relationship.

Healing between the two men had taken a leap forward when the conversation had ceased to be about the past and Archie asked to see the boat. Helen brought refreshments to the dock and Finn had proudly explained the boat's features and capabilities. Archie responded with appropriate awe and enthusiasm. Boat talk—it was a language both men understood and enjoyed.

When they reached the back porch, Ethan leaned against the deck rail and gave Helen a smile of encouragement. "So, what do you think? I'd say it went well."

"Yes, I think it did. I think Finn might still make your father jump through some hoops before he forgives him, but it will happen." She stood beside Ethan, her elbows propped on the railing, her chin in her hands. She watched as Archie opened the door to the cottage and she said,

"There are still strong ties between them. I don't think that storm washed them all away."

Ethan moved behind her, wrapped his arms around her waist and clasped his hands over her tummy. His breath tickled her neck below her ear when he said, "Old ties, new ties. There's no denying a strong connection exists between the Andersons and the Sweeneys."

She pressed her hand over his, over the place where the Bean lay protected inside her, growing by miraculous tiny cells every day. And still she shivered, because she knew what he meant by new ties. She and Ethan had formed a bond in the last weeks that on the surface was strong enough to endure into the future. It seemed stable, secure and real in its passion. But only Helen knew that this bond was as fragile as crystal, too easily shattered and impossible to mend.

She turned to see into his eyes, hoping to read the effects of the emotionally charged afternoon in his face. When his expression failed to provide answers, she said, "And what about you? You've been bombarded with information the last few days. Are you all right?"

"I'm fine," he said. "Maybe even relieved to learn that the deep sadness I always sensed about my mother wasn't only a result of what happened to me. The roots of her discontent reached all the way back to a stormy day in Heron Point."

He turned Helen in his arms. "You're trembling. Are you cold?" He automatically folded her in his arms and held her against his chest.

"No, I'm fine, too. For now."

He stroked his hand down her hair, capturing wind-blown strands at her nape and holding them there. "This has turned out to be a good day, after all, maybe the perfect day to tell you something important."

She leaned back, looked into his eyes and knew what he was going to say.

He wrapped his hands around her shoulders, held her gaze for a few seconds and said, "Helen, I'm aware we've only known each other a short while, but it seems like I've been with you for the best part of my life. Certainly long enough to say, without any hesitation…"

Her heart skipped a beat. *Not yet, Ethan. Not until…* She raised up on her toes and stopped his words with a kiss that expressed all the passion, frustration and regret she was feeling at this moment.

When she drew back, he smiled at her. "You definitely know how to make a perfect day even better," he said.

"I have to tell you something, too," she said, "and I want you to wait to tell me what's on your mind until you've heard me out."

His eyes creased in the corners, a sign of the confusion her statement had provoked. "All right, tell me now."

"Tomorrow. Tomorrow's soon enough. Can you meet me at the beach? We can go for a walk, just the two of us."

"Helen, is something wrong?"

She stroked his cheek. "No, but this is our fathers' day. What we have to say to each other must wait."

He pressed his lips on her forehead. "Till tomorrow, then."

Grateful to have her attention diverted from thoughts of the confession she had to make the next day, Helen pointed to the road. "Look, there's Pet's car. We'd better get back to the cottage before she begins staring daggers at Archie and talking about his aura."

A FEW MINUTES LATER, Ethan was turning into Dolphin Run. He looked at his father in the passenger seat. Archie had remained quiet during the short trip to the inn, perhaps reflecting on the afternoon's events.

"Well, this is it, Dad," Ethan said. "You're about to see the old place again."

Archie sat forward, staring out the windshield. "It's like old times," he said. "I'm feeling pretty damn good about things. It's going to be okay between me and Finn, maybe not in the next day or two, but soon."

Ethan stopped the car under the canopy of palm fronds. "And what about you? Can you finally let go of the past? Can you forgive yourself for not saving Hunter and admit that you weren't responsible for what happened to me?"

Archie shot a quick look at Ethan. "You sound like a psychologist all the sudden."

"It doesn't take a degree in psychoanalysis to see what's been going on with you all these years. Now that I've heard the whole story, I think I finally understand you." He smiled. "You may be the powerful Archie Anderson, but even you can't save the world, and when bad things happen, you have to live with the regrets without believing you could have prevented them. Simply put, Dad, the storm killed Hunter. And bad men took me. You were a victim of those circumstances just as much as we were."

Archie thought a moment. "Maybe I can learn to believe that, son. Lord knows, I want to."

"Good. And as your new self-appointed therapist, I'm advising you to let the past go, let your guards get on with their lives doing something meaningful so your son can lead his life. And when you remember the past, try to remember the good things, like that tape shows."

"I think I got a good start doing that today," Archie said.

Ethan resumed driving up the path to the inn. Just before the break in the trees, Archie said, "About Finn…"

"What about him?"

"There's something I can do for him. He misses the boat, going out like he used to. He didn't say it in so many words but I can tell."

"Dad, he's in a wheelchair. What can you do to solve this problem?"

Archie smiled. "I know a guy up north…"

Ethan laughed. "I'm sure you do."

"He's a boatbuilder in New Bedford, Mass. I think he can make adjustments on the *Finn Catcher,* maybe design a lift, special controls…"

"You're going to put Finn back in the captain's seat, aren't you?"

"I'm going to try. Damn it, son, it's where the man belongs." Dolphin Run came into view, and Archie's face broke into a wide grin. "Just like I belong right here."

CHAPTER SIXTEEN

THOUGH SHE DIDN'T HAVE a charter Friday morning, Helen still woke early, even before Finn. She lingered over coffee on the back porch of the cottage, her thoughts wandering to Dolphin Run, Ethan and Archie. Ethan had called her the night before to tell her that his father had been pleased with the progress Ethan had made in restoring the old hotel, and with the furnishings Helen had helped pick out.

"Truthfully, I believe he would have been happy to see the inn regardless of condition," Ethan had said over the phone. "In fact, even if I hadn't done any renovations, I don't think he would have noticed the peeling paint and layers of dust I found when I got here. He was that excited about coming back to Heron Point."

They had talked at length about the meeting between Finn and Archie, and both Helen and Ethan expressed optimism about the future of that relationship. And before hanging up, Ethan had once more asked Helen what she wanted to talk to him about during their walk on the beach the next day.

If he only knew, she thought now. The day had arrived, and Helen was much more concerned about her meeting with Ethan than she'd ever been about their fathers' reunion.

Andy rose from the straw rug that covered the porch floor and ambled to the screen door. He wagged his tail and lifted a front paw to scratch below the door handle, letting Helen know that Finn was in the kitchen.

She heard the refrigerator close and the wheelchair move over the wood floor to the table. "You out there, Helen?" Finn called.

She opened the door for Andy and stuck her head inside. "Yeah, Pop."

"Getting an early start, are you?"

More like building up courage. "In a way."

"You going into town?"

"Yes. I'm meeting Ethan about eleven o'clock."

"How long you gonna be gone?"

It depends how long it takes for me to get up the nerve to tell him about the Bean. After I do, I expect I'll be headed back home pretty quick. "I'm not sure," Helen said. "Do you want me to do something here?"

"I might need you to respond to a distress signal from the *Finn Catcher* this afternoon."

Helen went all the way into the kitchen and stood across the table from Finn. "What are you talking about?"

He set down his coffee mug and scowled up at her. "I must be crazy, but I let Archie talk me into letting him take the boat out, just the two of us."

Helen grasped the back of a chair and leaned on it. "What? You're letting Archie captain the *Catcher?*"

"He got me in a moment of weakness. But I made him promise he'd do everything just like I tell him. He may run the controls, but I'm still captain."

Helen bit her lip to keep from chuckling. "I'm sure everything will be fine, Pop. After all, you and Archie used to steal boats together." When Finn's eyes widened in shock, she confessed, "I heard a little of what you said to each other yesterday. Anyway, taking the boat out will be like old times—minus the threat of being arrested." She pulled out the chair and sat. "Shall I get fresh bait out of the freezer before I go?"

Finn frowned. "Might as well. The old buzzard will probably need me to show him how to fish again, too." He shook his head. "I'm sure I'm going to be sorry I ever let him talk me into this."

"Don't feel bad, Pop. You might not be the only Sweeney who's sorry for tangling with an Anderson at the end of this day."

He wheeled closer to the table and set his elbows on top. "Why do you say that?"

She rubbed her belly. "I'm going to tell Ethan today."

"Oh, Lord." He glanced up at the ceiling before giving Helen a concerned stare. "Get me the phone and the number to Dolphin Run."

"What for?"

"I'm canceling this trip and going with you. You're not going to face Ethan alone."

"Don't be silly, Pop. I don't want you to cancel with Archie. Besides, what good will it do for both of us to blurt out the news? Only one of us is pregnant."

"But, Helen, you really care about this guy…."

"Yes, I do, and that's why I've got to tell him the truth, just me and Ethan hashing it out." She laid a finger over Finn's hand. "But I thank you for the offer. It will mean a lot to me at the end of the day to know I've got you waiting to cheer me up." She smiled. "Just don't count on me to clean a bunch of fish. With my stomach the way it's been lately, this baby and I are on strike from that job."

She stood up, went to the cupboard and took out a frying pan. "Now then, breakfast. I'll cook, for once. Eggs okay?"

He stared off as if he hadn't heard her, and she took butter and eggs from the refrigerator. She didn't know what Finn was thinking, but she was trying to visualize the contents of her closet. What did a woman wear to plunge headfirst over an emotional cliff? She dropped a tablespoon of butter into the skillet and decided that a clothing choice was the least of her problems.

AFTER SOME DELIBERATION, Helen decided to wear the blouse with the blue ribbon she'd worn when Ethan first kissed her. It was pretty and feminine, and he seemed to like it, and her, when she last had it on. Not that any frilly accessories would minimize the effect of what she was going to tell him, but in this situation, she had to boost her confidence any way she could. Besides, before long she wouldn't be able to zip up the jeans that completed the outfit.

She drove into town an hour before she was scheduled to meet Ethan and immediately noticed a hum of activity on Island Avenue. A crew of men consisting of her neighbors and friends were wrapping twinkle lights around all the lamp poles on the street and hanging colorful decorations from the old-fashioned light globes. She waved to Stan from the Lionheart Pub as she walked toward Claire's shop. He called out a greeting from atop an eight-foot ladder and returned to the task of affixing a candy cane to the old cast-iron grillwork.

Christmas! For the first time, Helen realized the holiday was only a few weeks away. She certainly wasn't in the mood to haul boxes of decorations from the attic crawl space and begin decorating the cottage. Of course, she would do it. Finn appreciated her efforts every year.

How different the holiday season would be next year when packages under the tree would include toys. She would have fun picking them out. In fact, just thinking about a trip to Toys "R" Us in Micopee made Helen smile. As she continued down the street, she even experienced a renewed confidence. Current problems didn't seem quite so bad when there was something to look forward to.

She paused in front of Wear It Again when Claire tapped on the window and gestured down to a miniature Christmas village she had set up inside a border of colored lights.

"Looks great," Helen said, and waited for Claire to come outside.

"Thanks," Claire replied. "Don't you love Christmas?"

"Sure. I just can't believe the holidays will be here so soon."

Claire chatted while she hung a wreath on the shop door. "I heard everything went well yesterday. Jack dropped by the inn last night to see Archie. He said Archie was celebrating the success of seeing Finn again." She adjusted the wreath so it hung just so and turned to face Helen. "I'll bet you were relieved that the two of them got along as well as they did."

"Absolutely, I was. I think those two men will recover much of what they lost all those years ago. In fact, I get the feeling they almost might be good for each other."

Claire crossed her arms over her chest and gave Helen's

face a thorough perusal. "If that's the case, then why do you look so unhappy? Aren't you feeling well?"

Helen stared at the tiny porcelain people enjoying the quaint atmosphere of the New England town square in Claire's window. At this moment, she wished she could shrink down, go back a hundred years and experience the simple pleasures of holiday excitement with them. When she felt Claire's gaze still focused on her, she turned away from the idyllic setting and brought her attention to the present and her friend's anxious expression. "I'm feeling fine," she said.

Claire's eyes narrowed with worry. "Then what's going on with you?"

"I'm meeting Ethan soon in front of the Green Door," Helen said. "I'm going to tell him."

Claire gripped Helen's arm. "Oh, honey, good luck. I hope this works out the way you want it to. Do you know what you're going to say?"

Helen released a trickle of nervous laughter. "I've re-hearsed this scene a hundred times," she said. "I know my lines by heart, but it's Ethan's part of the script that has me scared half to death."

Claire gave her a smile of encouragement. "I understand, but don't despair. Ethan's a good man. He loves you, I know he does."

Helen blinked back tears. How many times was she going to cry before the Bean finally made an entrance into the world? She pulled a tissue from her pocket and dabbed at her eyes. She hoped her voice wouldn't betray her with a new flood of emotion when she said, "I love him, too. I've never felt this way about a man. Ethan is everything

I've ever dreamed of...." She stopped talking when her breath hitched in her lungs.

Claire tightened her grasp on Helen's arm. "Think good thoughts, Helen. You're doing the right thing, no matter how hard it is to do or how it turns out."

Helen sniffed, stuffed the tissue back in her pocket. "I know. I just wish that thought made it easier."

"Come back here if you need to talk," Claire said. "I'll kick everyone out and put on a pot of tea."

"Thanks." Helen started to walk away but stood a moment before the shop window. "Your Christmas village is really pretty, Claire," she said. "Makes me think that life was so much simpler back then."

"Life is what we make of it, honey," Claire said. "It doesn't matter when we were born. We all make mistakes. We try to correct them, and we live with the consequences." She looked down at Helen's tummy. "And you've got one consequence growing in there that's going to make up for a whole lot of disappointment."

Helen smiled. "You're right. Wish me luck that the words come out of my mouth the way I intend them to."

Claire crossed her fingers. "They will. Just be honest and be yourself. It's all *I've* ever needed to love you."

WITH THIRTY MINUTES TO spare, Helen arrived at the Green Door Café. She planned to go into the restaurant, order a raspberry iced tea and chat a few minutes with Pet if she wasn't busy. It seemed like a good plan, a way to take her mind off the overly practiced lines she'd have to deliver soon.

She'd just reached for the door handle when a familiar voice called her name. She spun around and looked into the seemingly painted-on features of Missy Hutchinson's cheerful face. Perfectly groomed as always, Missy's chin-length brunette hair shone with attention and skillfully applied auburn highlights. Her gleaming smile was framed in glossy bronze lipstick. "I'm so glad I ran into you," she said, leading Helen a few feet from the café entrance.

Wondering what in the world possessed the snooty gallery owner to show such exuberance to the town's fishing expert, Helen could only conclude that she'd done something *again* to offend Missy. "What's this about?" she asked. "If you're ticked off at me, now is not a good time for a lecture."

Missy forced a ripple of laughter. "Don't be silly, Helen. I'm not upset with you. I have a question, that's all. Have you seen that handsome Ethan Anderson recently?"

"Yes, a few times."

"Oh, good. He told me you were helping him decorate the inn." She gave Helen a conspiratorial smile. "I'll bet it's hard to keep your mind on business when he's around. So good-looking. So suave. He reminds me a lot of my Floyd."

Ethan Anderson compared to Floyd Hutchinson? Helen decided that *suave* must have a variety of definitions. Checking her watch and relieved to see she still had time, she said, "So what about Ethan?"

Missy drew Helen close to the exterior wall of the Green Door, as if what she were about to say was highly confidential. "As you probably know, Helen, Ethan was quite taken with my photographs, especially the sunset scenes."

Helen remembered Ethan's reaction quite differently, but she let Missy continue.

"He bought several, and I was hoping he might be interested in purchasing a few more. Since you and I are both businesswomen here in town, we should support each other. I'd appreciate it if you'd talk up my work, maybe encourage him to come to the gallery. I'm prepared to offer a ten percent buying incentive."

Helen sighed. "You'll have to approach Ethan yourself about this."

"But you're influencing his decisions, aren't you?"

Being in no mood to continue this conversation, Helen replied bluntly, "I'm furniture. Ethan does wall decor."

"Still, it wouldn't hurt if you put the idea in his head that he could use more Missy Hutchinson originals." She leaned in so close, Helen wrinkled her nose at the cloying scent of floral perfume. "And you'd better do it soon. You don't know how much longer Ethan will keep you in his employ."

Helen retreated a step. Her back hit the restaurant's rough wood siding. "What are you talking about?'

Missy spoke intimately into Helen's ear. "I know about your little secret."

Helen's heart tripped. She broke out in a cold sweat. The possibility that Missy knew about the Bean almost caused her knees to buckle. How in the world…? Who had told this woman, of all people? On the slight chance she was mistaken, Helen swallowed, took a shuddering breath and said, "What exactly do you think you know?"

Missy grinned, a catlike curving of her lips that lacked any sincerity, and spoke in her most triumphant voice. "About the baby, of course. You're pregnant!"

Helen jerked back even farther from Missy, as if the woman had burst into flames. She darted a quick glance up and down Island Avenue. They were alone. At least no one had heard the outburst. "Be quiet," she hissed. "Someone will hear you. Worse, someone will believe you!"

Missy stared at Helen and made an annoying clucking sound with her tongue. And despite her best efforts to return an equally fierce glare, Helen cringed. Could Missy see the panic she knew must be etched on her face?

"You're not denying this, are you?" Missy asked. "I know for a fact it's true."

Helen released a shattered breath. Her shoulders sagged. What was the point of lying about it now? "Who told you?"

Missy rolled her eyes. "Does it matter?"

Does it matter? Only the people closest to Helen knew about her situation, so of course it mattered! "Tell me right now, Missy, or I swear I'll leave rotting fish carcasses all over your precious azaleas."

"Oh, all right. You can be so crude."

Helen squeezed her eyes shut, temporarily blocking the image of Missy's smug face. Otherwise, she might not have managed to keep her hands from choking the woman's scrawny neck.

"I found out on my own," Missy said.

Helen forced her eyes open and waited.

"It was all a giant coincidence. Bernard came down with the sniffles yesterday. Turns out it was nothing serious, but I kept him home from school. Knowing it's better to be safe than sorry, and with the holidays coming on us now…"

"Missy!"

"Okay, okay. I took him to Dr. Tucker's office, and when we went into the reception room, I heard Maddie in Sam's office. She was asking him if she should call you to remind you of your appointment on Monday. He said yes, she should, that you probably wouldn't remember."

"And did she say what the appointment was for?"

"Well, no, but your folder was on her desk."

Helen blinked rapidly and told herself to breathe. "You looked in my patient record?"

Somehow Missy pulled off an indignant scowl. "No, of course not. I was just standing there with Bernard, as I told you. The file was open on Maddie's desk. I didn't snoop, if that's what you're implying, Helen. I simply looked down and there it was, the results of a pregnancy test in black and white."

Helen pressed her hand to her forehead. Damn small towns. And technophobic doctors who refused to use a computer to store confidential patient information. When she realized Missy was still talking she tried to concentrate.

"...mostly I was concerned about you, Helen. I thought you might have an illness. Now I realize that you are expecting a blessed event." Missy shrugged. "Though perhaps not so blessed considering your current unattached status. I'm assuming the father is that folksinger who played at the Lionheart Pub for a while." She tsked as if she were speaking to a troublesome child. "I don't know how you could have let this happen with a *transient*. I know how these entertainment types are. Why, the man is practically a gypsy! He certainly left you with a predicament, didn't he?"

Predicament. And to think, Helen had once thought of the Bean in just that way. Yet hearing the word spoken so casually from Missy's mouth made her nauseous today. "I don't think of this baby as a predicament, Missy. And I don't appreciate your use of the word, either."

Missy pouted. "Oh, dear, I've insulted you. Bad me. And here, all I wanted was to see if we couldn't help each other out. And to assure you that babies are an utter delight."

Helen nearly laughed out loud. *Oh, no, Missy, you wanted to be the one to tell me that I screwed up again.*

"I don't know what I'd do without Bernard," Missy rambled. "He's just the apple of my eye. I hope you'll feel the same about your child…if you have it."

Helen couldn't believe she hadn't walked away. But listening to Missy was like witnessing a car wreck and staying to see its miserable conclusion. "I'm sure I will," she said, "though I haven't yet started to think of him as fruit." She almost smiled. *As a bean, maybe, but only in the fondest way.*

Missy droned on as if she hadn't heard Helen. "Of course, your circumstances are quite different from mine. Floyd and I desperately wanted a baby, and when we found out I was expecting Bernard, we shared our joyous news with everyone." The bridge of her nose wrinkled between expertly plucked brows. "I'm sure you don't feel like doing that. It's why you've kept the news a secret. But, Helen, people will talk. No doubt, some of them will even be cruel enough to bring up your past indiscretions with men." She pointed her index finger at her own chest. "I wouldn't, of course, but some insensitive people surely will."

She took Helen's arm again and lowered her voice. "But then, I'm jumping to conclusions, aren't I? Perhaps you're not even considering having the baby. In your situation I wouldn't blame you. It won't be easy wheeling it around town when there is such an obvious stigma attached to the birth." She focused wide eyes on Helen and said, "So, what have you decided?"

Helen's anger was like a living thing that threatened to consume her and everything around her, including Missy. She wrenched her arm from Missy's grasp and balled her hands into fists at her sides. "What have I decided? Two things. One decision I made just now. I've made up my mind to do my darndest to never lay eyes on you again and to never let you and your scorching tongue within a mile of my baby."

Missy's eyes rounded in shock. "I might have expected such rudeness from you when I was only trying to help. I was actually going to offer to take you to have the problem dealt with. But you can forget it now. I wouldn't help you…"

Ignoring her, Helen continued. "The second decision I made a while ago." She pressed her hand fiercely over her abdomen and spoke firmly and loudly so Missy would have no doubt as to the future of the Bean. "I'm having this baby. I'm keeping it and raising it to the best of my ability. I can't wait until my child is born."

Helen barely noticed when Missy's focus suddenly switched to a spot over Helen's shoulder. She was relentless now, and wanted to make certain that Missy would have no misconceptions about her decision. "My baby and I are going to be just fine!" she added with extra emphasis.

Missy sucked her bottom lip between her teeth and tried to smile. Helen found the reaction strange and unsettling, until Missy leaned around her and spoke in her best polished gallery voice. "Good morning, Ethan. How nice to see you again."

CHAPTER SEVENTEEN

HELEN LOOKED INTO ETHAN'S EYES, saw shock, disappointment, even anguish—all the emotions that she was experiencing herself. After a moment she turned to Missy and said, "Will you leave Ethan and me alone, please?"

"But, Helen—"

"Missy, go. Now."

After a squawk of indignation, Missy took a few steps, but stopped in front of Ethan, who hadn't moved, not so much as a twitch of a finger or a blink of an eye. "How's everything progressing at the inn?" she asked. "If you need more photographs…"

His attention riveted on Helen's face, he said, "I'm good."

"Okay, then. You have my card." She glanced at Helen before heading down the street toward her gallery, pausing every few steps to look back.

Making certain Missy was out of hearing range, Helen moved cautiously toward Ethan. He thrust his hands in his pockets and remained still as a statue.

"How long have you been standing there?" she asked.

"Long enough."

"You're early."

"I was anxious to hear what you had to say." His eyes

sparked with chilling comprehension. "I guess that's been accomplished."

Finding it difficult to draw enough air into her lungs, Helen managed only clipped sentences. "We could start over. Take a walk on the beach. I could explain the way I'd planned."

"Would it change anything?"

"Not ultimately."

"Right. We'd talk at length about the situation, you'd still be pregnant and I would have sand in my shoes."

"I suppose." Desperate, she reached out a hand to him but let it fall to her side. "You have to know, Ethan, I wanted to tell you myself. I'd planned what to say. I certainly never wanted you to find out like this."

He rocked forward on the balls of his feet. "Is the father the folksinger?"

"Yes."

"How long have you known?"

"A while."

"A few days?"

She stared down at the sidewalk a moment before looking into his cold eyes again. And she confessed the truth. "I found out the day I ran into your rental car on Gulfview Road."

He made a sound like a cough and sent her a look of disbelief. "You've known for weeks? Since the day we met? Since the first time I kissed you, all those hours we worked together, the times we made love, for God's sake? You didn't think I had a right to know you were pregnant?"

A choking sob came from her throat before she somehow gained control of her emotions. Even if she had her reasons for keeping the secret, he was right. What she'd done was unforgivable. But how could she tell him the real truth behind her deceit? She took a deep breath and stated instead the rationalization she'd lived with for days. "I didn't think I should tell you until the problem with Finn and Archie had been straightened out."

He took one hand from his pocket and rubbed the nape of his neck. "Oh, here we go. Another example of Helen Sweeney's excuses to make everyone believe that her actions are always justifiable. I suppose you didn't think you should tell me until I'd given up the idea of starting our own charter operation, as well. You weren't quite through manipulating me on that score."

"That was part of it. I couldn't let you take business away from the *Finn Catcher*. I need *more* customers now, not fewer."

He stared blankly across the street and nodded once. His voice was bitter when he said, "I think I get the whole picture now. I'm putting the pieces together."

"What pieces?"

"The night Jack and I found you hurling cans at the sailboat…"

"That was the day I told Donny about the baby. He left town a few hours later. The sailboat was the only concrete target I had for my anger."

"So Donny not only ran out on *you*, he knew he was leaving you high and dry with a baby."

"Pretty much."

"That explains a lot."

Thinking she was finally getting through to him, Helen said, "I hope it explains why I was so insistent that you not start your own charter."

"That's not what I mean. It explains why you kept this little secret until…" He stopped. "Never mind."

But suddenly she knew. He didn't have to say the words. She saw the awful suspicion in the cold glare of his eyes, the stiffening of his spine. She almost couldn't form the words that were so far from the truth. "You think I was trying to trap you into marrying me?"

He released a quick, gut-deep breath. "In the last minutes, the idea has occurred to me."

Helen's thoughts tumbled in so many directions, she couldn't sort them out in her mind. Part of her—the stubborn, scrappy woman who'd grown up in a man's world—wanted to defend her actions against his mistaken conclusion. The self-righteous fighter in her wanted to slap him. And deep inside, the wounded, guilt-ridden woman wanted to sink to the sidewalk and cry out all her frustration. In the end, she defended herself, because she was Helen Sweeney, and she'd spent her life standing up to anyone who questioned her.

She strode to within a few feet of Ethan, tilted her face up to his and said, "How dare you make such an assumption? Do you think I didn't hear you on Thanksgiving when you announced that you don't want children? What kind of a husband and father would that make you? How desperate do you think I am?"

He stood his ground and glared right back at her. "I don't know. Pretty desperate, from the looks of things."

Anger boiled inside her. "I'm not desperate for you, Ethan. This may come as a shock to you, but I can manage on my own. I always have." She clenched her hand over her belly. "For *this* I'm desperate. And I'd raise this baby myself and work three jobs rather than trap you or any man into marrying me."

"If that's true, then why didn't you tell me about the baby before this?" A vein throbbed at his temple. "And why the hell did you sleep with me?"

A fraction of the cool disdain melted from his eyes, and somehow the awful, hidden truth finally found its way from Helen's heart to her mouth. Without forethought, she blurted out, "Why didn't I tell you? Because, Ethan, it wouldn't have made any difference."

His eyes widened. "No difference?"

She bit her lips hard, an attempt to staunch the tears scalding the backs of her eyes. "Right. Because someone like you would never marry someone like me. You know it and I know it. You could never really love me. Oh, you might talk yourself into believing you did for a few weeks of hanging out in Heron Point. But after a little fling with the town's female circus act, you'd have gone back to your real life, to who you really are. So when all's said and done, whether or not I'm having a baby is no concern of yours, is it?"

His breathing was suddenly ragged, as if each intake of air was forced and painful. "You think you know everything, don't you, Helen? You've got everybody figured out, all us square pegs in our square holes. That's how you explain everything you do, the choices you make. Well, I've got news for you. You just might be wrong once in a while, though a man, any man, would have a hard time convincing you of that. You clearly made a choice in this matter based on those preconceived notions that help you sleep at night. I hope your decision this time makes you happy."

He turned and walked away. He was done talking. And the pain in Helen's heart told her he was done with her, as well.

ETHAN COULDN'T REMEMBER ever working so hard in his life to accomplish a goal. For the next week he labored alongside hired crews to paint every wall in Dolphin Run. He helped make woodwork gleam with a fresh coat of white and, assisting the carpenters, he sanded and stained all the doors to the suites, and cleaned and varnished the oak plank floors.

He ordered new appliances for the kitchen and arranged for cable and Internet hookups for every room. Using a catalog, he chose furnishings for the rest of the accommodations. Placing phone orders with an impersonal sales representative wasn't as much fun as shopping in a funky little store in Gainesville and following that up with a gator burger. And it wasn't nearly as satisfying as watching Helen haggle over prices. But it was efficient, and delivery trucks arrived nearly every day.

By Thursday night, Ethan was dog-tired, in a gloomy mood and not even close to experiencing the level of satisfaction he'd expected to enjoy after completing so many tasks so quickly. He was half-asleep in a newly shampooed easy chair in the lobby when his father tapped him on the shoulder, jolting him fully awake.

"Look alive, son," Archie said. "I'm picking up Finn and Jack, and we're going to the Marina Tavern for beers and wings."

Ethan shook his head. "Thanks, but I'll pass."

Archie walked around the chair and perched on the edge of the coffee table. "You've got to eat."

"I'll get something here."

"No, you won't. Lately, you've been trying to kill yourself by either overwork or starvation. Both are effective, but hell, Ethan, I'll miss you when you're gone."

Ethan almost smiled. "Then get ready to pine away, Dad. I plan to be back in New York by this time next week. This job is practically done."

Archie expressed his admiration for the improvements all around him with a subtle nod. "True, everything looks good. The way you put this old inn back together would have made a hell of a reality TV show. Don't know whether I'd have called it the country's fastest makeover, or the compulsive labors of a jilted lover."

Ethan scowled. "*I* wasn't jilted."

"Does it really matter who did the deed?" Archie said. "You're as miserable as if you were."

Ethan leaned his head back against the cushion of the chair and stared at the ceiling. "You have the most irritating habit of bringing up subjects I'm trying to avoid."

"Hey, I've dropped the topic of twenty-four-hour guards. But you can't expect miracles. I have to talk about something." Archie propped his elbows on his knees. "Here's what I think. I have a twofold plan." He extended his index finger. "One, come out to eat with us and two, drive Wayne's car so you can leave when you want and go see Helen."

Ethan clamped his arms over his chest. "I've got nothing to say to her."

"Actually, you've got too much to say but no idea how to go about it." Archie stood. "Are you coming?"

"Nope."

Archie shrugged. "I tried. I'll bring you back an order of wings."

Five minutes later, Ethan carried a bottle of beer out to the dock. He sat on a bench and watched the full moon rise over the fading horizon. Soon blackness surrounded him, broken only by the pole lights which were now operated by an automatic timer. He took a long swallow from the bottle and silently cursed the effectiveness of the security lights. He would have preferred utter darkness.

His cell phone rang. When he recognized his sister's number, his mood improved negligibly. "Hey, sis."

She said three words. "You're a dope."

The mood-enhanced moment vanished. "Fine, thanks. How are you?"

"I mean it, Ethan. Have you always been this obtuse or has being in love made you take leave of your senses?"

"Cam, no disrespect intended, but this is none of your business. I don't care what Dad told you...."

"Okay, forget Dad. This is just you and me talking. *Do* you love her?"

Ethan sighed. Camille had always been like a dog with a bone, and her favorite choice of marrow was all too often her brother's misfortune. Since he knew there was no escaping her inquisition, he said, "Yes, I did love her."

"That's not what I asked. Do you love her?"

"How can I after what she did? She's pregnant, Cam. She's known about it for weeks. She never told me."

"Did you give her a reason to?"

Since when was it the injured party's responsibility to provide a reason for a manipulator to be honest? "What are you talking about?"

"Did you ever tell her you love her?"

"In words?"

"Of course, in words. If you only said it with actions, then that's just sex—good, satisfying, but certainly not the same."

"She should have known, and even so, she never once hinted that she was carrying a child."

"Maybe she should have. I'll grant you that…"

"Gee, thanks."

"But she was under no obligation to, unless you had confessed some obligation to her. For all I know you gave her that speech about not wanting children of your own." Camille paused, waited for his reaction. Hearing none, she said, "Did you, Ethan? Did you tell her that?"

"I might have mentioned it in passing."

"Oh, for heaven's sake. For a woman who's pregnant, there is no such thing as learning about a man's aversion to children in a 'passing comment.' It's a life-altering declaration."

He tried to defend himself. "I don't have an aversion…" Then, knowing his defense sounded lame, he sighed deeply. "It doesn't matter now, anyway."

"Why? Is one of you dying?"

"Don't be ridiculous. But I said some things I can't take back. And the baby she's having—from all I've heard, the father is a first-class jerk."

Camille's voice rose with impatience. "So you don't want to have anything to do with the baby because his father is a jerk?"

"You don't have to make me sound so callous, but I'm not at all certain about my feelings on this matter. I have concerns, yes."

"Okay, I understand. But may I remind you of a certain fifteen-year-old nephew of yours."

"What does Alex have to do with this?"

"How do you feel about Alex?"

"You don't have to ask. I love him as if he were my own kid."

"Why? Because he's mine and you love me?"

"Of course. Certainly not because of his father, who I barely knew, but who was a horse's ass…"

Camille chuckled. "What's that, Ethan? The man whom I mistakenly allowed to plant the seed in my womb was a horse's ass? Or, put another way, a jerk?"

He practically snarled. "You have the most annoying way of…"

"Getting to the heart of an issue?"

"I was going to say twisting my words around, but…" He smiled to himself. "I get your point."

"Were you happy with Helen?" she asked.

"Only every minute of every day," he confessed. "Though she confounded the hell out of me."

"Are you happy without her?"

"You know the answer to that or you wouldn't have called."

"Then do something, before it's too late."

He thought a moment. Could he go back? Could he change a basic truth about himself that he'd held to be true ever since he'd seen the effects of his kidnapping nearly destroy his mother? Could he do what he'd convinced his father to do? Bury the past and forge a bright future? If so, could he love Helen's baby as he loved Alex? Give her baby what every child needed and deserved? He gripped the phone tightly. "I'll think about it," he said.

"You do that. The right answers will come. No matter

what happens, I love you, little brother, and whether or not you say it back to me now, I know you feel the same. You have a lot of love inside you to share, and I believe you may have found someone worthy of it."

He heard her smile in her next words. "Just my two cents, for what it's worth."

"It's not that simple," he started to say, but Cam had already disconnected, leaving him to ultimately figure this out for himself.

AT SEVEN-THIRTY THURSDAY NIGHT, Pet pulled into the parking lot of the Marina Tavern and parked her car under the blinking red neon light that announced the bar's operating hours. When Finn had called an hour before and asked her to meet him, Jack and Archie for dinner, she was happy to come. Claire and Jane were working on Christmas decorations for Jane's classroom, and since Pet had stayed after the lunch hour at the Green Door to string garland around the ceiling, she was grateful for any excuse to avoid more Christmas cheer.

She stepped inside the tavern and noticed that the employees of the local watering hole had already prepared for the holidays according to the tavern's yearly tradition. A vintage 1970s aluminum tree rotated on a color wheel in a corner of the room in all its glorious and garish splendor.

Finn waved from a booth across the room. He was flanked by Jack and Archie, the two men that Pet never would have expected him to call friends. The transformation hadn't happened overnight, but it had happened. And though Finn had never formally forgiven Archie in specific words, he'd allowed the presumption to grow degree by satisfying degree. Now, only weeks after Jack's arrival in town, and eight days after Archie's, the two New Yorkers and one native islander had become a recognizable trio on the streets and waters of Heron Point. Pet often thought Finn should wear a sign pinned to his back proclaiming the old adage Never Say Never.

She sailed over to the large booth, her layered linen skirt billowing around her in a cloud of gold and orange batik design. She sat beside Finn's wheelchair and draped her braid over her shoulder. Its tip nearly reached the fringed scarf she had tied as a belt this morning.

Archie filled all the glasses on the table from the pitcher and motioned for a waiter to bring another. "Damn, Petula," he said when he poured her a drink, "you are definitely one fine-looking rose among all us thorns." He raised his glass and added, "To Pet, the best darned catch in all the Gulf islands." He looked at Finn before taking a long drink. "You're still a lucky man when it comes to the ladies, Captain."

Finn picked up his glass and scowled over the rim.

Pet waved off the compliment, since she'd long ago left the blushing to a younger generation, and ordered from the menu. "Where is Ethan tonight?" she asked, suspecting the answer but needing to be certain that Finn and Archie were aware of the emotional upheaval going on with their offspring.

"We've just been talking about him," Archie said.

Finn nodded. "And we've decided he's probably doing what Helen's doing."

"What's that?" Pet asked.

"He's at Dolphin Run, no doubt staring out over the

water like he does every night, with a sour enough puss to make the angels weep," Archie said.

"While Helen is doing the same thing back at the cottage," Finn added.

"But don't despair," Jack said, tipping his glass first at Finn and then Archie. "These two Dr. Phils think they've come up with a plan to turn this situation around and put Helen and Ethan back in each other's arms."

Pet smiled. "Well, I hope so. I have a sixth sense about love. I can always tell when it's the real thing." She sent a coy grin at Jack. "I'm mighty proud of the part I played in bringing Claire and Jack together. I have the same feeling about Helen and Ethan." She stared at Finn and Archie. "Don't be shy, boys. Ask for my help if you need it."

"I think we've got it worked out," Finn said, "as long as Archie can accomplish his part of the scheme."

"Don't worry about me. I'll make sure Ethan's on board the *Finn Catcher* tomorrow night as planned." He set his chin on his fisted hand and leaned toward Pet. "But as for that generous offer of help, Petula, I can think of more ways than one where your services could make a man happy his heart's still beating."

Finn aimed his index finger at Archie's chest. "Stop right there, Mr. Big Shot. You may have my permission to operate the controls of the *Finn Catcher*, but you've got no rights as far as this woman is concerned."

Astounded that these old enemies might risk their renewed friendship by fighting over a woman again, Pet passed a glance at Archie, warning him not to proceed with this conversation. He lifted his glass and responded with a mischievous grin.

Hoping she had interpreted Archie's hint correctly, Pet nodded once and turned back to Finn. "You'll not speak for me, Finn Sweeney," she said. "I'll associate with whomever I choose, whenever I choose."

"The hell you will." He set his glass down hard enough to slosh beer onto the table. "I still believe in a few old-fashioned values." He glared at Archie. "It might interest you to know, Anderson, that I'm going to marry this woman."

Pet smiled to herself but frowned at Finn. Okay, maybe she could still blush. A fluttering heart did that to a woman. "It might interest *me* to know it, as well."

"Well, now you do," he said. "Pick a day. I'll show up. Just don't make it the same date Jack and Claire are getting hitched. We don't want to upstage them with our own to-do."

"Fine," she said smartly. "I'll think about it." She darted a quick glance at Archie and almost burst out laughing when he boldly winked at her. At that moment Pet was definitely glad Archie had come back to Heron Point. And she didn't even feel too bad that he and Finn had once had an old rivalry over a woman in their past—or that they were sort of having one in the present.

She didn't know if Lottie had enjoyed the competition for her affection, but Pet was having the time of her life, even if Archie was only playing a part. She reached over, took Finn's hand and said, "You win, you silver-tongued old goose. After all that sweet talk, how can I say no? So I guess I'll marry you."

CHAPTER EIGHTEEN

FRIDAY WAS HECTIC. Many jobs had to be completed before the weekend or Ethan would have to pay his work crews overtime. Still, despite the pace, on several occasions during the day he found himself picking up the phone and dialing Helen's number. Each time he was interrupted before completing the connection, either by one of the laborers who needed his attention or by his own muddled thoughts.

Helen was driving him crazy, even more now that he wasn't seeing her than when he was. After talking to his sister, Ethan had spent a sleepless night being honest with himself and admitting that he loved Helen. At least he could find no other explanation for the abject misery he'd suffered since hearing her news and interpreting it as a betrayal. He definitely wanted her back, not just now but for always. But was he willing to have her on her terms, with all the complications she brought to the relationship? And was he willing to relinquish any ground he'd gained the day of their argument?

Damn it. She'd deceived him, tricked him and then rationalized her behavior by applying her own false interpretations of the type of man he was. Now he just wanted to shake her until she fell into his arms muttering all sorts of heartfelt apologies. But waiting for Helen to apologize was like waiting for the next solar eclipse. It might happen in a person's lifetime, but wasn't very likely.

The quandary Ethan found himself in on that Friday evening was worse than any he'd encountered in the business world or in his mostly meaningless past relationships. He had questions that seemed to have no answers the longer he pondered them. Did he want to be a traditional family man with kids? Could he live his life with a woman who would rather swallow turpentine than admit she was wrong? Could he erase her doubts and make her believe that he'd been nuts about her from the moment she'd helped him out of his mangled rental car? Could he forgive her everything and trust her forever?

Ethan had always compartmentalized his problems, made mental lists in his mind of the pros and cons of any puzzling situation. So, after weighing his options, for today at least, he'd pretty much decided that he and Helen weren't through yet. Soon, maybe tomorrow, maybe the next day, he was going to have to face her and his own feelings. But not today. He had work to do. And his pride was still too wounded. And truthfully, he didn't know if Helen even wanted to see him again. It had been a week and she hadn't called. The phone worked both ways. Still, eventually he'd have to give in to the yearnings that were about to drive him over the edge and settle this matter once and for all.

Unfortunately procrastination only made a miserable night an even more miserable day. A pall of gloom had settled over Ethan when his cell phone rang. Reluctant to answer and learn of another dilemma, he jabbed the connect button. "What is it, Dad?"

"I'm over at the Sweeneys'. I need you to meet me here."

Well, hell. The one choice Ethan *had* made was that he wouldn't see Helen tonight. He barked into the phone, "Can't. I'm busy."

"I don't care. Drop everything. Anyway, she's not here. She and Finn took off a few minutes ago. Won't be back for hours."

Ethan tried to shake off a totally irrational stab of disappointment. "Then why do you want me to come over there?"

"Remember that boatbuilder I told you about? The one in Massachusetts?"

"You thought he could make the *Finn Catcher* handicapped accessible."

"Right. He said there'd be no problem putting Finn in the captain's seat again. He's going to rig a couple of lifts and swivel chairs, mount some special rod holders to the bridge, build a ramp to the galley."

"That's great," Ethan said.

"Yeah, it is, but I need to take a bunch of measurements and I need your help. Bring a measuring tape and some paper. I want to sketch a layout of the deck."

"Now?"

"I can't do it when Finn is here, can I? It would spoil the surprise."

Ethan's shoulders slumped in resignation. "Okay. I'll be right there."

THE SUN WAS CLOSE to setting when Helen walked through the back porch carrying a bucket of cleaning supplies. Finn looked up from a sports magazine. "Sorry to have left the boat in such a mess this afternoon," he said. "Archie and the other guys had to run off somewhere or I'd have made them clean up. Darned irresponsible of them, if you ask me."

Helen held her temper as she swung the bucket ahead of her down the porch steps. Finn and Archie had been out on the *Finn Catcher* all afternoon along with two members of Heron Point's police department, Jack and Billy Muldoone. From the number of coolers Helen had seen the men carry on board, she figured she'd find the boat littered with food wrappers and empty cans. Now, it was left to her to make the boat presentable for her Saturday-morning charter. "It's all right," she said, grumbling the response under her breath so Finn would know she meant the exact opposite.

Unfortunately, her expectations were realized when she climbed on board. "Men!" she muttered as she crumpled the first sandwich wrapper into her fist and shoved it into a garbage can. "Such pigs!" She added several empty chip bags to the basket.

She next began picking up soda and beer cans from the deck. She'd crammed a half-dozen empties under her left arm and had two in her right hand when she looked up and saw someone coming across the lawn toward the dock. Not just any someone. Ethan.

He saw her at about the same time, paused, glanced around the property and resumed walking to the boat. When he reached the dock, he stopped and stared at her, seeming to take in her disheveled appearance and the similar condition of the boat. His lips twitched as he pointed to the cans in her right hand. "Are you going to throw those at me?"

Having totally forgotten the recyclables, as well as the instinct to keep breathing, she followed his gaze, focused on the cans and said, "What? These?" She tried to smile, but her lips felt as if they were made of cement. "I might if you provoke me. If not, I'll just add them to my cache of weapons."

He smiled, and her heart melted. "Have you seen my dad?" he asked.

"Not since he left here with his grubby fishing buddies about an hour ago."

Ethan's eyes rounded with surprise. "He's not here? He asked me to meet him. Actually, he said you and Finn weren't home."

Helen tried to ignore the regret that Ethan hadn't come to see her. "That's funny. Finn's on the back porch. He just told me to come out here and clean up the mess." She peered at the house, realized her father was nowhere to be seen and decided that she and Ethan had become the victims of a rather obvious ploy. "It seems our fathers have performed a timely disappearing act."

"And with a specific purpose in mind," Ethan said.

"It appears so."

"Maybe you ought to fast-pitch a couple of those cans at me in case the old boys are watching out a window. We ought to at least give them a show."

"I would, but my aim has been a little off lately. I couldn't hit the side of a boat."

He walked to the edge of the dock. "Mind if I come on board? It doesn't seem fair for you to get stuck with cleanup duty all alone."

She moved aside, waited for him to step onto the deck. When he was close, she gave herself a moment to study his features. He looked tired, maybe even a little thinner.

But still so darned good she thought she might disintegrate into a puddle right there on the *Catcher*'s deck.

He bent down, scooped up some litter. "So, how have you been?" he asked. "Is everything okay with the…" He paused as if searching for the right word.

"The baby?" she filled in for him.

"Yeah, the baby. You feeling okay?"

The new improved Helen Sweeney, which she'd tried to become over the last miserable, lonely week, had decided to leave deception out of her repertoire, so she told him the truth. "Actually, no. I've been feeling pretty lousy."

He held scraps over the trash can and stared at her as if forgetting his hands were full. "What's wrong? It's not the…?" Again that telling silence. Couldn't he even say the word?

"The baby?"

He nodded.

"No. This baby and I have been getting along great lately." She took the crumpled papers from his grasp. Her fingers brushed the backs of his hands, and she felt the tingle of the brief contact all the way to her stomach. "It's other interpersonal relationships that have kept me out of sorts," she said, dropping the trash into the can. "Ones on a more adult level."

"Ah, do you want to elaborate on that?"

She gave him an intensely serious look, hoping to mask the trembling that seemed to have taken over every inch of her body. She'd lain awake nights imagining what it would be like when she saw Ethan again. Heron Point was a small town, so unless he left in the dark of night, which she'd prayed he wouldn't, she knew it would happen eventually.

And now he was here, face-to-face, and all the words she'd rehearsed suddenly flew from her mind.

As much as she'd ached to see him again, longed to hear his voice and feel his arms around her, she hadn't expected that coming this close again would so tear her up inside. Instead of speaking confidently and logically, she found that every breath she tried to take caused a sharp pang in her chest. Every blink of her eyes threatened to unload a stream of tears down her cheeks. She felt so weak she didn't know how she managed to stand.

And then, oddly, Helen had a quick mental vision of the love poems her high school English teacher had assigned. Helen had found them tender, heart-wrenching, inspiring. Now, she figured she could write a few herself, telling the world the truth. Loving someone so deeply, so uncompromisingly, and so unsuccessfully, was horrible.

But he'd asked her a question, and she was obligated to answer it. So the new, wounded, weary Helen straightened her back and said, "Sure, I'll elaborate. I've missed you. And I'm sorry for what I did."

He gave a halfhearted grin. "Wow. All of it?"

"Well, no. But the pregnancy part, for sure."

"Okay, I'll settle for that. The car incident was just a lot of crumpled metal. The fishing trip was humiliating but kind of funny." He shifted his weight from one foot to the other, looking, for that moment, as uncomfortable as she was. "As long as we're confessing," he said, "is there anything else you want to say?"

So, he was laying this whole emotional mess right in her lap. Not quite fair, but perhaps deserved, so Helen decided to risk it all. This meeting was unexpected, but she might never get another chance to tell the truth. In a soft, wavering voice, she said, "I suppose at one point I was sort of beginning to fall in love with you...which," she added quickly, "made everything I did that much worse."

He relaxed his stance and even chuckled. "Then I guess I can tell you that the same thing was sort of beginning to happen to me, too."

A kernel of hope sprouted deep inside her, maybe right next to the Bean, where all blessed beginnings seemed to originate. "And did it stop?"

"I willed it to," he said, "but no luck. My attraction to you kept battering me like a damn hurricane, relentless and powerful."

She scuffed the toe of her sneaker along the deck. "Wow. You felt that strongly about me once?"

"Why not you? Until..." He paused, smiled ruefully. "So, what should we do about this situation?"

She pressed her lips together, pretending she was actually trying to eke a logical thought out of the chaos in her brain, and said honestly, "Darned if I know."

He shrugged one shoulder as casually as if he were about to suggest that they have peas instead of corn for lunch. "Maybe we ought to get married and play this thing out to the end."

She released a sputter of laughter. "Right. Like that's going to happen." When he didn't respond with amusement, she sobered instantly and said, "Look, Ethan, the problems haven't disappeared just because our fathers decided to act as matchmakers and we played truth or consequences." Aware that his gaze had dropped to her abdomen, she added, "The baby exists. It's going to be born."

He continued staring as if trying to find a place in his controlled world for the disruption growing inside her. Amazingly, his features were nonjudgmental. Instead he seemed interested and perhaps even slightly puzzled. "I was just imagining the baby," he said. "Her sunny blond hair and that little dimple like you have."

Helen moved her hand caressingly over her tummy. "Why, Ethan, those sound almost like positive comments. You're not getting all soft and squishy on me, are you?"

"Don't kid yourself. Mostly I was thinking about how this kid will come into the world and, just like her mother, pull a fast one on me during her first twenty-four hours of life."

"She could, you know. She could even be born a boy. That would really confuse you."

"Nope. No chance of that. Pet told me the sex when I went to the Green Door asking for you the other day. I assumed she'd already told you, too."

Helen laughed, feeling pretty good about Ethan's confession that he had thought to inquire about her this week. "Pet's prognosis is not scientific," she said.

"She sounded convinced to me." Ethan settled an intense gaze on Helen's face. "But it doesn't matter. I'll like your baby no matter what sex it is. Hell, I'll love her, with all her quirks, because she's yours."

Helen's internal security system went on full alert. Was this Ethan talking? The man who'd announced that fatherhood wasn't in his future? She frowned at him. "Aren't you still the same man who admitted on Thanksgiving that he didn't want children?"

"A slightly altered version of that guy," he said. "In the

past week, I've done a lot of thinking, and I've come to a rather shocking conclusion about myself."

"Oh? What's that?"

"I'm a great talker. For years I've told my father what to do, how to feel." He smiled. "It was good advice for the most part. A person shouldn't dwell on past heartaches or live in fear of taking risks. Life itself is a risk, every day. Just standing on this boat, you and I could get struck by lightning."

She started to smile at the remoteness of his example, and he chuckled. "That's the thing about risks," he said. "You gotta take them once in a while because most often everything works out okay."

"So, what are you really saying?"

"I'm trying to tell you that I have a problem. I'm great at handing out advice, but lousy at taking it myself. My arbitrary decision to not have kids is just my version of my father's decision to keep guards around me for the last two decades. Only, his guards were real. Mine were mental barriers. But they accomplished the same thing—kept us both tied to the painful memories of the past and prevented us from living in the present. In our own ways, we both avoided taking a risk on life."

He stared at her. "I'm not going to do that anymore. I want to take a risk with you and your baby. I believe the odds are overwhelmingly in favor of a lifetime of happiness."

All at once the *Finn Catcher* seemed to rock, just as if they were miles out to sea, and Helen was being taken on a wild ride. Only these waves were emotional ones that both thrilled and frightened her. She inhaled deeply and said, "Are you really serious, Ethan? Because you're creating a situation here where all the soft and squishy feelings are suddenly attacking me. And that scares the daylights out of me because I can't help thinking you don't truly mean what you're saying."

He laughed softly. "Oh, I mean it. And I'm a little scared, too. But not nearly as scared as I would be if I were faced with going back to my life without you in it. In the last week, while we've been apart, and I didn't know if we'd be able to get past the words that were said, I've had to force myself to think about leaving here, leaving you. I didn't like considering that. Since before this argument, or whatever it is we had, I'd been growing pretty comfortable imagining you with a permanent spot right beside me for years to come."

Helen swallowed, fumbled for words and hated her inability to come up with anything, a phrase, a thought, to adequately express her feelings at what was turning out to be the pivotal moment of her life. What she said now could possibly end everything between her and Ethan, or take her to that happy ending she'd always dreamed of but never thought she'd attain.

But she couldn't just agree, could she? He hadn't exactly dropped down on one knee with all the gallantry she'd come to expect from him and confessed an all-consuming love that would prove to her that he spoke from his heart. Helen couldn't ignore the nagging possibility that she was still just a diversion that fascinated him on several levels but might one day grow ordinary and no longer fire his imagination. Maybe, as horrible as it was to consider, he was proposing on a lark, thinking they could make it work, convincing himself that he could love another man's child. Helen had a right to know what lay in the deepest part of Ethan's soul, and so did the Bean.

When he wrapped his hands around her arms, she lifted her face to his, making her aware that she'd been focusing on a spot on the deck, afraid to meet his gaze head-on. Afraid of the truth she might find in his eyes.

"What is it?" he asked. "What's wrong? You don't want to marry me?"

Oh, I want to marry you! I've never wanted anything more in my life, and I'll never want anything more for the whole of the rest of it. Your words are the promise of the future I've always wanted, and you are the one man, the only man I know, that can make it happen.

But she didn't say those words. Past resentments, stupid mistakes, old scars clawed their way from her wounded ego to taunt her now, and Helen didn't think her fragile heart could survive another direct hit. "It's not that," she said, and swiped angrily at a tear that rolled from her eye.

He smiled down at her, the kindest, gentlest smile she'd ever seen. "Then what? Tell me, so I can make this happen for both of us—all three of us."

She sniffed and cowardly returned her attention to the deck between their nearly touching shoes. Her breaths were shallow, painful, as she drew from a well of strength and said the words that expressed half of the remaining doubt that kept her from leaping into his arms. "I…I don't know if you really love me enough."

He paused before cupping her chin and raising her face. "Do you love *me* enough?" he asked.

This was it. Helen's moment of truth. She nodded. "More than enough."

That beautiful, comforting smile stayed on his face, though his eyes grew dark and intense. "Then why can't you believe I feel the same about you? I know there have been a few times when you and I haven't exactly been on an identical course." He placed his hand over his heart. "But here, where it counts, we've been running side by side on the same track since we shared that piece of chocolate cake." His grip on her arm grew tighter as his other hand coiled into a fist that lightly thumped his chest. "I love you, Helen. More than enough to want to spend my life with you. More than enough to want to be the man to make you happy for all the years ahead of us."

He lifted his hand from his heart and laid it over hers on her abdomen. "More than enough to tuck this little being into the part of my heart that isn't already overflowing with you and keep her safe and warm and loved."

He'd said the words that made the remaining doubt vanish from her mind on a flood of tears and a shudder of emotion. "You really, *really* mean that?"

He rolled his eyes in feigned impatience. "What do I have to do to prove it to you? These past days all I've been doing is trying to think of a way to convince you that I'm not the jerk I seemed to be when I heard the news—"

She immediately interrupted him. "You weren't a jerk. How could you have reacted any differently? You were blindsided. I was wrong. I should have—"

He put his finger over her mouth. "Let me finish. We'll assign blame later—or never. It doesn't matter. What does matter is that I've come up with a preliminary parenting guide."

She sputtered a bark of laughter. "What?"

"Yeah. You and I will play to our strong points. You'll teach Little Helen to fish…" His brows arched in amusement. "Only no games, no tricks. Just skill and technique. And you must promise never to tell her about the ice bag."

Catching on, Helen said, "Agreed. And you'll teach her mergers and acquisitions."

Ethan grinned. "Something like that. And if, despite our best efforts, she comes home one day with a guitar she picked up at a garage sale, well, we'll consider the genetic pool then and pay for her lessons."

For the first time in her life, Helen realized that happiness was more than an emotional high. It was a gut-level physical reaction that warmed the insides, tingled fingers and toes and sent a person's senses soaring. She crushed her body against Ethan's, wrapped her arms around his waist and was thankful for the boundless sky and open sea. For it seemed that no room, no one place could contain the utter joy she felt at this moment.

He held her close and kissed her temple. "Can I assume from your body language that this is a yes? That you'll marry me?"

She leaned back, looked into his eyes and drew a long, trembling, satisfied breath of pure contentment. "You can."

His mouth claimed hers with all the promise of his words. And as he kissed her, Helen heard voices floating across the lawn. She squinted one eye and, peeking over Ethan's shoulder, saw Archie and Finn halfway between the cottage and the dock. Archie raised a glass in the air and said, "I think that Lottie is one happy angel, don't you, Finn?"

Her father raised his glass, too. "I do indeed. It's like she wrote the script."

EPILOGUE

ETHAN'S CAR PULLED IN FRONT of Helen's cottage at nine-thirty, a half hour earlier than expected, which suited Helen just fine. It was December twenty-fourth, and they had a list of errands to run that would take most of the day. Thank goodness Christmas Eve dinner was being held at Dolphin Run for the Sweeneys, Andersons and Claire and Jack's family. With everything going on this season, no one had time to host a big dinner at home.

Helen mentally retrieved her calendar of upcoming events. Claire and Jack were being married in two days. Pet and Finn were taking the plunge two weeks later followed by Ethan and Helen's wedding at the end of January. Love was definitely in the air in Heron Point.

Ethan strode to the front door, something he insisted upon lately even though Helen was perfectly capable of meeting him at the car. "We men feel so useless during these nine months," he'd told her. "You're doing all the work, so at least let me walk you to the curb."

He stepped inside, kissed her good-morning and asked if she was ready. "Wow," he said while draping her sweater over her shoulders. "It looks like you've added another dozen packages to that stack under the tree."

His guess was pretty accurate. She'd stayed up late the night before wrapping gifts, including several more for him. She'd never enjoyed shopping as much as she had this year. With a bright future ahead, she'd actually withdrawn a few precious dollars from her savings account. The result was that everyone she loved had specially chosen gifts this year. There were even a few for Ethan's sister and nephew who would arrive in Heron Point in time for dinner. She smiled at him over her shoulder as they walked outside. "I know. I've had such fun."

Once in the car, they breezed across the bridge and along the two-lane road on the mainland. She expected him to turn into the largest supermarket in Micopee so she could pick up her orders for cookies and cakes and the huge spiral-sliced ham she was bringing to dinner. "Whoa, you passed the turn to the grocery," she said when he drove onto the four-lane.

"I know. We'll have time to pick up the order on the way back."

She sent him a questioning look. "Back from where?"

"You'll see."

He was smiling, and she knew something was up. "Ethan, what have you done?"

"I got you a present that's too big to fit in the car."

She pictured the colorfully wrapped packages with her name on them under the tree and said, "You've already bought way too many gifts. I can't imagine what this could be."

His smile broadened, and he nodded at the dashboard. "Why don't you slide in that CD of Christmas music? We should be there by the time it's over."

The carols ended when they reached the town boundaries of Gainesville. "Why are we here?" Helen asked, fondly recalling the time they'd shared gator burgers in The Swamp at the university.

"Your present. It's just around that corner."

Helen read the street sign as he turned. Live Oak Place. She admired the narrow tree-shaded lane bordered with mature trees and trim, well-kept older homes. "What did you do? Have a tree named after me?"

He laughed. "Not quite." Halfway up the block she saw her gift. There was no way to miss it since a huge red bow was attached to the peaked roof of a wide veranda. Christmas lights twinkled from garland wrapped around each porch column.

Helen flattened her palm against her chest and gasped. "You bought a house?"

"Subject to your approval, of course. But I left a small deposit with the Realtor so I could sort of wrap it up for you. The final decision is yours."

Helen had never loved material objects in her life. She meticulously cared for the *Finn Catcher*. She was grateful for the old Suburban, which always ran no matter what. But possessions were merely necessities, not objects of endearment. All that changed when Ethan stopped in front of the modest Victorian with its gabled windows, stained-glass doors and sparkling gingerbread trim at the roof eaves. Helen stared at the scrolled numbers by the front door and immediately fell hopelessly and completely in love with 2917 Live Oak Place.

"What do you think?"

She threw her arms around him and squealed, something else she'd never done before. "I can't believe it. I love it!"

"I figured that since you've always liked this town, you might want to spend some time here. I can work out of the house except for when I'm traveling for Dad."

"And I can go to Heron Point on weekends and still help with the charters…" At Ethan's scowl, she added quickly, "…for a few months, anyway."

"Right. Since Finn and Archie took the decision about a charter company for Dolphin Run out of our hands by starting up A and F Charters, they're the bosses, remember?" He withdrew a set of keys from his shirt pocket. "I suppose you want to see inside. It's not furnished, but you're good at doing that."

She grabbed the keys and started to open the car door.

"Wait a minute," he said, leaning over her and searching in the glove box. He took out an envelope and handed it to her. "This goes with the house—again, subject to your approval."

Her hands trembled as she lifted the flap and removed a letter. She immediately recognized the Gators logo on the stationery. Her heart pounded when she saw her name at the top.

Dear Helen Sweeney. It is our pleasure to inform you that you have been accepted…

She skimmed the page before tears blurred the words, forcing her to fold the letter and place it on her lap. When she looked at Ethan, his smile was as wide as her heart. "Oh, Ethan, I'm going to college! I'm going to be a teacher."

"You sure are, sweetheart. You didn't think I'd carry this family all by myself, did you? If our dads are taking the charter business away from you, I've got to see that you're gainfully employed doing something."

She laughed and cried at the same time. Stroking her hand down his cheek, she said, "You really are the dream-come-true guy."

He took her hand and kissed her fingers. "Back at ya, sweetheart." He opened the driver's door, but leaned over to her before getting out. "It has four bedrooms, by the way."

"Four?"

He grinned and shrugged. "Well, you never know what the future will bring."

She got out of the car, the keys jangling in her hand. He was so right. You never know.

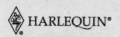

HOTEL MARCHAND

**Four sisters.
A family legacy.
And someone is out to destroy it.**

A captivating new limited continuity, launching June 2006

The most beautiful hotel in New Orleans,
and someone is out to destroy it. But mystery,
danger and some surprising family revelations
and discoveries won't stop the Marchand sisters
from protecting their birthright…
and finding love along the way.

SPECIAL PRICE!

This riveting new saga begins with

In the Dark

by national bestselling author

JUDITH ARNOLD

The party at Hotel Marchand is in full swing when the lights suddenly go out. What does head of security Mac Jensen do first? He's torn between two jobs—protecting the guests at the hotel and keeping the woman he loves safe.

A woman to protect. A hotel to secure. And no idea who's determined to harm them.

On Sale June 2006

HARLEQUIN®

Super Romance®

A GIFT OF GRACE

by Inglath Cooper

RITA® Award-winning author

In a moment of grief, Caleb Tucker made a
decision he now regrets. Three years later,
he gets a second chance. All because
Sophie Owens walks into his store with her
little girl—a little girl who looks a lot like his
late wife. But in order to get his second chance,
he'll have to ruin Sophie's world.

On sale June 2006!

*Available wherever books are sold, including most
bookstores, supermarkets, discount stores and drugstores.*

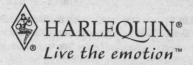

HARLEQUIN®
Live the emotion™

COMING NEXT MONTH